It Will Come to Me

EMILY FOX GORDON

SPIEGEL & GRAU

New York

2009

Published in the United States by Spiegel & Grau,
an imprint of The Doubleday Publishing Group,
a division of Random House, Inc., New York.
www.spiegelandgrau.com

SPIEGEL & GRAU is a trademark of Random House, Inc.

BOOK DESIGN BY AMANDA DEWEY

Library of Congress Cataloging-in-Publication Data

Gordon, Emily Fox, 1948–
It will come to me / Emily Fox Gordon. — 1st ed.
p. cm.
1. College teachers' spouses—Fiction. 2. College teachers—Fiction.
3. Domestic fiction. I. Title.
PS3607.O593618 2009
813'.6—dc22
2008029338

ISBN 978-0-385-52587-9

PRINTED IN THE UNITED STATES OF AMERICA

1 3 5 7 9 10 8 6 4 2

First Edition

For Emma Adelia Constantine

Though it was really one laugh
with a tear in the middle,
I counted it as two.

—J. M. BARRIE

It Will Come to Me

CHAPTER ONE

P rofessor Blau!" the student cried out, bounding up the steps.
A frenetic session of handshaking ensued, but Ruth could
see by Ben's warm vague smile that this young man had him at a
momentary disadvantage.

The student, or ex-student, was sandy-haired and sunburnt.
His aviator sunglasses hung from a braided leather cord around
his neck. Now he was telling them about his year as an intern
in a senator's office and how he'd gotten into the Stanford program. Remember Alison, his girlfriend? She was in med school
and they were getting married in December. Here he glanced
shyly at Ruth.

A pause. The preliminaries had been gotten through, and
Ruth knew all too well what would happen next. The student
would ask Ben's advice and Ben would dispense it. Ruth would
stand there, trapped and excluded, shifting from one foot to the

other in an ecstasy of boredom. Twenty minutes, forty minutes. At some point the conversation would begin to wind down. After a long diminuendo of farewells the student would excuse himself. But even then, the danger would not have passed. It had happened more than once that even as Ben's interlocutor had turned and taken several steps away, Ben remembered some final piece of advice—a colleague to look up, a course to avoid—and actually called the student back. The coffin sprang open and the grinning corpse of the conversation sat bolt upright.

Now was the moment to slip away. She smiled her quick sideways smile at Ben, who was too involved in talk to notice, and withdrew to the stone railing. Looking down, she saw a scene of young people standing in conversational knots. This place, known as Nirvana, was the graduate-student bar, a beer-dispensing station operating out of the basement of the chemistry building. Patrons descended into that dank grotto to order their seventy-five-cent bocks and lagers and carried them up into the light of late afternoon to drink them under the dappled shade of live oaks. They arrayed themselves around the grounds of the building, sitting on benches, leaning against brick, ranged along the steps of the external stone staircase leading to the second floor. Nirvana was a chronically endangered institution. For years, a counselor at the Wellness Center had been waging a letter-writing campaign against it in the student paper, and the proprietors had recently been put on notice that it would be shut down by the university if a handicapped ramp was not installed.

Ben liked to spend an hour or two here on a Friday afternoon perched at the very top of the stone steps, where he could pick his students out of the crowd, or those of his colleagues—not many showed up—to whom he wanted to speak. Ruth had pointed out

several times that he was just as visible to people down there as
they were to him, but the panoramic view seemed to make him
feel secure. On these occasions he drank one beer, two at most.
Ruth drank two and wanted two more.

She looked down directly on the neatly parted blond head of
a young woman who stood flanked by two tall young men. One
was carrying a sleeping newborn in a front pack. The other had a
receding hairline and an Adam's apple like a swallowed anvil. The
patrons here were mostly graduate students, some as old as forty,
but their faces were so unmarked as to seem hardly human. Faculty members tended to stay young too, she'd noticed—perhaps
it was the sea of youth washing over them year after year. And
when they did begin to show age the effect was often stagy and
unconvincing, as though they'd achieved it by powdering their
hair and applying grease pencil to the lines around their mouths.

Ruth stole a glance at Ben, who was listening to the student
with unfeigned interest. How the student glowed in the light of
his attention. Or perhaps that was just his youth, just his health.
Ben had turned sixty a few weeks ago, but he was still broad in
the shoulder and trim at the waist. Standing in shadow he could
almost pass for a graduate student. Could she? Certainly not,
though she dressed as though she hoped to, in black jeans and
clogs and dangling silver earrings.

As faculty brat and faculty wife (or spouse, as the euphemism
had it) and occasional adjunct instructor, she'd always been a
member of what the administration liked to call the "university
community." Though she was permitted to use the gym and the
libraries and included under the umbrella of the university's medical and dental insurance, she was not, apparently, covered by the
stay-young policy. She was fifty-six, and looked it. But recently

she'd discovered one of the benign perplexities of aging: despite the increasing efforts she made to conceal them, the cosmetic changes didn't bother her terribly. In the last few years she'd watched the pleating of the flesh under her chin and the deepening of the seams that ran down her cheeks with a certain dismay but also with an oddly detached sense of satisfaction. It was very much the way she felt twenty-five years ago when she was pregnant, standing nude in front of a full-length mirror, assessing the swelling of her belly. *It's coming along,* had been her thought then, and that was her thought now too. *Coming right along.* How was it, then, that most nights she lay awake at three in the morning, brooding about age and death?

Looking down again, she counted three toddlers in the crowd. One slumped in a backpack, blankly mouthing a pacifier. Two staggered unsteadily through a forest of adult legs. They made a pleasant enough sight, she supposed, if one was in a mood to find it so. She wasn't. Instead, she was feeling irritated, as she often did these days. Why, she asked herself, does nothing ever happen? This was a drinking establishment, but no place could be safer or duller. The presence of children made it duller still. Somebody should tell the wellness counselor not to worry: in all the years she and Ben had been coming here, she'd never seen anyone betray even the mildest symptom of intoxication. It was as if some odorless gas had been released into the air, rendering all these fit young people perfectly placid and well behaved. There were no brawls, no loud laughter, no raised voices, none of the intense intellectual talk Ruth would have liked to become embroiled in. Or would she? She used to think of herself as an aggressive debater, but she'd grown shy in recent years, conscious of all she didn't know, easily flummoxed by a challenge.

. . .

None of Ben's students knew it anymore, and neither did most young faculty, but twenty-five years ago Ruth had been a writer of some small note. Her first book, published by an academic press, was a collection of carefully crafted short stories in the *New Yorker* style which got little attention and was reviewed only in the local paper. Under the influence of Alison Lurie's *The War Between the Tates,* she went on to try her hand at a short novel—a novella, really—about an assistant professor of ethics with a bullying, womanizing chairman and a passive, contemplative wife. *Moral Turpitude* was its title, and it happened to catch the attention of a prominent reviewer, who called it "sharply observed." Encouraged, she produced another, *In These Halls,* with the same cast of characters. "Refreshing!" a second critic said, so she wrote a third, *Getting Good.* Her publisher packaged the books as a trilogy under that title, which was duly hailed as "acid," "biting," and "caustic." The volume sold surprisingly well and Ruth was summoned to New York and fed cold salmon at lunch by her publisher.

Then Isaac was born, and in the milky dreamy years of early motherhood she found she'd lost access to whatever capacity it was that had called forth all those low-pH adjectives. She looked for it again when he started school, and discovered it was still gone. Not that she stopped writing entirely. During Isaac's early adolescence her time was divided among part-time teaching, volunteer work, and consultations with his therapists and teachers, but even so, she produced three hundred pages of an unfinished novel. Three years ago, at the advice of her own therapist, she enrolled in a local writing program, where she was the oldest student in all her workshops. She dropped out in the middle of her third semester. For a year after that she worked in fits and starts on another novel, *Whole Lives Devoured,* two hundred pages of which now lay ignored in a disordered pile on her desk.

The paperback of the *Getting Good* trilogy had long since gone out of print, but you could find it in secondhand bookstores, sometimes in the dollar bins out in the street. She could spot it on a shelf fifty yards away, a compact, chunky book with a pastel three-stripe cover design, like a slab of Neapolitan ice cream. Every once in a while—less and less frequently as the years went by—she would be introduced to someone who would stare at her hard for a moment and blurt out, "You wrote *Getting Good,* didn't you?" Ruth would blush violently and say yes. Yes, that was me.

Now, with Isaac out of the house, she found she could summon forth any amount of useless bile. At a Philosophy Department potluck dinner last spring she had posted herself in the kitchen doorway and observed. How, she asked herself, would she make use of the scene she was watching? If she squinted hard enough to blur the identities of the guests, she could imagine, just for a moment, evidence of sexual tension in the interaction between a statuesque graduate student and a married faculty member. But it didn't last. There was nothing predatory in his posture, nothing seductive in hers. Could she hope at least that they were sharing confidences? Probably not. More likely they were complaining about the delinquencies of the registrar's office or the campus parking situation.

That party. It was like a hundred others. The table was laden with the ruminant foods brought by faculty members (quinoa salads and lentil casseroles) and the childish sweets contributed by graduate students (lopsided cakes and giant cookies embedded with M&M's). Guests grazed at the table, milled through the rooms of the house, paused to take inventory of the books on the shelves. Looking at these people, many of whom she liked, she felt a mild astonishment. My, they were dull!

It wasn't that Ruth wanted to promote adulterous liaisons between faculty members and graduate students. All she asked for was a world where the expectations of her childhood might be borne out—a world of background and foreground, light and shadow, up and down. One day when she was ten or eleven, a pair of lovers, both faculty members, both married to others, had come to her parents to confess their intention to run away together. They literally appeared on the doorstep after lunch. Ruth's parents led them into Ruth's father's study—he was a classics professor at a small New England college—where all afternoon the lovers petitioned for their blessing. Ruth's parents gave them a sympathetic hearing but refused to sanction their plan. There were intervals of shouting, a few blasts of anarchic laughter from the man, much quiet sobbing from the woman. Pressing her ear against the door, Ruth heard it all.

What she needed was a world in which such excitements were at least hypothetically possible. It wasn't that she wished to enter into them herself. That was in fact exactly what she didn't want. She was entirely dependent on other people to act it out for her, to provide her with something to observe, something to record, something to speculate about. She didn't require anything splashy; at this point she'd settle for a malicious glint in somebody's eye, a quick exchange of sympathetic glances. But here on this quiet Southern campus she was apparently living at the end of history. There was nothing to write about, no affairs, no scandals, no feuds of any but the pettiest kind. There were

misfortunes, more and more of them medical, but misfortune is
not the stuff of novels, at least not the kind she wanted to write.
There were a number of difficult people, certainly, but in most
cases they were discreetly ignored. The expectation was that eventually, like tired children, they would learn to comfort themselves
and go to sleep.

Dull. Dull dull dull. Nirvana was dull. Potluck dinners were
dull. Convocations were dull, but luckily she was excused
from attending them. Lectures were almost always dull. The department picnic was so dull—four hours of desultory softball in
the blazing late-May sun—that she pleaded with Ben to be let
out of it. She herself was dull. The other day Ben had run a finger
along her cheek and told her she had a pleasant face. A pleasant
face!

Of all the dull events in the academic calendar, the annual
dinner honoring university chair holders was, in the end, the
dullest. It was also acutely frustrating, because it got her hopes
up. The chair-holder dinner was the only dress-up occasion of the
year. It held the promise of a little glitter, a little transcendence,
and every October, in spite of herself, she found herself looking
forward to it. There was a cocktail hour with real bar drinks and
white-jacketed waiters (they were undergraduates, but so what?)
circulating with trays of hors d'oeuvres. Ruth genuinely enjoyed
the early part of these evenings; she welcomed the chance to observe people from many different vantage points, all removed
from the action. She liked to patrol the outskirts of the party on
Ben's arm, pointing out to him the latitude with which some of
the honorees and their spouses interpreted the term "black tie."

Even so, there were always a few striking costumes to admire. Last year a quiet little wren of an Indian molecular biologist elicited gasps when she made her entrance in a midriff-baring white satin sari. And there were notables to be spotted—a very new dean, backed up against a wall by a pack of sycophants, or a recent hire in Anthropology with a shaved head and a tattooed neck. Not that there was anything particularly exciting about that: trendy academics were the tamest of exotics, utterly habituated to the academic preserve, declawed cheetahs paraded on jeweled leashes by the department chairs who acquired them.

Later, sitting at a round table in a partitioned-off section of a commons room, eating hard-to-identify morsels served in nests of frisée lettuce, she paid for her earlier pleasure. Typically she found herself seated next to a professor emeritus of engineering with two hearing aids. On her other side would be a mathematician, or an empty chair. Ben generally had better luck. His dinner partner was usually the conversation-starved wife of the engineer, who kept him occupied with anecdotes about her grandchildren.

Dessert was served and watery decaf was poured. The president of the university clinked his glass with his fork and bade various faculty members to come forward to receive praise and parchment scrolls. Then it was time to introduce the speaker, always an academic with a vaguely recognizable name and a long history of coziness with the president. "Now I don't want to tell tales about Old Joe here," the beaming, swaying president would begin. He'd throw an arm around Old Joe's shoulders, launch into a story about Old Joe's paradoxical modesty, his self-effacing collegiality, his heroic integrity. He'd detail the many presidential commissions to which Old Joe had been named.

Then Old Joe (who was on alternate years a female) would

rise to speak. Last year's Old Joe had been a physicist, an academic of the spare, ascetic type, a perfect complement to the stout florid president. His topic was "The Role of the Arts in a Science-Oriented Curriculum." Ruth looked down at the collection of empty plates from which she had just fed. How could she have left herself no solace? Not a sip of wine remained, and the waiter who had filled her glass repeatedly during dinner had gone off duty. She saw him leaning insouciantly against a wall, a napkin drapped over his forearm. Not a crumb of cheesecake either. Across the table some anorexic had abandoned hers after taking two bites.

All through Old Joe's address her consciousness flickered, but she came to for long enough to register his rhetorical strategy. He was plowing through the arts, detailing the ways that each "keeps us human." She dropped off again, jolted awake at intervals by the muted detonation of one thuddingly inevitable phrase after another. Universal language. Vibrant tapestry. Enrich our spirit. But what really kept her from sleeping soundly through the after-dinner harrumphing and speechifying was an idiot voice that kept piping up inside her. What about me? this voice demanded. I know about *you*, Old Joe, but what about *me*?

At last there came a gentle rain of applause. Ben was standing at her back, a hand on her shoulder. Groggy and enraged, Ruth shrugged it off. It was the polite clapping that infuriated her, and Ben's complicity. How could these people sit still for this? They should be hurling water glasses, overturning tables. It wasn't just that Old Joe had subjected them to a collection of dozy platitudes. He'd also insulted their intelligence with his assumption that the arts serve a merely restorative function. Not that her dinner partner would object. And not, come to think of it, that she'd be any happier if the speaker had reversed his ordering of the importance of the arts and sciences. She was no arts booster. The ones she knew were irritating in their own right. There were many flavors of academic dullness; at this university it happened that the flintily dull taste of science predominated.

The guests rose. The president bellowed out his farewell and a reminder to guests to check under their chairs for the numbered sticker that matched the one on each table's floral centerpiece. Ruth won, as she often did. Clutching her prize she followed Ben through the crowd and out the door into the clarifying air of the evening. She had a throbbing white-wine headache, and on the way to the parking lot she hissed her complaints. Holding her arm tightly, Ben hustled her along, smiling tightly as they passed people they knew. Once the car doors were closed he turned to her and told her in a low steady voice how angry he was that she'd spoiled his pleasure in this occasion—which was, after all, intended to honor him. "You know what?" he said. "I don't like you when you drink."

It was true. Drinking made her angry. That was more readily apparent now than it had been fifteen years ago when she was angry all the time. These days she was relatively calm. Since menopause had taken her off the wheel of premenstrual instability she no longer shrieked at Ben for breathing audibly or flossing his teeth in front of the television. In some ways she'd gotten crankier, but it was a broad, level, abstract kind of crankiness. She could see a long way, standing here on this high plain of middle-aged equanimity, and what she saw disappointed her.

The fact was that she actually drank less than she used to, or at least less often, partly because now there was a physiological price to pay—heartburn, disturbed sleep, a flattened depression the following day. She knew a few women her age who had given up drinking entirely, but somehow it seemed essential to keep her hand in. Most nights she abstained entirely. But once a week, occasionally twice, she drank, always a little more than she should. She might drink a big martini, for example, followed by a beer. Or she might drink four glasses of wine. Or two beers followed by two glasses of wine, or the other way around. Many permutations, but always the same result: the genie of grandiosity was born in her chest. You're too intense, it told her, too original, too *brave* for these careful people. This meant Ben, so she picked a fight with him.

Time for another beer. She moved over to Ben and tapped him on the shoulder, holding up her plastic cup. "Get you one?" "Oh yes," he said, pulled back into the scene, "yes please." She turned inquiringly to the student, who flashed her a smile, held up his water bottle and mouthed, "I'm good." No you're not, she muttered to herself as she descended the steps from the second-floor terrace, stepping gingerly over pairs of outstretched legs. You're just conventional.

But not quite gingerly enough, because her foot caught on something that threw off her balance enough to send her lurching down several steps with her arms outstretched, breaking her fall against one student's chest and another student's shoulder and finally the stone balustrade at the foot of the stairs. She took a moment to examine the abraded palms of her hands, then turned to see what it was she'd tripped over. A purse? A bike helmet? No. Apparently it was a baby, a very small one, strapped into a car seat. A company of young couples had risen as a body to surround the baby's mother, who was sitting with her knees drawn up to her chest, cradling the baby in its car seat. Through a stand of heads and shoulders Ruth could quite clearly see the baby's face, an enraged knot of negative capability. All was eerily silent for a long moment, and then a great wail rose up and out of it.

"Oh, I'm so sorry," Ruth cried, pushing up the steps against a tide of concerned murmurers. A few faces turned her way. "Please!" she called out. "Let me through. I want to see . . ." The baby was crying lustily now. "I'm so sorry," Ruth repeated. "I just didn't see it. Is the baby OK?" The look the baby's mother gave her was not so much one of blame as of nonrecognition, as if she were unsure how to respond to a being that had yet to be classified and described. "I'm sorry," said Ruth again, but now a move was afoot to shoo people away so that the mother and baby could make their way down the stairs to the access road and into a waiting car, driven by a weedy young man Ruth assumed was the father. In a moment the crowd had closed up around the hole the resolved event had left. There was nothing for it but to climb down the remaining steps and make her way around the corner, stonily ignoring what she took to be looks of disapproval, to the wide-planked wooden door that led down a final flight of stairs to the basement where the kegs were kept.

The barroom, if it could be called that, made her think of a festive antique submarine; it was a dark, smoky, air-conditioned cylinder with pale-green plaster walls, hung year-round with twinkling holiday lights. Down here was where the electricians drank, the maintenance men, the guys from buildings and grounds— the proles. A space alien happening to wander down from the upstairs aspect of Nirvana might conclude that he'd stumbled upon an entirely distinct species, like the underground Morlocks who terrorize the gentle Eloi in H. G. Wells's *The Time Machine.* Up above among the academics, the rule was quiet and moderation; down here it was noise and excess. For every beer the academics drank the proles drank three. At a recent dinner party the topic of alcohol abuse downstairs at Nirvana had come up—Ruth, in fact, had been the one to raise it. One of Ben's colleagues made a prissy observation about how it certainly couldn't be good for anyone's health to drink that much, and a sociologist mumbled something about shortened time horizons.

The proles smoked and guffawed. When they threw back their heads in laughter she could see that they'd lost molars. They coughed wetly and hung on one another, stumbled a little as they dismounted their stools to head for the bathroom, flirted lewdly with the occasional stubby female who joined them at the bar. Whenever a young woman from above invaded the proles' territory they fell awkwardly silent, but when Ruth appeared among them to order her three beers (one for Ben, one for her now, one for her later) they seemed hardly to register her existence. She was neither one thing nor the other to them, she supposed, neither daughter nor wife. Though once, a few years ago, a redheaded prole resting his head on the bar had peered up at her craftily and told her she looked like Carol Burnett.

Clutching her three beers to her chest, she shuffled across the floor Geisha-style, doing her best not to spill. Even so, several ounces sloshed down her front. She found a seat on a bench in a quiet corner where the chess players sometimes sat. These were representatives of yet another nonfaculty tribe, the computer technicians and audiovisual specialists, who signaled their class affiliation by wearing button-down short-sleeved shirts and hooking their cell phones to their belts. The walls around the chess corner were rich with graffiti. There were the usual offers of sexual favors attributed to third parties, accompanied by the phone numbers of those third parties, the usual crude drawings of phalluses. There was also a kind of minimalist poem, written out vertically in spidery pencil:

BOB
CAN
SLOB
ON
MY
KNOB

Sitting here, an unobserved observer, she took note of the scene: the LET'S OBEY THE LAW, PEOPLE sign painted in bold letters on the tented ceiling above the bar; the proles swarming around it like piglets on a sow; the two aging, enigmatic hippie proprietors manning the taps. This was exactly the kind of vantage point Ruth instinctively sought: a wall at her back, a pocket of shadow in which to take shelter, an unobstructed view. She wished she could stay down here all evening, enjoying the cool darkness and the tranquilizing thud and shake of the jukebox.

An idea came to her. Perhaps here, right here in downstairs Nirvana, she'd found the material she'd been looking for in vain upstairs, the elemental stuff, the mother lode of passion and con-flict. And wouldn't it be interesting to make a study of the proles, to investigate their lives. She could see the research stretching out ahead through the fall and winter months, and then in the spring she could start the actual writing. But could she really sustain this vision of the proles as embodiments of Dionysian vitality?

How much passion and conflict can be generated in a life spent waxing and buffing cafeteria floors or driving a gnome cart? She felt a little ashamed to catch herself entertaining such a fatuous notion. The proles worked harder than she could imagine. It was unbecoming in her to envy them the solace of boozy camaraderie, to entertain fantasies about infiltrating their society.

And besides, she'd never get up the nerve to approach them— not unless she drank a very great deal. And what would happen then? The last time she'd spent a lot of time in a bar was more than thirty years ago, before she was married. She and a friend had rented a cabin in the Adirondacks. They fell into a habit of spending evenings at a lakeside roadhouse, where the locals bought them round after round of beer and told them tales of unfaithful wives and children lost to custody disputes. Boredom and curiosity had been the rationale for this early fieldwork, and the result was that she was backed into several dark corners and several tongues were thrust down her throat. That wouldn't happen now, would it? Not that she'd want it to, but perhaps it was the price of access. She hadn't appreciated then how universally accepted a passport her nubility was. She saw that only in retrospect, as she was seeing so many things. How dim she'd been then, how unable to assess herself! If telepathic communications could be directed backward through time, she'd whisper a message to the Ruth of 1972, the one who used an army-surplus shell canister as a purse and wore her luxuriant auburn hair in a badly maintained long shag: *You are sexually adequate.*

She'd heard it said that you don't feel old on the inside, and it was true. She didn't feel old or even middle-aged. Instead, she felt every age she'd ever been—every age, that is, except the age she was. Her variously aged selves were so active within her that she pictured herself as a kind of human lava lamp; the glowing mass of self-stuff continually heaving and stretching into twin and triplet blobs and then into great bubbling litters which reconvened and merged once again, if only briefly, into one. What was the age of that reconstituted self? About thirty-four.

It cost her an effort to remember that the proles were not older than she was, as those men at the roadhouse had been. They were not even her contemporaries. They were younger—a lot younger. Hard living and poverty and self-neglect had aged them at a much faster rate than the academics, but the fact was that she had fifteen years on most of them, twenty years on some. Yes, she was neither daughter nor wife. If anything, she was mother, but not the kind of mother they'd have in mind. If she was mother she was a tall, angular, bluestocking kind of mother who wore a lot of black—a hag, in other words. But no, she wasn't a hag. Nothing so definite as that. She was simply unplaceable, and hence invisible.

Carrying a full plastic cup of beer in one hand and a slightly less full one in the other, she climbed the basement stairs and rejoined her own kind. The cast of characters who had witnessed the baby-upending incident had been replaced. She was once again merely an arty-looking faculty wife, the object of quick, mildly curious glances, mostly from women assessing her clothes and jewelry. Climbing the steps, she saw that Ben and the student were gone. They'd been replaced by two preteen girls who sat front to back and cross-legged on the landing at the head of the steps, one French-braiding the other's hair. She suspected they were the children of somebody she knew. Should she greet them? As she registered this small social worry, a larger anxiety displaced it. Where *was* Ben? It wasn't like him to disappear. Why hadn't he come looking for her? Was he angry? Fed up in a final kind of way? Had he never existed at all and had their thirty years of marriage been a hallucination, as in the plot of a made-for-TV movie she'd watched the other night when she couldn't sleep? She stopped, turned in a slow circle to look for Ben, drained the slightly less than full beer in one long pull.

She walked up the exterior steps to take up her old post on the terrace by the stone railing, the backs of her knees aching. It was dusk now and the air had cooled. The hazard lights of the cars parked along the inner campus loop made a long blinking chain and the branches of the big live oak overhanging the chemistry building rustled faintly in the evening breeze. Looking down, she could see that the gathering had swelled to half again its earlier size. Something had shifted; the change in light had become a change in tone. The faces of its constituents obscured by darkness, the crowd below her had taken on a sluggish malevolence; it seemed to Ruth that it was beginning to seethe and shudder like water coming to a boil. In her present dilated and paranoid state it was easy to envision the graduate students as a zombie army or a convocation of pod people. She could see them trickling in from all directions, appearing from out of the shadows at the summons of the Hive Mind, assembling to take up torches and stagger stiffly across the campus and out into the world, where they would find new campuses in which to take root and propagate.

Where was Ben? She wanted to tell him about this fantasy. He would find it amusing, and she would take comfort in his willingness to point out the obvious—that of course the graduate students were not undead but living human beings with emotions and aspirations. She would say yes, but that was just her point.

They were people, young people. So where were the extremes in their natures? They were a stunningly docile bunch. It was as if they'd been deprived of some vitamin since birth—or, more likely, given too much of one. Not only did they not compete with one another; they seemed to do their best not to distinguish themselves. Their idiosyncrasies were superficial—trademark hats, nicknames, the occasional tattoo. Their entertainments were childlike, green beer on St. Patrick's Day, heart-shaped cakes on Valentine's. The girls liked to bake and tended to gain weight. The boys watched sports and moped.

They were utterly unlike the wolfish, haggard, chain-smoking graduate students of Ruth's youth. She found it hard to remember that the ones who belonged to Ben were studying philosophy; to all appearances they might have been working on MBAs or degrees in physical therapy. They were very kind to one another, much more so than her own peers had been, and touchingly polite to their elders. But where was their complexity? Where was their angst? And—this was really baffling—where was their lust? It seemed to Ruth that they shied away from one another sexually. Ben disagreed; he was quite sure they got up to plenty because, he said, young people always do. You just want them to, said Ruth—you wish *you'd* gotten up to plenty. But they won't oblige you. They're too careerist.

You could find them in the library at all hours. Their dedication to their goals was steady and dogged, but what drove them was a desire for security, not distinction. They were working for a place of their own in the academic preserve—that, and tenure. They wanted to be marsupials, creatures with no natural enemies who could look forward to living out their days in absolute safety. The graduate students were good children. It was unfair to compare them to zombies. If anyone was undead it was their professors.

The graduate students were anxious. Ruth could sympathize with that. But it was hard to tell what motivated some of Ben's colleagues. Their emotional repertoire was extremely limited, the spectrum ranging from blank contentment to donnish amusement to agitated peevishness. They were peaceable souls—apart from the occasional mystifying temper tantrum—and utterly undefended.

Twice, over the years of Ben's career at this university, a throwback had appeared, a creature with a full set of claws and teeth and an inclination to use them. The first, a Simone Weil scholar in the Religion Department, sued the university when she failed to receive a prize. In the process, she publicly accused two of her male colleagues of sexual improprieties. The result was a cascade of marital breakups, some directly traceable to the accusations, others less so. That had happened twenty years ago, the university's last major scandal, remembered now by almost nobody. The Weil scholar, her lank blond hair gone gray, continued to walk the corridors, though she wasn't given a lot of committee assignments.

More recently a Kant specialist in Ben's department defamed his colleagues to the dean when his demands for a large raise and a reduced teaching load went unmet by the chair. The department's reaction—Ben's too, though he raged privately—was to roll onto its back and expose its belly. Ben and his colleagues humored this man, whose name was Dwight Fremser, worked around him. They managed this without complaints, without spiteful asides; their forbearance was extraordinary. Eventually he left to take a chair at Emory. Ben had just taken over as chair and Ruth had to host a farewell dessert party for the Fremsers, who were sweet-toothed teetotalers. She and Ben had the worst fight of the second half of their marriage that night. This had happened only three years ago, but already the department's collective memory had gone dim. Academics, it seemed, have trouble holding the idea of human evil before their minds. By now, the era of Dwight was only a Bad Time Long Ago.

A small flurry of activity pulled her eyes to the sundial plaza across the access road. Under a streetlamp, two small boys were bedeviling a golden retriever with sticks. The scene reminded Ruth of one of those side panels in an illuminated medieval manuscript, meant to portray a minor saint undergoing some incidental scourging. "Bad boy!" they shrieked in unison. "Bad boy!" The dog sank slowly onto its haunches, its tail still thumping. The children continued; the dog ducked its big head to one side and winced. Ruth clutched her ears. It was cruel! Somebody should *do* something. Tears sprang to her eyes and a noise escaped her that might have been a theatrical scream of protest, but was in fact a creaking groan audible only to herself. As if in answer a young woman in khaki shorts—presumably the children's mother—trotted across the street and took them by their wrists, leaning down to remonstrate with them softly as she led them away from the dog, which shook itself briefly and trotted off, the stupid resilient thing.

Ben's hand was on her shoulder. "Look who I found," he said.

Ruth turned. It was Ben's colleague Bob Bachman and his wife, Barbara, and no wonder he sounded triumphant. The Bachmans were not often seen at Nirvana. They were chamber-music devotees, gallery-opening attenders. Discovering them here was like sighting a pair of flamingos in New Hampshire. Ruth gave her damp eyes a quick swipe with the back of her wrist and extended her cheek to be kissed.

The Bachmans were a very small couple who lived in a large house with the youngest two of their four very good children. Bob was a historian of science. Ruth had nothing against him. Barbara had trained as a psychologist, but had given up her profession when her children were born. Recently she'd taken a part-time position as a researcher in the Medical School.

The Bachman family had never owned a television. The Bachman children, whose names were Maya, Noah, Joel, and Ariel, were exemplary; their science-fair projects were the stuff of legend. They all played stringed instruments and every November the Bachmans rented folding chairs and invited the humanities faculty to a family musicale in their living room. For years, Ruth had been waiting for one of the children to manifest signs of mental illness, but in abrogation of all the laws of action and reaction, it hadn't happened. Not only were all four of them accomplished; they were sane and happy and genuinely nice, and Ruth was left to chew the bitter cud of envy and resentment. The bill for her own apparently incorrect child-rearing practices had come due. She'd been wrong, and even if twelve-year-old Joel Bachman was picked up for cocaine possession, she would not be vindicated.

"What brings you here?" she asked, and was relieved to hear that it sounded like a plausible conversational gambit. "Well," said Bob, "do you remember Frames for Less?" He was a confiding, vole-like man, famous for the puzzling way he began at the periphery and moved elliptically toward the center of any thought.

Barbara was equally famous for the vigorous way she stepped in to make sense of his orphic utterances. "We're meeting an old student of Bob's and then we're having dinner at that new Afghani place where Frames for Less used to be. Can you join us?"

Ben gave their excuses—tiredness, teaching day tomorrow, casserole defrosting. Barbara registered these by nodding once, emphatically. Then, pivoting on her heel, she turned toward Ruth, effectively forcing her to step back a few inches. Barbara was one of those people with no regard for the rules of personal space. Tiny though she was, she stood her ground so squarely that in her presence Ruth felt weak and wavy, like some pallid underwater plant. "So," Barbara said, crossing her arms in front of her chest, "Ruth. Looking well. Up to what?"

"Not a lot," said Ruth. Name, rank, and serial number was her rule with Barbara, but sometimes she found herself saying more than she had intended and then, to explain or qualify the too much she had said, she felt compelled to say still more, giving Barbara material to exploit in future interrogations.

"Ah," said Barbara, in her characteristic I-know-you-better-than-you-know-yourself tone. "Now that I don't believe. You are one person who is *always* up to something, at least up here." She tapped her temple. "Weren't you telling us about some fascinating idea for a novel? About Alzheimer's?"

Ruth had been afraid she'd remember this. Six or eight months ago the Bachmans had hosted one of their entertainments, a blind wine-tasting followed by parlor games. At the end of the evening, when she and Ben were standing in the foyer in a crowd of guests attempting to get past Barbara and out the door, Barbara asked her what she was writing these days. Feeling exposed and embarrassed and suspecting that Barbara knew quite well she wasn't writing anything, Ruth mumbled that she'd been working on a novel about Alzheimer's entitled *It Will Come to Me.*

"What's that?" Barbara had asked, sharply enough to turn heads. "A novel about what?" "Alzheimer's," said Ruth. Suddenly she was at the center of an urgent buzz of discussion. Everyone had something urgent to say. Stories about relatives who suffered from the condition. Reports of new research pointing to the benefits of fish oil. Other reports implicating the heavy metals found in farm-raised fish. Millicent McCordle, an elderly classicist married to another elderly classicist, tugged at her sleeve and confided that she'd been worrying recently about forgetting names. "Oh, I'm no expert, Millicent," said Ruth. It was another twenty minutes before they got out the door.

"I'm sorry, Barbara," she said now. "That was a joke." "Ah," said Barbara. "I see. A joke." A small puzzled smile played around her lips. "A joke. About Alzheimer's." As she considered this she allowed her gaze to wander out over the twinkling night campus. "Oh yes," she said, as if recalling herself from an absence. "I've been meaning to ask you. How's Isaac? Just the other day I saw a study . . ."

CHAPTER TWO

B en's office was on the third floor of Horace Dees Hall, newly built in memory of Horace Deming Dees, former director of the board of trustees. Horace Dees was the great-nephew of Lola Dees, founder of the university which began ninety years ago as the Lola Dees Institute. To the world these days it was LDI; to residents of Spangler, Texas, it was Loladees, emphasis on the third syllable; to students and faculty it was Lola. As the LDI Raptors loped onto the football field the brass section of the marching band blared "Whatever Lola Wants, Lola Gets." And when, as sometimes happened, the Raptors scored a touchdown, the crowd rose to its feet and bellowed out a chorus of the old song by the Kinks:

Well I'm not the world's most masculine man
But I know what I am and I'm glad I'm a man

And so is Lola.

Lo-lo-lo-lo LOLA, lo-lo-lo-lo LOLA . . .

Even if athletics was not its strong suit, Spangler was proud of Loladees. "The Harvard of the South," they called it. The school was highly rated and hard to get into; the students were earnest and well behaved. If they were geeks, Spanglerites loved them all the more for it, as they would have loved an odd bright late-born child. They smiled indulgently at the tame university-sanctioned pranks that were part of orientation week every fall. They treated the faculty with a deference usually found in German university towns; Ben never tired of hearing himself addressed as *"Doc*tuh Blau." The university was strongest in the sciences, particularly in physics and engineering and microtechnology. A few years earlier a study committee had been appointed to consider how better to balance the curriculum, and when it was decided to free up a portion of the university's considerable endowment to build Horace Dees Hall, it was also decided that the building would serve as the new home of the humanities departments.

The doors of the new building had opened a year ago, admitting a stream of historians and metaphysicians and Chaucer scholars. All of them had come from a diaspora of small dark offices in departmental rabbit warrens, where secretaries were wedged into spaces between filing cabinets, junior faculty banished to carrels in the basement of the library, graduate teaching assistants forced to conduct student conferences in the halls. The space and light and palatial proportions of the new building were almost too much for them. They wandered blinking into the great ground-floor lobby with its marble floors and mosaic murals and made their dazed way through wide, gracious hallways to their new high-ceilinged offices, all of them carpeted in smart beige-and-black tweed and fitted with mahogany desks and commodious built-in bookshelves. Each had its own upholstered reading chair and Swedish-designed reading lamp. A few had fireplaces.

Even now, the building smelled faintly of new plaster and paint. As Ben walked along the hall from the elevator to his office he passed a display of photographs of the university's first four graduating classes, groups of seven and twenty and thirty-five and fifty, standing in black frock coats and ankle-length white dresses in front of the lone brick building that was the Lola Dees Institute in those days, surrounded on all sides by tuffed prairie. Peering into these pictures, examining the stern young faces preserved under glare-free glass, Ben found it impossible not to feel a little thrilled at how far the university had come, and how far he had come as well. He was probably a fathead, he admitted to himself, to feel this way; his colleagues would scoff if they knew. Their attitude toward the new home the university had provided them had advanced very quickly from gratitude to skepticism, and in some cases from skepticism to resentment. The grumbling in the halls had started before Thanksgiving: How was it that all the humanities departments—including political science and sociology and anthropology, which for reasons no one could remember had long been members of the division—were expected to occupy a single building when physics and chemistry and engineering each had their own? Hadn't they been relegated to a golden ghetto? Wasn't there a marginalizing impulse at work here, hiding behind the show of largesse? It was undeniable that the results of throwing them all in together had been mixed. Old enmities had been exacerbated by new proximities. Somebody was probably making notes for a study even now.

Ben's office—a chair's office—was half again the size of his colleagues' and equipped with a mini-fridge stocked with bottles of mineral water and a modular leather couch and a Brobdingnagian glass coffee table mounted on a pitted concrete pillar. One wall was all but taken up with a multipaned, floor-to-ceiling window looking down over a park of live oaks run through with brick walkways. Ben tended to keep his distance from the window: its size and clarity frightened him. He never felt quite comfortable in the office, never quite unobserved. He'd found that he was unable to do his own writing in this bright room; since the move to the humanities building he'd been working on his altruism manuscript at home in the mornings and coming into the office in the afternoons. He found it difficult to read here as well. The light was excellent and the armchair quite comfortable, but for some reason he couldn't bring himself to fling his leg over its armrest. He felt obliged to sit stiffly upright.

This morning, the first day of classes, he was sitting in that armchair inching his way through an article entitled "Hard and Soft Duties" in *Acta Ethica Scandinaviensis.* After twenty minutes he flung the journal aside and moved to his desk to sort through the conference fliers and lecture announcements and publishers' catalogs he'd found in his mailbox. Checking his e-mail, he found a communication from his editor at Priggers Learning, reminding him that the third edition of *Social Ethics: Problems, Principles, and Prospects,* Blau and Federman, editors, was due to go into production in less than a month. Bruce Federman was one of those academics who spends most semesters on leave in pleasant places like Florence or Geneva. At the moment, he was in Majorca, having left all the work of putting together the third edition to Ben.

Next came four requests for letters of recommendation. Two of these had come from graduate students for whom he had letters on file that would take only a few minutes to adapt. The third was from an undergraduate major who'd gone on to do graduate work at NYU and was now on the job market. He remembered her as a capable but odd girl whose affect was so disturbingly flat that encounters with her left him feeling as if he'd just stepped out of a high-speed elevator. She suffered from chronic postnasal drip; her classmates complained about her disruptive snorts and swallowings. Hard to imagine what kind of teacher she'd make, but he'd learned how to leave a soft spot here and there on the otherwise tautly inflated surfaces of these recommendations to convey reservations he couldn't make explicit. The last was from a student he'd apparently taught eleven years ago, of whom he had no memory. There were no computer records from that era and the physical files had long since been moved from academic offices to a morgue in the basement of the administration building. The days when he could have wandered down there and looked through the files himself were over; he'd have to go through an elaborate procedure to initiate a search for this student's transcript. Or Dolores would, if he could bring himself to delegate such a small task, or perhaps the work-study student.

Finally, there was a memo from Roberta Mitten-Kurz, the humanities dean. "Dear Colleague" it began:

As you may remember, the on-site review team from SCAC will be visiting campus this fall. This is the next step in the accreditation process. As you were cautioned last spring, these visits can occur anytime during the semester. Please be aware that members of the SCAC team have been charged with the task of interviewing faculty members and staff and visiting classes unannounced.

SCAC was the acronym for Southern Collegiate Assessment Commission, an initiative aimed at enforcing accreditation standards according to a purportedly objective set of criteria. Grades, he understood, wouldn't do—too subjective—and neither would student transcripts. Instead, the dean's office barraged department chairs with forms and questionnaires and charts and long explanatory memos, all of which Ben had been ignoring for months. There had been some mention of keeping writing samples for entering freshmen on file and comparing them to writing samples produced at graduation, but that seemed so manifestly unfeasible that he'd forgotten it instantly.

Ben's style as chair had always been minimalist and laissez-faire. He had no particular interest in special programs or cross-disciplinary dialogue, only in maintaining the department's day-to-day functioning and, when necessary, making sound hiring decisions. His colleagues didn't seem to mind. He'd heard a rumble or two about administrative dissatisfaction but that hadn't bothered him. Fine, he thought. Let them find another chair. Muriel Draybrooke, for example, who wore the same egg-yolk-encrusted seersucker jacket day in and day out, or Stuart Dilbert, who raised pointless objections in faculty meetings and whose toneless bray put everyone's back up. Ben had no great investment in the job. He was doing it, in fact, for the fairly unselfish reason that he was the only member of the department both capable and willing. He'd seen no reason to pay the SCAC business much attention. He'd understood it as yet another ambitious bureaucratic scheme, the kind that blew in and out of Lola with the regularity of storms from the Gulf.

But the mention of a "next step" in the process alarmed him. What had the previous one or ones been, and how had it or they escaped him? And when had he been "cautioned"? He didn't recall being cautioned. The memo continued:

It is crucial that every member of the Lola community understands that these visitors from SCAC have been trained in best assessment practices. Any inappropriate affect or failure to identify with the aims of the assessment process may result in long-term adverse consequences.

"Inappropriate affect . . . long-term adverse consequences"? Ben was staring at these words when Dolores leaned into the room. "Excuse me," she said. "We've got a little problem. Maintenance can't go into Irv's office." Ben raised a temporizing finger. He wanted a moment to absorb the import of this memo and think through its implications, and he wanted to do that without consulting Dolores—though he knew quite well that eventually he'd cave and ask her for help.

Dolores was a Jeeves of a secretary, calm and methodical, able, if necessary, to run the department with very little assistance from Ben. Without her he would never have been able to keep the banker's hours that made it possible for him to prepare for his classes and make any kind of steady progress on *The Necessity of Altruism*. Inside her small neat head was a history of the university going back to the late sixties, a map of its labyrinthine bureaucracy, a glossary of acronyms in current use, a file of medical and marital case histories. She could be trusted to keep these last to herself, except when some grave faux pas was about to be committed. Nobody was better at placating students with grievances, discouraging persistent textbook salesmen, showing the door to the Sephardic nut who cruised the hallways looking for Ashkenazim to berate. She was the envy of all the other humanities chairs, many of whom were saddled with snippy timeservers who could never be fired. On the occasion of her twenty-fifth year of service to the university, the dean gave a reception in her honor. Five of her seven children and a dozen of her grandchildren attended. Her husband, a retired AT&T lineman, held her purse as she accepted flowers and praise and a commemorative plaque.

Dolores lingered in the doorway; evidently this was a problem that couldn't wait. Ben got up and followed her into her office, where an unfamiliar custodian stood waiting. "Professor Blau," said Dolores—Ben had trained her to call him by his first name, but she insisted on using his title in the presence of students and workmen—"this is Roman. He's new in the building." Roman looked to be roughly Ben's age, about six inches shorter, but powerfully built. His gray hair was full and springy, his shoulders broader than Ben's, his feet in lace-up work boots larger. Ben extended his hand—he'd been raised to consider a handshake a wholesome, egalitarian gesture, appropriate in any circumstance. Roman's grip was deferentially gentle, his palms impressively calloused.

The formalities accomplished, Dolores and Roman resumed what was evidently a broken-off discussion. His tone was respectful but vehement, hers almost theatrically exasperated—Ben had noticed before that an entirely different Dolores emerged when she spoke Spanish with underlings. Eventually Roman threw up his hands, nodded to Ben, and left the room. "He says he's sorry," she explained. "They're not allowed to get involved with this kind of thing. Only basic cleaning. Come." She squared her shoulders and led him down the hall to Irv Dorfman's office.

The door to the office was open. Ben and Dolores stood at the threshold for a long moment. Ben's first impression was that a heavy spring snow had somehow accumulated on every surface, but in a moment he saw that in fact the office was knee-high in paper, layers and layers of it, corners curling in the low current of the air conditioner, which Irv had apparently left on when he departed for Heidelberg at the end of June. It was strange and marvelous and a little sad, this shifting, trembling field of white that seemed to generate its own hush. It put Ben in mind of a documentary he'd once seen, a handheld camera panning silently around the deserted squares of Chernobyl.

After a moment he noticed a faint sweetish odor, like mildly bad breath. On the windowsill was a row of small tarry heaps that had been peaches or plums in June. Irv had evidently left them there to ripen. And there was another smell; something subtly but pungently organic, a bass note that gained power as Ben and Dolores stood there at the threshold of the office, drawing its preserved air into their nostrils. Was it Irv himself, dead under the paper? He was an insulin-dependent diabetic, and lived such a lonely life that for a moment it seemed possible. But no; Ben had seen enough crime dramas on TV to know that a dead body would produce an overpowering stench, detectable throughout the building.

Dolores was standing well back in the hall. Her eyebrows were raised, her nostrils flared, the tendons in her neck visible. "Rat," she said.

.   .   .

They moved through the room in a slow spiral, Ben doing the stoop work, Dolores following with a plastic garbage bag. The idea was to start by removing any trash that came immediately to hand—food wrappers, Styrofoam cups, cardboard packaging. Under their feet things crunched and crackled. They'd been working for half an hour when Dolores stepped on a syringe. She waded out of the room to find Rhoda, the work-study student, who jogged across campus to the B&G building and borrowed two pairs of utility gloves. These turned out to be so bulky they made it impossible to sort through the paper. Ben took his off. "It's not as if he has HIV," he observed. Dolores gave him a quick startled look and removed hers.

The second phase of the job was more painstaking and intricate—the separation of important papers from miscellaneous mail and flyers and loose pages from *The Chronicle of Higher Education*. Their chief concern was to reconstruct the scattered manuscript of *The Technology of Being: The Being of Technology*, which Ben recognized from Irv's vita—ever since he could remember, it had been forthcoming from Modernahaus. Under a heap of those pages, January's issue of *The Journal of Speculative Cosmology* lay belly-up, opened to an article entitled "Taxa, Semi-Frequent Events, and Balescu Strings." Interspersed throughout were class and grade rosters, student papers, loose pages from student papers, pay stubs, and blank checks.

In the course of their excavations they disinterred a cheerful red-and-yellow-plaid couch and an ergonomic rocking chair. How odd, they both noted, that Irv had thought to buy his own furniture. What remained on the floor at this stage were the books, which they stacked neatly in a corner; a banana peel; a former avocado; several empty smoothie cups; and one smoothie cup half full of fulminating blue mold. There was a lot of loose change, a one-dollar bill, a five-dollar bill, several empty vials of insulin. Ben took a fresh garbage bag and began a last patrol of the room. "No," said Dolores. "Leave it. That's for Roman." The source of the bad animal smell turned out not to be a rat but a small bird, fallen into the fireplace from the chimney. It made Ben sad to think of it fluttering helplessly. Dolores laid the little heap of feathers in a Kleenex box and covered it with a layer of tissues.

The job nearly done, they came to a simultaneous, unspoken decision to sit down. After a moment Dolores got up and left the room, reappearing with two mugs of coffee—she remembered that Ben took his with a few drops of milk and no sugar. The two of them sat in companionable silence, surveying the room. The carpet was gritty and littered with detritus and glittering bits of broken things, but they had made order, and made it in an orderly way. Ben took satisfaction in that, and in knowing that Dolores took satisfaction in it too.

He couldn't help feeling close to her at this moment. She sat on the edge of Irv's ergonomic chair, ankles crossed, head modestly lowered. There was something touchingly childlike about the way she wrapped both hands around her coffee mug. It was rare to see Dolores in an attitude of unbustling repose, rare to get a chance to really look at her. She was small, with a round head and a sweet round face and plump, dimpled knees—smiling knees, he thought, and the thought made him smile. Her style of dress reminded him of his mother's tweed skirts, low-heeled shoes, heavy flesh-colored stockings, or panty hose, he supposed.

Whatever the weather, she always arrived at the office in a fully buttoned raincoat, a scarf tied under her chin. What did she make of the undergraduate girls, the ones with studs in their navels and jeans cut down to their pubes?

The raincoat and scarf put her in the company of the older women he remembered from his youth, the ones who seemed to spend their lives in grocery checkout lines, clutching coupons and counting out change. To his adolescent mind, no woman over forty seemed to have a reason for living other than a purely economic one. In unguarded moments that was still how he saw them. (But never Ruth; her wrinkles and sags seemed as accidental and nonessential as his own.) How old was Dolores? Somewhere between fifty and seventy. It was quite possible that she was younger than he was, perhaps younger than Ruth.

It seemed presumptuous to try to guess her age, but as he sat there facing her, the silence between them growing thick, it occurred to him that he could turn his mind to something more presumptuous yet. What would it be like, he asked himself, to entertain a sexual fantasy about Dolores? He was relieved to find that her rectitude was a force field strong enough to repel any such speculation. He had only to think about thinking about this to find his thought instantly rejected, like a crinkled dollar bill from a vending machine.

It seemed time to say something, so he said, "What do you think Irv would say if he walked in right now?" That was a blunder; he could see her shrink back a little in her seat. She must have thought he was inviting her to make fun of Irv. "Oh, I don't know," she answered, turning a faint smile toward the window, self-deprecation giving cover to her withdrawal.

"Maybe he'd just say thanks," said Ben, though he thought

it more likely that Irv would go pale with rage. He tried again. "How are your kids?" he asked, and then remembered that there were too many of them for a blanket inquiry. "How's Hector doing?" Hector was her youngest, in law school, the repository of much maternal pride. "Oh Hector is fine," said Dolores, looking up, smiling warmly. "He's taking his boards in December. We're keeping our fingers crossed."

"He'll do great. Still engaged to the same girl?"

"Brenda, yes. They're waiting to be done with school, both of them. She's in nursing school."

"And that'll make—how many of your kids are married?"

"That'll make seven. All seven."

"And maybe more grandchildren?"

"Yes! More!" Dolores threw out her arms. Her smile was roguish, glorious.

A pause. "And how is . . . ?" Dolores hazarded.

"Isaac." It was a measure of his habitual reticence on this subject that Isaac's name appeared to be missing from Dolores's exhaustive database. How often had it happened—in restaurants, at dinner parties, at halftime during basketball games, wherever his fellow academics congregated—that the conversation turned to the doings and accomplishments of adult and near-adult children? Every one of these, it seemed, was a fledgling lawyer or surgeon, or would be after a year spent building latrines in Central America. Whenever this topic came up, he and Ruth exchanged quick furtive looks: let this cup pass from us! But soon enough the assembled inquiring eyes would turn to them.

And then what would they say? That Isaac was twenty-four and not only had never attended college but had failed to graduate from high school? That the only job he'd ever held for more

than a week was as a dishwasher in a cantina where for some reason the proprietor had taken pity on him? That he was a great
shambling Goth with a spiked dog collar and a long filthy black
coat who mooched around the city streets—Ben had seen him
just the other day, coming out of a movie theater at four in the afternoon—wearing a pointed Merlin hat and a pair of split tennis
shoes? That he haunted the aisles of pornographic anime stores?
That Ben and Ruth hadn't spoken to him in nearly two years—
not entirely their fault, as Isaac's therapist (paid for by Ben) had
forbidden them any contact with their son. That his last communication before he went to ground had been a crudely addressed
envelope containing one of his own decayed molars? That this
was his response to Ben and Ruth's campaign to persuade him to
see a dentist—to *at least* see a dentist?

They had tried. They continued to try. They enclosed friendly
notes in the monthly checks they sent to him through his therapist. They called, allowing the phone to ring and ring, passing
the receiver off to each other. Ben had gone to his apartment,
knocked and then pounded on the door, shouting, "Isaac! Isaac!"
Eventually the door creaked open and a young Mexican woman
peered out. "He is gone," she said. And he was. By the time Ben
got a lead on the place he'd moved to he was gone from there too,
and then he was gone from another apartment, and then living on
the street. It was possible, Ben and Ruth had discovered, to lose a
child and to have no recourse.

"Isaac," he said in answer to Dolores's inquiry, "is troubled.
He's had a lot of trouble." Why was he telling her this? He never
told anyone. "Oh yes," she said. She leaned forward in her chair,
her sympathy instant and unstinting, her forehead knotted with

fellow feeling. "I know sometimes . . . my Evelyn, you see, she was also very troubled. We were at our wits' end for many years . . ."

But someone was standing in the doorway.

Two people, actually. One was a young girl, very small, with red ringlets. The other, standing a little behind her, a proprietary hand on her shoulder, was a large middle-aged man, very ruddy, with a graying pageboy. Was this parents' weekend? No, that was in November. The semester, he reminded himself, was just beginning.

By the time he had gotten to his feet, Dolores had crossed the room and was asking, "May I help you?" in a familiar vigilant tone. Never a quick reactor, Ben stood there, conscious of his arms hanging heavily in their sockets. For some reason his attention was riveted by the male intruder's great paunch, which strained against the buttons of his pale-blue guayabera. The sight of it seemed to paralyze him.

"This is Ricia Spottiswoode," said the man. His voice was startlingly deep and cultivated, an FM radio announcer's voice. "I'm Charles Johns. I'm afraid we're early."

"Oh yes," said Dolores. "So sorry. Welcome! I hope you've had a good trip."

"Very pleasant, thanks," said Charles Johns, peering around the room with puzzled consternation. Ben broke free from his freeze and joined the group, extending his hand. "Ben Blau," said Ben. "I'm philosophy chair. Glad you could make it." (Glad you could make it?) Charles Johns's answering grip was strong enough to hurt. He was evidently a handshaker of the old school. "I hope we haven't put you on the spot. We thought we'd take a few extra days to get settled." His voice made Ben's fillings vibrate.

Charles Johns was the future inhabitant of this office, the visitor who would replace Irv for the year. The woman (woman?) was not his daughter but his wife, the English Department's new writer in residence. They had been expected to arrive day after tomorrow. Ricia Spottiswoode was actually famous, Ben had gathered, a cult figure of sorts. The English Department considered her a great catch for their fledgling MFA program. One of her requirements had been that an academic perch be found for her husband. The dean had approached Ben and asked him to find a course for this man to teach—he had some kind of background in philosophy, or at least some kind of interest. Ben had resented this pressure, but there was no principled way to say no. More than once he had observed that over the course of the last thirty years nepotism had gone from being forbidden to being obligatory without ever having become merely permissible.

He realized that he'd forgotten to introduce himself to Ricia Spottiswoode. This was potentially a major gaffe, one he had to correct. But somehow she had gotten past him and wandered all the way across the room to the far window, where she stood in profile, her hair blazing. Whether this was an impulse of shyness or a bid for attention was hard to guess. Perhaps it was both. He walked toward her a little tentatively, as he might have approached a wary cat or a skittish colt, one hand extended. She offered hers and let it lie in his like a resting dove. To shake it would have been a violation. "I love the room," she said. Her voice was a confiding whisper; he had to lean close to hear it. She waved a vague hand at the floor—the banana peel, the glimmering scatter of change, the frothing smoothie cup still lying on its side.

"Oh," said Ben, "we were just cleaning up in here. The ordinary . . . inhabitant . . . is a bit of an eccentric. We didn't know he'd left such a mess. The cleaning staff—"

"No," she interrupted. "I meant it. I like messes. I often wish things were messier."

She was young, but not as young, seen close up, as she had seemed at first. Perhaps thirty. Her face was long and pale, with an oddly belligerent jaw. It made him think of a sea horse's face. Her eyes were a deep unfocused blue. Her artlessly tangled hair was a remarkable new-penny red.

"Has the English Department been helping you get settled?" he asked. "Have they found you a place?"

"Well yes they have," said Ricia, "but I'm afraid we're not sure we like it. It's kind of sterile. We like things to be old."

"You're here from where?"

"Providence."

"Oh," said Ben. "You'll find it's very different—"

"We understand, but we thought they might have found us something . . ."

"Yes," said Ben. "My wife and I like old places too, but nothing goes back very far around here." It was true. A New Jersey boy himself, he'd grown tired of apologizing for Spangler. The city was cosmopolitan; it was quirky; its cheap ethnic restaurants were unrivaled by those in any city he could think of, and that included New York and Los Angeles, or so he said when he defended Spangler to East and West Coast visitors. In parts it was oddly beautiful. But there was no denying its gargantuan chaotic sprawl, its flatness and rawness, its eternal newness—or at least its failure to age. The Texas sun peeled paint, the hemorrhagic rains rotted wood. It was almost as if the elements were doing their best to "distress" Spangler, to create the illusion of age. But only the slow moldering of centuries creates charm; new decay makes ugliness.

"Where have they put you?" he asked.

"Oh, I don't know. Some big condominium complex. Charles!"

She had a voice when she chose to use it. Charles left his conversation with Dolores and joined them. Clearing his throat thunderously, he reached into his breast pocket and produced a small notebook. "It's called the Waters on Shadyside" he said, his voice filtered through phlegm. "It's on the 215 access road."

"Oh yes," said Ben.

"No water in sight and very little shade," Charles Johns observed, clapping the notebook shut and re-pocketing it.

Ben knew the Waters on Shadyside. It had been written up in the paper when two floors of its parking garage had flooded after the last gully washer. "That's a Spangler thing," he said, "naming places after nonexistent geological features. There's a Lake Spangler and a Mount Spangler."

Charles Johns smiled blandly. Ricia looked dismayed.

"There really are some very pleasant areas," Ben went on, feeling himself pressed into service as a representative of the Spangler Chamber of Commerce, "but nothing much older than the turn of the century. You might want to have them show you the Museum District. There are some very appealing . . ."

He had been about to say "bungalows," but out of the corner of his eye he saw that Dolores was shaking her head vehemently. Once again she'd saved him from stumbling into error. In this case he'd been on the point of encouraging the Spottiswoode-Johnses to demand that the English Department rehouse them. The dean would have heard about that, and he was already in trouble with her. Elias Wertmuller of the Religion Department had taken him aside recently after a Curriculum Committee meeting and warned him that she'd been making ominous noises about the Philosophy Department's less-than-positive attitude toward university service and the perception, on the part of some, of its "elitism." "There are some very appealing exhibitions," he began again. "I believe they've got some woodblock prints up right now—a show of, ah, I believe, nineteenth-century woodblock prints."

Dolores was bidding for his attention again, raising her eyebrows and pointing at her wrist. "Oh," said Ben, "I'm afraid you'll have to excuse me. I seem to be late for class." He re-shook Charles's hand, and then Ricia's, murmuring the conventional expressions of goodwill that the office of chair had forced him to memorize.

He'd drawn a new room, too big for this class. A bank of audiovisual devices, baffling and useless to him, blinked and hummed above the central desk. The students had distributed themselves in the usual way; four or five keen-eyed boys and two earnest girls sat in the first semicircular row of seats, directly in front of the desk. These could be assumed to be the most ambitious of what was always a hardworking bunch. They'd already purchased the packet of course readings and they'd be lined up outside his door ten minutes before tomorrow's office hour. The rest—the average and the unclassifiable, from whose ranks he could expect to discover at least a few interesting minds—had spread themselves out rather thinly through the rows. As always, the athletes sat in the back, six healthy specimens this season, up from four last fall. Looking down at the roster he noticed the names of two promising football recruits. Over the years he'd become known as an athletic supporter. Not because he'd ever given a jock an unfair advantage; more likely because he could be seen in the stands at nearly every home game in every sport, even women's basketball.

Ben was a good teacher, not an inspired one. In his thirty years of teaching he'd learned to expect his students to like and trust him. Generations of them had imitated his habit of rocking back and forth on his heels like a davener. Though generations of students had written warmly respectful comments on his teaching evaluations, he'd never won an award, never drawn the kind of adulatory attention that some of his colleagues seemed to inspire. Writing came more naturally to him than teaching, though writing too was a great effort.

Even so, he kept trying to improve. He offered conferences. He wrote extensive comments on papers. He revised his syllabus every few years, tried consciously to refurbish his stock of illustrative anecdotes in the face of what seemed an ever accelerating process of cultural turnover. In the mid-eighties he'd jokingly accused a graduate student of being a nattering nabob of negativism. A what? said the student, but a few others in the seminar remembered. Last year he'd alluded to the Jonestown massacre. Jonestown?

These were Lola freshmen, and he knew they would prove to be bright and conscientious enough, but this morning they were gaping at him like guppies in a tank. As he stood over his notes and roster, giving the introductory silence a moment to settle in, he scanned the rows, searching for an answering human gaze. There it was, unmistakably, directly in front of him in the second

row, emanating from the lively, kohl-rimmed eyes of a big tattooed person in black leather shorts with a stiff ridge of pink hair
running down the middle of his or her otherwise shaven scalp.

"This is Contemporary Moral Issues, Philosophy 101," Ben
announced. "Is everybody in the right place?"

The front-row students snapped opened their notebooks.
Some of the athletes put away the sports page. The big pink-
haired person smiled at Ben. It was a generous smile, utterly undefended, showing a pierced tongue and much gum tissue and
many small teeth. Who are you, *compañero*? thought Ben. And
what is your gender?

"Let me start by saying a few general words about philosophy," he began as he always did when teaching an entry-level
course. "Does anyone happen to know what the word means?"
Silence. Nobody ever knew, or if they did they were too cowed to
speak out. Ben turned to the blackboard, writing PHILO in bold
block letters. " 'Philo' means love," said Ben, "or 'love of.' " Below
PHILO he wrote SOPHY. "Or," he added, erasing the Y and replacing
it with IA, " 'sophia.' Can anyone guess what that meant in the
original Greek?" he asked over his shoulder.

"Wisdom," called out a voice as gender-indeterminate as Big
Bird's.

"Right," said Ben. "Philosophia. Love of wisdom. How do we
show our love of wisdom?"

Silence.

"How do we *seek* wisdom?"

A girl in the front row raised her hand. Ben nodded. "We ask
questions?"

"That's right," said Ben. "And this semester that's exactly what
we'll be doing."

. . .

What in hell kind of name is 'Ricia'?" asked Ben. Ruth was sitting at the desk in his study in front of the computer screen; he was standing over her. They'd gotten onto the subject of the Spottiswoode/Johnses at the dinner table and decided on the spot to do some research. With Isaac out of the house, they could leave the remnants of their omelets and salad on the table, act on this kind of impulse. The computer was taking its time to boot up.

"It's short for Patricia. Pa*treesha.*"

"Pat is short for Patricia. Patty is short for Patricia. I never heard of Ricia."

"What's she like?" asked Ruth. "Is she attractive?"

"She's ethereal-looking," said Ben. "Ophelia-like. Not beautiful." She wasn't, it was true, and it was always wise to make this kind of stipulation when he could do so without lying. "She does have amazing red hair," he added after a moment.

"Affected?"

"I thought so. I don't know poets. She could be a regular Will Rogers by their standards."

"She's not a poet. She started out as one but now she's a memoirist. That's how she made her reputation. And then she wrote one of those spiritual how-to-write books. What's the husband like?"

"He's big, like a bodyguard. Much older. He could be my age." The computer gave its "I am born" electronic trill.

"Here we go," said Ruth. "Amazon first, or Google?"

"Come on," said Ben. "Let me do it. Let me sit."

Grumbling a little, Ruth stood. Ben sat down, drew himself closer to the desk, squared the mouse on the mouse pad, and brought up the Amazon home page. "What's her memoir called?"

"I'm Nobody."

Ben tapped in the title. The page materialized, and the book. "Enlarge it," said Ruth. The cover was a full-body photograph of Ricia lying submerged in water. She was shown from above, eyes wide and blank, vague garments spreading, hair billowing. The title was rendered in watery script above her head. The subtitle, *Who Are You?*, floated between her collarbone and her décolletage.

"Very effective," said Ruth.

Next came the blurbs. "Ricia Spottiswoode," Howard Richards had written, "has undertaken the fabulous journey from poetry to memoir. She has survived the trek—survived it, I might add, triumphantly. She returns to us bearing messages from the underworld of childhood trauma—messages that we ignore at our peril."

"Oh please," said Ruth.

Ben scrolled down past the book's Amazon ranking number, a respectable 1,067 three years after its publication. He moved on to the newspaper reviews, a long parade of ellipsis-studded raves—". . . coruscatingly brilliant . . . ," ". . . courageous and poignant . . . ," ". . . heartbreaking . . ."—and from there to the seventy-nine reader reviews. A quick survey of these found that roughly two-thirds were positive ("I cried!"), one-third negative ("Gag me!").

Ricia Spottiswoode's most recent book, *The Divining Rod: Feeling Your Way Through Writers' Block*, was number 178 on Amazon. Once again, Ricia appeared on the cover. This time she sat on a wooden stool in a short black skirt and a violet sweater set. Her legs were fetchingly crossed, her arms folded under her breasts. Her hair had been pulled away from her face, one bouncy lock left free to follow the line of her cheekbone. She was smiling a conventional lipsticked smile. She looked friendly, and undeniably pretty.

"It's the *sane* Ricia," said Ruth. "It's Ricia the role model." On to Google: 220,000 hits for Ricia, 230 for Charles Johns. On closer examination nearly all of these were for other Charles Johnses—a Charles Johns recorded as present at the raising of the colors at the VFW lodge in Schoharie, New York, on Veterans Day in 1999, for example, or a Charles Johns rounded up for vagrancy in Spokane. There were only a few hits that clearly applied to the Charles Johns whom Ben had met that afternoon, and they all involved Ricia Spottiswoode.

One of these was a *Poets and Writers* interview that followed the publication of *The Divining Rod,* featuring a spread of photographs of the Providence, Rhode Island, loft she shared with Charles Johns. He was shown in the kitchen in a chef's apron, peering at the photographer over half-glasses as be boned a fish. Ricia appeared in profile in front of a Victorian stained-glass window at the head of a staircase, her hair a cloud of fire. In another photograph she reclined on an antique love seat, a cat draped along her hip, her head leaning against Charles's shoulder. The rest of him had been cropped out of the picture.

"Ricia Spottiswoode," said the *P&W* interviewer, "what has changed in your life since *I'm Nobody?* What has made the difference?"

"Well, I married Charles."

"And that's made the difference?"

"Charles is my muse. Did you know that there's such a thing as a male muse? Charles's love for me is unconditional. He makes me feel safe, for the first time in my life. I feel taken care of. I feel treasured."

I am *not* being unfriendly," said Ruth. They were lying on their sides in bed, Ben facing Ruth's back, Ruth facing the wall.

"It's Ricia Spottiswoode, right?"

A silence followed, and then a violent stirring of bedclothes and knees and elbows. Ruth was hauling herself up into a sitting position, jamming a pillow behind her back. "Yes it *is* Ricia Spottiswoode," she said, "but not the way you think."

"What way do I think?"

"You think it's conventional . . . sexual jealousy. It's not. Don't bother trying to tell me you're not attracted to her, by the way, because I know you are."

"I am not attracted to her," said Ben.

"Not even a little?"

"Not even a little." Not quite true, but close enough. The attraction he felt for Ricia Spottiswoode was only the baseline erotic interest he took in any nubile female, augmented slightly by the titillation of her fame.

"That's not the problem anyway."

"What is the problem?"

"Well," said Ruth, sliding back into a prone position. Ben could feel her agitation diminishing. "Well, there *is* a little bit of sexual jealousy, but it's not really personal. I'm sorry." She rested a hand on Ben's chest. He took it and squeezed it. "Sorry," she said again.

She went on. "It's a whole swirl of things. It's more envy than jealousy. It's her youth and her fame and my age and my non-fame. But even that's not quite it. It's that thing of the world being divided . . ."

Ben knew this theory well. Ruth divided the world into those able to work their will on others and those on whom the will of others was worked. She placed herself in the second group and moved Ben from one to the other depending on her mood. He had repeatedly pointed out to her that these categories were both overly broad and needlessly restrictive, that this distinction lacked explanatory usefulness and served only to justify her fatalistic passivity. Tonight it seemed best to let it go.

"And I can't help resenting how far she's gotten on how little actual talent. If you saw her books you'd be amazed. They're artful, in their own way, but they're so arch and so manipulative—"

"Have you read them? I haven't seen them around."

"I've seen them. I've looked through them in bookstores."

"You know what you need to do, Ruth."

"I know. Get back to writing." Her intonation was singsong. This was not the first time they'd had this conversation.

Ben drew a deep breath. He'd memorized this litany. "You're a writer, Ruth. Isaac's gone. You gave the faculty-wife busywork thing a try. You need to be writing. There's nothing stopping you. There's been nothing to stop you for years."

His exhortation was having no effect, he could see, or rather it was having only a soothing effect. She had heard it so many times that now she found it reassuring; she engineered their conversations to solicit it. That was all to the good, he supposed. Twenty years ago, the arrival of Ricia Spottiswoode and Charles Johns

would have been the occasion of a giant fight, one of those ruin-
ous all-nighters that woke Isaac and continued even when they
heard him shrieking in his crib. As their marriage aged, the spiky
line of argument running through it had become an undulating
path of theme. They had simply moved beyond the possibility of
resolution to find that their marriage had endured.

"Oh," said Ruth, "I almost forgot. There was a message from
Martinez on the machine." Eusebio Martinez was Isaac's therapist.

Ben made an acknowledging noise. Ruth was lying on her
back, one hand resting on his upturned wrist. Her breathing had
grown regular and his own brain waves were beginning to relax
into swells and troughs. In a moment they would simultaneously
flip onto their sides, each to begin the solitary descent into sleep.

"Ben?"

"Yes?"

"You treasure me, right?"

"Yes," said Ben. After a moment he added, "I do."

CHAPTER THREE

~⌒

At four forty-five on the morning of the day she was to host the welcome back potluck dinner, Ruth rolled out of the cocoon of sleep and fell awake. She eased slowly out of bed—Ben was jealous of his rest—and padded downstairs to the kitchen and started the coffee.

It was too early for her walk. Turning on a light seemed rash, so she sat at the kitchen table in the dark until the coffeemaker had ceased its gurgling. She felt around in the cabinet for the round-bottomed mug she liked to use—the shape mattered to her—and poured coffee and carried it out onto the renovated screened-in porch. Then she stretched out on the wicker chaise where she did most of her reading, turned on the TV, and groggily watched the weather report. A blender-blade symbol representing Tropical Storm Denise was whirring across a stretch of flat blue representing the Atlantic, followed at a distance by a smaller blender blade named Gary. Too early, the local-color weatherman was saying, to know yet whether either of these would attain hurricane status and whether either might pose any threat to south Texas. "But look. Lookie here," he went on, pointing to a whorled swelling off the coast of Africa. "That's Tropical Depression Three formin' up there, gettin' ready to get in line."

As she drank her coffee she watched the dawn pick out the details of the backyard, the humanoid limbs of the crepe myrtles, the sagging garage they still meant to convert someday into a study for Ben, the sun-scorched patches on the lawn. The lights in the house across the way went on and she settled back in the chaise to watch the yuppie breakfast scene she'd been monitoring for the past ten years. The cast of characters consisted of two tall blond parents, three rangy blond children, and an ever changing nanny. She'd never met this family, never even seen them outside of this view, but she'd made as thorough a study of the children as was possible, considering that she couldn't quite make out their faces. She remembered two from the time they were toddlers and the youngest as an infant. The parents she knew only as slender bending figures in the periphery of the picture, the father in pale-green surgeon's scrubs and the mother in a narrow skirt and blazer, leaning down to distribute goodbye kisses. Many years back, when the children were small, she'd felt an automatic stab of disapproval at these daily leave-takings. In recent years she'd come to acknowledge that she was in no position to pronounce judgment.

The nanny attrition had sped up recently; two had come and gone in the last year. Ruth knew why. The eldest blond child was a preteen now, and his transformation from child to adolescent was well under way. She saw it in the abject hostility of his slump

and the way he turned his body away from his siblings. In her
mind's eye she could picture the look on his face—that princely
contempt disguising queasy panic, as though it had just occurred
to him that perhaps it was he and not the world that was the
source of some smell he couldn't get out of his nostrils. It was
Isaac's expression, the one she first noticed when he was ten or
eleven.

She kept a group of framed photographs on the table beside
the chaise. Here he was a few minutes after delivery, a pugilistic-
looking newborn with a squashed nose. His face was covered
with livid purple and yellow blotches; he squinted hard under
the delivery-room lights and hunched his shoulders like a miniature ogre. "It's Chuck Wepner," was Ben's remark, addressed
to a young intern, one of a group of five or six clustered around
the delivery table as the dripping, wailing, mucus-smeared baby,
umbilicus just severed, was laid on Ruth's chest.

"Who?"

"Chuck Wepner," said Ben. "The Bayonne Bleeder. A heavy-
weight from the seventies." Ben was wearing regulation scrubs
and paper turban. He'd taken out his camera, but for the moment
seemed disinclined to use it. This was the first Ruth had seen of
him in a while; he'd been pushed far back in the crowd of onlook-
ers during the delivery.

"He's Isaac," Ruth announced. Nobody seemed to hear her.
She propped herself on her elbows and took a look at the baby.
On his slimy cheek, she noticed, was an adult-sized pimple with
a hard white pustule at its center. "He already has a pimple?" she
asked the nurse who was taking her blood pressure as another
nurse lifted Isaac away to be washed and weighed. "Oh, that's *real*
normal," said the nurse in a soothing-nurse voice. "Maybe he's

precocious," said Ruth, but this seemed to go past her. "What do you think of your son, Professor?" asked the other nurse. "Ten pounds, six ounces. Here, hold him." Ben took the howling, tightly swaddled Isaac in two spread hands, as if receiving a football. "You don't need to be scared of him," said the nurse.

The newborn Isaac was not pretty. Nor was he friendly. He went rigid with rage and shook his fists when he was hungry, and he was always hungry. But for the four days that he and Ruth were kept in the hospital because of Isaac's mild jaundice, Ruth had the distinction of being the mother of the biggest baby in the nursery. "What a big guy," murmured one of the other mothers, sidling up to her as she stood over Isaac's bassinet. "How was the delivery?" "A little rough," said Ruth, "but we got through it." "Well, bless your heart," said the woman. "Here's your big big boy," cooed the nurse who carried him into her room to be fed. "Feel how solid he is!" The candy striper who distributed the daily menu form giggled at his noisy nursing, the grunts and growls and smacking noises he made at the breast. On her second day in the hospital a young black man came to Ruth's bedside to draw her blood. Isaac was deep into a feeding—once he'd attached himself to the nipple there was no tearing him away. "I'm a man," crooned the technician, smiling down on Isaac as he wrapped a rubber strap around Ruth's upper arm. "I spell M-A-N."

She'd had the room to herself for the first two days, but on the third she awoke to find that the curtain around the other bed had been pulled shut. She never spoke to her roommate, never even saw her except for a glance at her inadequately covered backside as she limped into their shared bathroom. She did get a look at the baby when the nurses brought it in and noted that it was a very small girl in a pink preemie cap. Apparently the mother's milk hadn't come in fully—from behind the curtain Ruth could hear a steady low hum of concerned consultation and an occasional faint ululation from the baby.

After a lunchtime feeding, when Isaac was milk-drunk and ready to drape himself compliantly across her shoulder, Ruth heaved herself out of bed and hobbled down the corridor to take them both for a turn around the solarium. She needed to get out of the room to allow herself to enjoy the surge of triumphalist joy that had been gathering in her. For his first two days of life she'd viewed Isaac as an evil Golem, intent on making her nipples bleed. She flinched when the nurse brought him to her; it wasn't easy to form an attachment to a hideous frog-legged thing that seemed to want to eat her. But on the third day her feelings changed. Suddenly she was proud of him, proud of his size and voraciousness and his very ugliness, which she now understood to be a source of a repellent protective power, like the grotesque masks and amulets prized by primitive peoples. It was a power in which she shared. She was the mother of a big, big boy, a battered, heroic survivor of the birth canal, and unlikely as it seemed, that made her the reigning queen of the *Totem and Taboo* land that the delivery floor had turned out to be. Maybe Freud was right, she thought. Maybe it was true that the only truly unambivalent human connection was the relationship between mother and son.

Here was Isaac at eleven months, in his high chair. He'd mastered the pinching motion necessary to pick up a Cheerio between thumb and forefinger and he was offering one to Ruth, who was leaning into the frame in profile, her face lit with an adoring smile. Was she even capable of that smile now? And here he was at three, sitting cross-legged on the floor in the children's room at the library with Ben, working on one of the advanced puzzles the librarian kept aside for him. He was as pretty as a little boy as he'd been ugly as a baby, with curly dark hair and girlish eyelashes. By the time he was two he was no longer particularly large—only a little over the sixtieth percentile. People smiled down at him when Ben and Ruth took him on stroller outings. He was an altogether appealing and promising child, solemn, conscientious, confiding. He put away his toys methodically. He sang on key in a high sweet voice. He listened to stories with intense concentration and retained long passages in his memory. Was it possible he'd be an early reader? As it happened, no. He learned to read at six, but quickly. Soon he was ahead of all the others in his first-grade class.

If Ruth had a particularly clear and detailed recollection of Isaac's preschool history, it was because she'd been asked to recapitulate it so many times by doctors and therapists. Her memories rarely satisfied them; they pressed her to bring back anything unusual, anything she might have forgotten. But to all appearances he'd been an entirely normal infant and small child. He began to talk at thirteen months, to walk at fifteen—her pediatrician told her that big babies were often slightly delayed in their gross motor development. Apart from that he scored well above age level. Perhaps his many allergies or his refusal to eat anything except peanut butter sandwiches and carrot sticks had had some insidious cumulative effect on his development that she'd failed to anticipate or understand. Maybe the anxious intensity of his will to do things right presaged something—at the time it had simply reminded her of Ben. Illnesses? Nothing outside the usual, except for the case of periorbital cellulitis he developed when he was four. Here her interlocutors brought out their clipboards and pens. When she told them that the cellulitis had been brought under control by antibiotics in a few days the pens were returned to breast pockets.

The troubles began in first grade. No, better to say that certain tendencies began to manifest themselves. Any change in the classroom configuration upset him. When one wall was being painted and the reading circle was moved to the other side of the room, for example, Isaac refused to join the class. He planted himself on his usual cushion in his customary place and howled. And when the lockers in the hallway were carted off to make room for new ones he pummeled the workmen with his fists and shrieked. The principal—an idiot, like most of his kind—actually threatened to call the police. That sent Isaac into a state of shivering hiccuping catatonia. Ruth was summoned to take him home.

He was not a sociable child. When Ruth suggested that he share his blocks with another boy in the library children's room he simply shook his head and gathered the blocks close to his body. When she insisted, he stamped his feet and shouted. Other mothers looked up. She had to carry him—kicking hard and gnawing on her shoulder—out to the little yard in back. By the end of second grade he was no longer receiving any birthday-party invitations that were not extended to the whole class.

And yet he did very well in school during those early years. For the most part he was healthy and in his self-contained way he seemed happy, particularly at home. He was content to sit at his parents' feet in the evenings and look at picture books, or shuffle around the carpet on his knees pushing a plastic car and making quiet urrr-urrr noises. And she, Ruth, was happy too, even later, when things began to go wrong. The truth was that she almost welcomed his problems, if only because they gave her a way to stay involved in his life. She'd never quite felt able to wear the mantle of successful motherhood, at least not for long. The smug, tranquil maternal style was not for her. She felt more like herself when she had reason to serve as his defender and advocate, to intervene on his behalf, to lurk in the hall waiting for a word with the teacher.

Before Isaac she had ruined every photograph taken of her by smirking or lowering her eyes or turning her head. The "candid" shots from her wedding reception made her wince; how had she managed to contort her mouth that way, and why? But in pictures taken with Isaac she was rarely self-conscious. Even in poses where she was deliberately mugging—squatting behind him as he blew out the candles on his birthday cake or trotting after him as he wobbled along the sidewalk on his first bike—she looked relaxed and sane. She looked like any young mother. Her message to the viewer of these photographs was no longer the insupportable "Here am I." Instead it was "Here is Isaac, and here am I, his mother."

Naturally, the happiness of those years had a converse side. Over the course of Isaac's first year she called the pediatrician's office at least twice a week. There was the incident at four months, when Isaac ate an ant. "A little extra protein," said the pediatrician's famously patient nurse, but Ruth couldn't get the words "formic acid" out of her mind. There was the late-night trip to the emergency room when she was sure she'd discovered a lump in his armpit. And there were dozens of other panics, not all of which prompted her to call the doctor's office. Sometimes fear of seeming crazy stayed her hand.

And there were the fights with Ben, which had always been bad but got worse after Isaac was born. His first attack of night

terrors happened during one of their late-night kitchen shouting matches. That episode was followed by many others, most of
them seemingly cued by raised voices. Ruth called the pediatrician's office and arranged a consultation. "What's the nature of
the problem?" asked the nurse, an edge of asperity in her voice.
Ruth told her she'd rather not say. "Are you *sure* this isn't something I can help you with?" asked the nurse. Ruth told her no, her
voice quavering. She wanted to talk to Dr. Mead privately.

She arrived alone and was shown into a treatment room, where
she wedged herself into a child-sized rocker and leafed through
back issues of *Parents* magazine for forty minutes until Dr. Mead
arrived. He was a buoyant, exhausted-looking man with a green
pipe-cleaner puppet riding in the pocket of his lab coat. This
was the first time she'd talked to him outside of Isaac's presence.
"Mrs. Blau," he said, "how can I help you this afternoon?" Ruth
burst into tears and blurted out something about fights and night
terrors. She hadn't brought it up in Isaac's twenty-four-month
checkup, she confessed, because there'd been a medical student in
the room. Dr. Mead went into listening mode, propping his back
against the examining table, removing his glasses, massaging the
bridge of his nose, nodding steadily—"Got it," each nod said.
Ruth struggled to give a rounded picture of the situation, but her
powers of articulation were squeezed by contrary pressures: it was
important to acknowledge that the fights were very bad and getting worse and that on more than one occasion she and Ben had
gone on screaming at each other for some time even after they'd
heard the eerie mechanical cries coming from Isaac's room. But
Dr. Mead should also understand that their marriage was stable
and actually very close and that they'd been together for several

years before Isaac's birth and had gotten used to feeling free to air their differences . . .

At this point she saw that he was stealing a glance at his watch, a big one with visible internal workings that had always fascinated Isaac. She allowed her account to run aground. Dr. Mead paused to make a note in Isaac's chart and sat down on a swivel chair, his widely splayed knees bracketing hers. Leaning forward, looking her deliberately in the eye, and speaking slowly and clearly, he explained that the thinking on night terrors had changed. They were no longer understood to have their origin in trauma or in any psychological problem, but instead were seen as a kind of sleep disturbance, a purely neurological phenomenon. They were very scary for parents, but also quite common and really nothing to be alarmed about. And Isaac—here he consulted Isaac's chart—at twenty-eight months, was smack-dab in the center of the average age of onset.

The nurse knocked softly on the door. Dr. Mead was instantly on his feet and Ruth was on hers too, thanking him effusively. Dr. Mead gave her a tired smile and a no-thanks-necessary shrug as he edged past her. When he was gone Ruth sat down heavily in the rocking chair for a few seconds, then got up again and gathered her jacket and purse. She walked down the echoing back stairs to the hospital lobby, empty at this hour except for an elderly couple peering inquiringly into a popcorn cart, and came out blinking into a bright fall afternoon. She found her car and sat in it for a few minutes, resting her forehead against the steering wheel.

Her many-layered reaction put her in mind of wine reviews she'd read in glossy food and travel magazines. She felt a certain relief—a light floral top note—at the news that she could not be held responsible for Isaac's night terrors, and also a certain resentment toward Dr. Mead, whom she'd always regarded with anxious deference and never quite trusted. Beneath all that was a prickly heat of shame: she was embarrassed more by the nakedness of her need to confess than she was by the content of her confession. And underlying that was a familiar substratum of dread, something that was always with her but whose presence she rarely sensed as strongly as she did now. For just a moment she was visited by the insight that her anxieties only represented a desire to propitiate that dread, which sat at the very center of her happiness.

TO DO:

1. Walk.

Ruth obliterated this item with a heavy application of pencil lead. It was hot already, or would be soon, and there really wasn't time.

2. Vacuum downstairs.

Ruth took a brief tour of inspection. The house was a bungalow built in the forties with a second-story half addition, furnished in the graduate-student style of thirty years ago. It was, in the words of a clipboard-carrying Realtor who'd nosed discreetly through the rooms over the summer, "dated," "tired," and in need of "sprucing up." Ruth found it hard to accept the idea that their low-slung, clean-lined, functional chairs and futons and coffee tables could age. They were modern, weren't they? That meant new, intrinsically youthful.

They'd consulted the Realtor when they were toying briefly with the idea of looking into the downtown loft condominiums into which many Lola faculty couples their age had been moving. "Sprucing up," Ruth muttered under her breath for days after the Realtor's visit, and in a short-lived burst of zeal she called in a cleaning service and bought four watercolor prints and two small, good Turkish rugs. The effect was negligible; any sprucing up, she realized, would need to be a revolutionary undertaking. It would require an overturning of the established order. The stained, tufted carpeting would be ripped from the floor; the futons and the coffee table and the canvas-sling chairs would be dragged out to the curb on heavy-trash day. The peeling wallpaper would be steamed and prized off with a scraper. The frayed lampshades would join the rest of the pile of historical detritus at the curb, as would Ben's flat-tired bike, which had been parked in a corner of the living room ever since she could remember.

They would begin again, and then what? What regime would replace the long-extended graduate-student era? (Was this what people meant when they talked about the dilemma of postmodernism?) The furniture they owned was worthless but irreplaceable; its kind was no longer manufactured, or rather it was, but it was cheap and people consciously identified it with youth—with starting out, not starting over. Any new era could only be a turning back to a much older one—the era of their parents—and oddly enough, Ruth sometimes longed for just such a reversion. Sometimes it struck her as unseemly that they lived the way they did, so oblivious (especially Ben) to their material surroundings.

By now, they should have cultivated an appetite for comfort, for polished furniture and soft surfaces. People their age should wear slippers, not pad around barefoot, as they had done in their twenties and continued to do now. They should suffer from age-appropriate ailments. They should own a looming breakfront and heavily upholstered sofas with matching club chairs. Their house should smell of brisket. Were they too young to live like their parents? No. That couldn't be the objection. They weren't too young for anything anymore.

Walking into the half bath adjacent to her study, she was reminded of a series of disturbing photographs she'd once seen of toilets in the Soviet Union before the advent of abrasive cleansers. Now here was a situation in urgent need of remedy. Vacuuming was beside the point; the graduate students wouldn't notice dust. (Barbara Bachman would, and a few other wives, but that would be the least of what they'd notice.) She crossed out "Vacuum downstairs" and wrote in "Scrub bathrooms." She paused for a moment, crossed out the final "s," inserted a carat between "Scrub" and "bathroom," and penciled in "downstairs."

3. Grocery store.

She'd assembled the ingredients for her chicken chili with white beans, though she'd had to substitute parsley for cilantro. She'd gathered two bags of tortilla chips, two bags of pretzels, two bags of potato chips, two jars of mixed nuts and one of salsa. Whatever Ben might say, she knew the graduate students could eat this and more, and if they didn't, any leftover food could be pressed on them as they went out the door. On impulse, she'd dropped a jar of wasabi peas into the cart; she'd eat them if nobody else did.

Now she was hesitating in the paper-products aisle. For a reason that remained obscure to her, she had consciously neglected to check whether they already had paper plates and cups and plastic forks on hand. Actually, she was sure they had plenty, left over from last year's potluck, and year before last's, and year before year before last's. Even so, she chose three cellophane-wrapped packs of shiny yellow paper plates and three packs of matching napkins and flung them defiantly into the cart. She did this every year, and every year Ben dragged the old paper plates and napkins she knew quite well were already there out of the cabinet above the sink and arranged them in a shaming row on the central island, like the bales of marijuana and blocks of hashish the DEA puts on display after a major bust.

On her way to the checkout, she remembered that she'd also intended to buy milk and cereal and a bottle of peroxide for Ben's periodontal routine, so she swung the cart around and picked these things up, snatching a bunch of purple tulips from the floral department while she was at it. This purchase would irritate Ben even more than the superfluous paper plates and napkins, but it would also soften him. At the counter she was careful to divide her purchases into two piles, the larger to be paid for by the Philosophy Department entertainment fund. "You fine arrythin' awry?" asked the checker.

4. Wash and dry wineglasses.
5. Polish silver.
6. Iron tablecloth.

In what alternative universe must she have been living when she made this list? She crossed these entries out and wandered into the kitchen where she turned to the more agreeable task of looking for a vase for the purple tulips and then out to the living room where she found a place for them on the mantel. She spent a few minutes choosing books to display on the coffee table—her own, of course, and one of Ben's and a few recent novels and the most recent Pushcart anthology. As she moved around the room, straightening and rearranging, she discovered that she was feeling something pleasant, a cool run of exhilaration along her veins. It took her a moment to recognize the sensation of anticipation, to realize that she was actually looking forward to the potluck dinner this evening. She hadn't felt this way about a party—certainly not one of her own—in many years. Apparently something in her still survived from a time when a glittering path of expectation lit up the days and hours before a party, when she rang a doorbell with the hope that the next three hours might change her life.

Ricia Spottiswoode and her husband would be coming. That, of course, was the explanation. She'd been maintaining a provisional skepticism about these two—especially about Ricia—but even so, she'd been dwelling on them continually, waiting for her chance to meet them. She imagined her house as she hoped it would look through their eyes—the house of a writer, who lived more in her imagination than in the world. In a back room in her mind where wishes were formed, she'd already invested them with the power to divine her languishing talent on sight, to restore her lost career. That was crazy of course. But even if Ricia was as affected and self-involved as Ruth had reason to believe she was, even if Charles Johns was the superannuated hipster Ben had described, they still promised to be more interesting than the blank young people she could usually expect to meet this time of year—the new graduate students and the newly hired epistemologists and metaphysicians. Interesting to her, at least, because they were emissaries from the exciting world she'd blundered into and out of all those years ago, a world in which the phone rang with news and the knock of the FedEx delivery man could be heard at the door.

Was it possible they knew her work? Charles Johns was of an age to have read it. Maybe he'd put Ricia onto it. Maybe they'd discussed it. That was unlikely, she knew, but even if they'd never heard of *Getting Good,* couldn't she, Ruth, seize the initiative to-night (for a change) and bring the talk around to it? Wouldn't it be natural, talking to a pair of writers at a Philosophy Department party, to let them know that she was a writer who had written about philosophers? Of course that was a risky proposition. On one or two of the handful of occasions when she'd tried the kind of self-promoting moves that seemed to come naturally to other writers, she'd lost her sense of timing and disgraced herself.

Ricia Spottiswoode: now there was a writer with no compunctions about putting herself forward. She could give lessons! (In fact she had: chapter eight of *The Divining Rod* was explicitly pre-sented as a primer in self-marketing.) Of course if Ruth brought up her own work—or even if she didn't—simple politeness would require that she equip herself with something to say about Ricia's. She hadn't been able to bring herself to buy *The Divining Rod,* but paging through it at Barnes and Noble she recognized it as one of those pseudo-books generated more by the publisher than the author, a wide-margined exercise in packaging written in chirpy journalese. She did buy a copy of *I'm Nobody* and spent an hour looking around in it. (And right now, before she forgot, she should take it off the shelf and put it out on the coffee table. To neglect to display it would be unforgivably rude.)

The incest sections were conveniently italicized, so she'd found it easy to avoid them. She was too sick with envy to sink very deeply into the narrative, but even so she found herself pulled in by an occasional passage. Ricia's writing was not without charm, she had to admit, especially when she dropped the dark portentous tone and used her own naturally light voice. Ruth had liked a passage describing a cheap olive-green enamel watch one of Ricia's aunts had given her and a subsequent brief meditation on how that color had opened up a territory of far-flung longings and associations. She remembered that phenomenon from her own childhood.

Back in her active writing days she'd learned the trick of letting the part substitute for the whole. All you had to do to satisfy even the most praise-hungry writer was to find a piece of text, even a very short one, about which you could express real enthusiasm. That was the ticket: she could see herself late this evening, standing with Ricia and Charles in the corner where Ben's collection of black-and-white photographs were hung, a glass of wine in her hand, carrying on rapturously, and more or less genuinely, about the olive-green enamel watch.

At ten after six, Ruth and Ben stationed themselves at the dining-room window facing the street. "Look," she said, standing clear of the window and pointing out to the street. "See what they're doing? They're waiting until somebody else gets here." For the second time, a hearse-like black Buick was circling the block. She could make out the pudgy silhouette of the driver, Todd Philby, a second-year philosophy graduate student. His wife, Melinda, was just out of ed school. They were a shy, precociously stuffy young couple, so consistently early to arrive at parties that Ben and Ruth had given up the practice of placing bets. "What kind of car is that for young people?" asked Ruth.

"A parent's car," said Ben. The phone rang. Ben took it in the kitchen. "Just a moment," she heard him say. "I'll put his mother on." Pressing the receiver into his chest he mouthed "Martinez." Isaac's therapist: for two weeks, Ruth had been trying to return his call. She carried her wineglass up the stairs, sat down at Ben's desk, and picked up the extension. This was the room where she liked to take potentially difficult phone calls; it was tidy and monastic and she could brace her elbows on the desk.

"Mrs. Blau, please." A starchy British accent she'd never heard before. The usual secretary had a bonelessly soothing drawl. Perhaps this was the night secretary. (Was there such a thing as a night secretary?)

"This is she."

"Will you hold for Dr. Martinez?"

"Certainly." Already she'd begun to imitate the secretary's accent. A pause ensued, perhaps forty-five seconds long. At one point she looked down and was surprised to find her wineglass empty.

"Hel*lo*, Mrs. Blau. We finally make connection. Forgive me, please. I've been out of town." Eusebio Martinez divided his time between Spangler and Mexico City. "All is well with you? And Professor Blau?"

"We're fine," said Ruth. Dr. Martinez's cultivated manner and breathy, intimate voice made her feel awkwardly forthright, an American rube. "Does Isaac need . . . something?" More money, she meant. That was the usual upshot of these calls.

"No," said Dr. Martinez. "But I have news of him." He delivered this announcement with characteristic drama, lowering his voice to a near-whisper, elongating the word "news" and pronouncing it with special relish—neeeyooooz. Ruth gripped the edge of the desk with her free hand. "He's OK," she said. This was a declaration, a demand.

"I should say rather that I have news *from* him. He has asked me to arrange a meeting with you and his father." Here he paused, allowing Ruth a moment to take in the information. Her first reaction was a choking rush of tears to the sinuses—she held the phone at arm's length so Martinez would not hear the wet noises she was making. She reminded herself that this was exactly the way she'd responded the last time Martinez had promised to produce Isaac, and failed.

Her second reaction—and this was new—was a wave of queasy anxiety. Isaac was a filthy street person now, a malevolent stranger who had captured and engulfed her child. She was afraid of his smell. This was a recently developed obsession. As she lay awake at night she'd imagined it. Somehow it seemed essential to get it right, to summon it so vividly that it became a true olfactory hallucination. She knew the smell template from her years in New York, when she picked her way around the bums who warmed themselves on the subway grates. It was a rich, blunt, yeasty odor at first, and then the frank reek of fresh urine poked through. For two years—longer than that, really, because even when he still lived at home he'd refused to wash—she'd been longing to run warm water in the tub and settle Isaac into it, just as she'd done when he was small, to sit on the rim and sing to him while he soaked, to welcome him into a dry towel when he was clean.

Just a month or so ago they'd seen him from the car. When

she begged Ben to pull over and stop, he refused. They'd agreed, he reminded her. They'd promised to stay away. They could set things back. Who was Martinez to keep them from their own son, Ruth demanded. They'd been over this ground again and again, sometimes switching sides, Ben taking the anti-Martinez position and Ruth defending him. These sessions usually ended with both of them wondering if it was possible that Martinez was skimming money from the monthly cash allowances they sent through him to Isaac.

What Ruth hadn't told Ben was that she'd seen Isaac herself, several times, and hadn't stopped the car. Actually, one time she did. She parked and got out and followed him at a distance, keeping a block between them, weeping all the while, unable to summon up a voice with which to call his name. Eventually Isaac ducked into a building. His destination was an office of some kind on the second floor; she saw an acronym and an arrow.

"This happened once before," said Ruth. "And it fell through." In her own ears she sounded abrupt and rude, a suspicious spoilsport.

"Yes," said Martinez. "For this I must chide myself. Isaac was not yet ready. It was too early. This time is different. He has something he wishes to tell you."

"What is it?" Ruth's heart was flopping irregularly.

"Mrs. Blau," said Dr. Martinez, "I appreciate that you are anxious. This is to be expected." (Real normal, thought Ruth.) "You have been disappointed, and you wish not to be disappointed again. It is Isaac's wish that he should be the one to tell. We need to respect these wishes. Shall we make an appointment?"

.   .   .

The young Philbys had been admitted. As she came down the stairs she saw that they were seated side by side on the sofa in the otherwise empty second living room. A contingent of three new graduate students had also arrived while she was on the phone. They were gathered in the kitchen in a cluster around Ben. Ruth poured herself a glass of wine, much fuller than she'd intended, and resolved to make it last until eight. She hovered for a few moments on the periphery of the group. The students were oblivious to her—social skills were not a strength in this discipline—and Ben could only shoot her anxious glances. He was constitutionally incapable of extracting himself from conversations.

The Philbys had left their contribution of meatballs in a Crock-Pot on the kitchen island. Turning the burner on low under her own pot of chicken chili, she caught sight of her reflection in the glass door of a cabinet. Her eye makeup had run and her hair had come loose; two graying sheaves of it lay flopped on her shoulders. She ducked into the half bath at the end of the hall leading away from the kitchen. Leaning into the mirror, she scrubbed at her eyes with a wad of dampened toilet paper. It wasn't easy to get the stuff off; mostly she was redistributing it, further darkening the bags under her eyes. What had she been thinking of, painting herself so heavily? Why hadn't Ben said something? It seemed she'd reached the age when nobody will tell a woman the truth about the way she looks. She thought of a local harridan who showed up for lectures and panel discussions in false eyelashes and a Cleopatra wig. Now there was a cautionary tale.

And why had she thought it appropriate to put on her most outré jewelry, the earlobe-stretching silver disks and the great clanking bedouin breastplate? The students would take her for a madwoman—some of them already did. Ricia and Charles would take her for what she was, a frustrated faculty wife desperate to impress. She unhooked the necklace and stashed it in a drawer. Better. She scrubbed her face some more, took down her hair from its armature of tortoiseshell combs and brushed it smooth. She looked at her face in the mirror. There it was, flushed and raw from rubbing but as always plain, long, "pleasant." Also younger.

Leaving the bathroom she noted that Ben was still cornered and that the Philbys continued to languish alone. She knew her duty. "Welcome," she called out, striding across the room. They shrank together a little at her approach. "How've you two been?" she demanded. Todd replied that they'd been fine. Melinda directed her gaze at Ruth's feet. She joined them on the couch, a foot away from Todd, bracing herself with one hand and pivoting on her hip so as to face them brightly.

"Ready for another academic year?" she asked.

"Guess so," said Todd.

"What are you signed up for this fall?"

"I'm taking Dr. Wendell's Ancient Philosophy and Dr. Johns's Ecstasy seminar."

"Ecstasy. Well, that'll be a change."

Todd surprised her. "Huh-yeh," he snorted. "*Real*ly." Ruth recognized an allusion to Beavis and Butt-Head—when Isaac lived at home she sometimes tried to join him in front of the television. She was grateful to Todd for this spark of irony, this flash of fellow feeling. It seemed to open up conversational possibilities. But she was distracted by Melinda, who continued to sit frozen in profile on Todd's far side, like a fugitive evading a searchlight beam. Was that really necessary? Was Ruth such an object of horror that this young female rabbit couldn't bring herself to make eye contact? She was visited with an urge to get on her hands and knees and scramble over Todd and push her face into Melinda's. That'd give her something to be afraid of.

"What are you reading for the Ecstasy seminar?" she asked Todd.

"Uh, Blake, Whitman, some others. I forget."

"Sounds like an English course."

"It's cross-listed with English. Religion, too."

"And Kinesiology," said Ruth. That elicited another faint chortle from Todd.

She saw that Ben had broken free of the graduate students and was easing across the room in her direction, stopping to greet new arrivals. She stood and lifted a finger. "Excuse me," she said. "I'll be back. Can I get you something to drink? Wine, beer, soft drink, fizzy water?"

Todd turned to Melinda, who mumbled something in his ear. "Do you have Diet Sprite?" he asked.

"Indeed we do," said Ruth in her best hearty-hostess voice. She'd reluctantly bought two big plastic bottles of it that afternoon.

Heading toward the kitchen, she encountered Ben, deep in conversation with Josh Margolis from political science. Unacknowledged, she waited for a break in their shoptalk. Just as she was about to give up and return to her Diet Sprite mission, Beth Mapes tapped her on the shoulder. Beth was a favorite graduate student of Ben's from many years back, a likable lesbian in her late thirties with an erect carriage and a neatly maintained buzz cut. Ruth always pictured her wearing epaulets and metal-rimmed spectacles, like the young Kropotkin. "Beth," she said, after they'd exchanged cheek kisses, "I'm so glad to see you. Tell me something: do I scare you? I seem to be scaring people tonight." Ben had taken notice now; something in the quality of Ruth's voice had made him abandon his conversation with Josh to monitor Ruth's with Beth. He was smiling—she hadn't yet gone too far—but his fingers were tightly interlaced and his thumbs were moving in agitated circles.

"Do you *scare* me?" said Beth. "Certainly not. Who'd you scare?"

"Oh never mind. A graduate student. It doesn't matter."

"Graduate students need scaring," said Beth.

"Excuse me, Beth," said Ruth. "I've been waiting to have a word with Ben." She took him by the wrist and led him out of the living room and up the stairs. She wanted to get into the bedroom and close the door, but Ben stopped her in mid-ascent.

"Tell me now. How much does he want?"

"He doesn't want money. He wants to see us," she said. "He wants to meet with us."

"Who? Martinez?"

"No, Isaac. With Martinez."

"Ah, this again."

"Martinez says he's got something to tell us."

"What is it?"

"He wouldn't say. He said he wants to leave that to Isaac."

Ben clutched his head in his hands. "For God's sake, Ruth, why didn't you insist? He has no business . . . Where are we supposed to go for this meeting?"

"His office. Martinez's office. Look, Ben, this could be very good news." (*Could it really?*) "I don't see why you're taking it this way." It would be just like Ben to dig in his heels when negotiations were at their most fragile.

"Do you think he's still there?"

"There? Who?"

"Martinez."

"In his office?" She had no idea. Maybe he'd gone home. Maybe he was seeing a patient.

"Call him back now. Demand to know what this is about."

"No," said Ruth. "*I'm* not calling. *You* call." The word "no," she realized, had come out as an indignant yelp. The low chatter of guests standing at the foot of the stairs went silent. She and Ben had been audible—and visible too, she realized, or at least their legs had been—all along. She looked down into a semicircle of faces, all blank, all curious. From left to right: Bobo Ernhardt, a bow-tied mathematician and bicycling enthusiast, not a member of the department but a kind of fellow traveler to the logicians; Roberta Mitten-Kurz, dean of humanities; Bob and Barbara Bachman and nine-year-old Ariel, who held a large Pyrex baking dish full of something she'd no doubt baked herself; two unidentified young women in jeans; and the Brautigans, a quiet couple who lived across the street.

In the midst of this silence, the doorbell rang—a loud, ripe, startling peal. Ruth made her way down the stairs; the guests parted to let her through. She opened the door to a stout middle-aged man in a Mexican wedding shirt, perspiring heavily and holding a giant bouquet of mixed lilies. "Charles Johns," said Ruth.

"The very same." He proffered the lilies and she took them, murmuring that they were lovely. Ben was right, she thought.

Charles Johns did indeed have a remarkable voice, with a timbre so deep it reminded her of the gargling devotions made by Buddhist monks.

"Will we be seeing your wife tonight?"

"She sends regrets. One of her migraines." *Me*graines, as he said it. The British pronunciation.

To the wondering remorseful Ruth of the next morning it seemed that the loss of control began when she squawked at Ben and drew an audience. From this moment onward her memories lost narrative cohesion and became episodic. She remembered offering Charles Johns a glass of the Australian shiraz she'd been drinking and finding that the bottle was all but empty. Deftly and efficiently he uncorked a new one and with a sommelier's twist of the wrist poured glasses for them both. This was her third, or perhaps her fourth.

She remembered her second encounter with the young Philbys, still marooned on one end of the couch. She'd made a mental note to bring them the Diet Sprites she had promised earlier, but instead found herself approaching them with a bowl of wasabi peas. Todd declined them, but to Ruth's surprise Melinda leaned forward to examine what was in the bowl, her nostrils quivering. "Have you tried these?" asked Ruth, encouraged by this show of interest. "I love them. I eat them all day long."

Melinda considered them for a moment, then shook her head faintly and leaned back into Todd's shoulder. "Really!" said Ruth. "Try some!" As if to demonstrate how delicious she found them, she scooped up a handful and brought it to her mouth, and then another and another, all the while chewing enthusiastically. Looking down, she saw that bright green peas and pea fragments and bits of mashed pea had collected on the carpet around her shoes.

She remembered giving Dean Mitten-Kurz a piece of her mind. She'd been meaning to do this for a year now, or at least she'd fantasized about it. She wanted to let it be known how outraged and disappointed she'd been when she learned that the Lola English Department had ended its relationship with Frank Muldoon, an eminent literary critic of Welsh extraction. She'd been surprised and excited when Muldoon moved to Spangler, apparently for complicated personal reasons. In her graduate-student days he'd been considered the preeminent literary critic of his time. His books and essays were magically insightful, rigorous, subtle, always clear, always accessible to the educated lay reader. Even as literary theory became entrenched dogma in one English department after another, the unfashionable Muldoon continued to write, and by sheer force of mind, to command a readership inside and outside those departments.

When he arrived in Spangler he was in his late seventies, but still brilliantly productive. People looked at him wonderingly, suspiciously. When would his powers begin to fail? He taught graduate seminars at both Lola and the local branch of the state university for several years. Just when Ruth had summoned the nerve to sign up as an auditor, the Lola English Department abruptly let him go in favor of a young American studies specialist. Muldoon left Spangler then and moved to Cambridge to teach a seminar at the Harvard of the North. Ruth had met him once, briefly, at a university reception, where he accepted her stammering compliments with gracious modesty. He'd been out on the balcony alone when she approached him, smoking a Players, looking for all the world like an elderly pensioner drinking his pint in an empty pub.

The dean was standing by the door, evidently trying to edge her way out of the house. She'd been snagged for the moment by Marv Plotkin, a grievance-mongering part-timer. Roberta Mitten-Kurz was an impressively obese woman in her early sixties, a plus-size clotheshorse who wore cleverly knotted hand-painted scarves and enviably expensive silver jewelry. Ruth had dealt with her on the two occasions when Ben had managed to wangle her adjunct lectureships in the English Department.

"Dean Mitten-Kurz," she called out. Suddenly it seemed she was speaking in a vibrant new voice, a Greer Garson–greets-the-faculty voice. "Ben and I are so pleased you were able to join us tonight." Mitten-Kurz's head swiveled toward her. Plotkin faded away.

"Lovely party," said Mitten-Kurz, backing away, "but I'm afraid I have a number of potlucks to drop in on tonight."

"Yes," said Ruth. "Tonight's the night for them, isn't it?"

"A wonderful tradition," said Mitten-Kurz, smiling warmly and reaching for the doorknob. "A Lola tradition."

Here was Ruth's chance. "Before you go, Dean Mitten-Kurz, there's something I've been wanting to talk to you about. I've been troubled about this for some time." Mitten-Kurz squared her shoulders and turned to face Ruth deliberately. This was a smoothly executed multistage maneuver like the wheeling around of a battleship. It involved the adjustment of various lengths of trailing fabric and gave the dean time to reassume the mantle of her deanliness. "I know I'm not a full-time faculty member," Ruth began, "not even a faculty member at all, technically speaking . . ." In her ears her voice sounded high and wheedling, so she did her best to deepen and steady it. "But I am a member of the university community," she went on. Mitten-Kurz nodded emphatically. "Yes, you are," she said. "And a valued one."

Here Ruth was distracted by tears, which had sprung into her eyes embarrassingly. "I am a member of the community," she repeated, her voice quavering, "and I believe we all lost something irreplaceable when we lost Frank Muldoon." (*Do I really care so much about this?* an internal critic inquired. In truth, she hadn't thought about Muldoon for months.) A shadow of dismay passed over the dean's undersized features. "I know I'm not the only one who feels this way," Ruth added. That was weak, she thought, unnecessarily defensive.

"I think we were all very conscious of how honored we were to have Professor Muldoon among us," said Mitten-Kurz.

"Well then why isn't he among us now?" said Ruth, registering in some remote cerebral listening post that with this bluntness she'd gone too far.

Mitten-Kurz sighed. It was a sigh she'd sighed before, Ruth could tell, the sigh a dean sighs when she is forced to deal with an unreasonable petitioner. "That . . . decision . . . came out of a long and complex and sometimes . . . difficult . . . conversation among the stakeholders."

"The stakeholders? Who are the stakeholders?"

"Well," said the dean evenly, "the stakeholders are exactly who you'd expect them to be."

"The tenured English faculty," said Ruth.

"Yes, and elements of the administration. And the board has a certain amount of input. There was a feeling among the English faculty that Professor Muldoon didn't entirely represent the current thinking in the field. As I think you know, I myself am a sociologist. When I don't know much about a subject I tend to defer to those who do."

Ruth felt the intended dig. She also registered a suspicion that in fact the dean knew quite a bit about the current thinking. So did Ruth, but something told her not to let on about that. If Mitten-Kurz could play the innocent, so could she. Best to stand her ground as an indignant amateur. "Am I," she asked, her voice once again quavering involuntarily, "am I not a stakeholder?"

"Well of course—"

"Do I not read? Do I not *think* about what I read?"

The dean had thrown up her hands now, and was smiling a tender, ironic smile in the direction of some imagined auditor. The *characters* we have here in our academic community, that smile said. The irritating characters who are nonetheless a vital *part* of that lively community.

"Stakeholders," said Ruth, who knew she was speaking too loudly and no longer cared. "Are not all we readers stakeholders?" (Should that have been "us," not "we"? She was stumbling over her own inverted syntax.) She tried again. "Why can't we all be stakeholders? In literature?" That didn't sound right either, but she'd be damned if she didn't get some use out of this appropriated trope, even though Ben, trapped in conversation across the room, had just shot her a look of horror. "Let me put it another way, Dean Mitten-Kurz. If academics are the only stake—"

But gentle fingers had closed around her upper arm. It was Marjorie Brautigan, her quiet across-the-street neighbor. "Ruth," she whispered—Marjorie was an anxious, tentative, helpful soul. "People are starting to get hungry? I've been trying to get the table organized? I don't know where you keep things?"

The potluck. Ruth had completely forgotten. It seemed a new dispensation had begun because in the twinkling of an eye Mitten-Kurz had melted away and now Ruth was sitting on a stool in her disorderly kitchen drinking another glass of wine while Marjorie and—to her slightly numb surprise—Charles Johns were taking charge of the chaos of casseroles and baking dishes and salad bowls on the central island. They had transferred what was salvageable of her chicken chili into a microwavable glass bowl and left the blackened pot to soak in the sink. "Thank you," she said to them a number of times as they methodically ferried the potluck offerings into the dining room, around which she could see that guests were beginning to cluster like deer at a salt lick. "Thank you so much. I can't tell you how grateful I am."

Then she was sitting outside on the back steps among a group of four smokers, holding in her hand yet another glass of wine. She could be sure it was new because it was white, not red as the previous ones had been. One of her companions was Brad Sonenshein, a veteran graduate student famous for being unable to complete his dissertation. Another was his chronically exasperated girlfriend, Danielle, whose last name Ruth had forgotten. The third was a chunky young man with a head of glossy dark curls. She'd seen him before but had never caught either of his names. The fourth was Charles Johns.

The conversation was languid and intermittent, touching on such topics as Internet movie rentals and the new sushi stand in the Student Union food court. It was the smoking ritual that was the main thing, the communal ritual of inhale and exhale and the wavering room of smoke that housed them all in the heavy warm air. How could she have forsaken the company of smokers? It seemed to her that a certain necessary kind of human intimacy had all but disappeared from the world, and that one of the few places it could still be found was among the members of these transient communities of exiles who huddle outside hospitals and office buildings and houses. The idea made her want to laugh, and so she did, deeply and inwardly but not inaudibly, because Charles Johns, who was standing apart from the group a little, began to laugh with her and also to cough.

She wanted to talk to him, to take advantage of the marvelous elision of transitions that drunkenness makes possible, but before she could edge over to where he stood, her attention was caught by the face of the chunky young man whose name she didn't know. He had turned so that the light caught his profile. Who was it he resembled, with that high forehead, those dark, liquid, exophthalmic eyes, those curls? Was it Beethoven? No. Was it Orson Welles? No. Then it came to her. "Byron," she blurted out. "Do you know you look like Byron? George Gordon Lord Byron?" This was her first conversational offering, and apparently it was unacceptable. The young man gaped at her. His companions smirked. Charles Johns, standing out of the light, seemed to be toeing the ground with his shoe.

Time had elapsed and she was sitting on the wrought-iron bench among the weedy flagstones at the very back of the property. She had no glass of wine and though she couldn't remember exactly what series of events had caused her to be here and not where she'd been before, she had the impression she'd been left alone in a condition of disgrace. She felt desolate enough to weep.

She had her back to the house and the light, so she was mildly surprised when Charles Johns settled himself on the bench, close enough so that she could feel both the fat and the muscle in the arm and the thigh that pressed companionably against hers. *"Zoë mou sas agapo,"* he said. His voice was a comforting rumble.

"Maid of Athens, Ere We Part" said Ruth. The region of her brain that stored titles and verses and song lyrics was unassailable. No amount of alcohol could shut it down.

Charles Johns had brought her a selection of miniature quiches and some slices of brisket and what looked like a mound of rice and beans, all piled on a sagging paper plate. "Have something to eat," he said. "Have you eaten today?" She hadn't, except for a spoonful or two of ill-fated chicken chili and the wasabi peas she'd force-fed herself an hour or so earlier. She took the fork he offered her and made her way doggedly around the plate. The food tasted of nothing, but already she'd begun to feel steadier and clearer. "Thank you," she said. "I think I'm a little better."

"Eat it all," said Charles. "Every bit. You need some buffering fats in your system when you drink." His accent, she realized, was not slightly British, as she'd thought, but slightly and aristocratically Southern—a Tidewater accent. She finished the food.

"At our age we can't push it as we once did," he said as he took the damp plate away from her and folded it into a tidy wedge. This from a man who must have weighed two hundred and eighty pounds. If she hadn't felt so grateful she might have bristled. "I've been looking forward so much to meeting you," she said. For the first time that evening her voice sounded sane and natural. "I've been reading Ricia's book and I was looking forward to talking to her."

"She was sorry—" Charles Johns began, but Ruth waved him off. "It's just as well," she said. "She would have been bored to death. I'm sorry I acted badly," she went on. "I had an upsetting phone call just before people started arriving. Do you have children?"

"I do," said Charles. "Two grown children, both estranged. And you?"

"One," said Ruth. Charles had firmly and deftly turned them off this subject. She rifled through her mental files to find another but nothing came to her, no question or remark that seemed appropriate to this odd encounter. How long could she sit here, like a patient under the care of an attendant? Finally she turned to face Charles Johns directly and blurted out, quite unpremeditatedly, "How do we grow old?"

This caught him by surprise. "Well how do we *not*?"

"No, I mean it. I mean of course we *can't* not, but don't you feel that people of our generation are singularly unequipped—" Here Charles lit a cigarette and offered her one, which she declined.

"—singularly unequipped to meet the fact of growing old? Don't you think that after we've reached a certain age, after fifty-five or so, there are no markers anymore? We no longer have any way to locate where we are in our lives? No sense of where we are in relation to the end? Just a long featureless glide and none of the traditional signs along the way. When I think about somebody like Mamie Eisenhower . . ." But no. Forget Mamie Eisenhower. That was a tiresome way to illustrate her point. "How old are you, by the way? May I ask?"

"You may. I'm fifty-two." Ruth was surprised. She'd taken him to be her senior by at least five years.

"Does that sound familiar to you? The glide path? Maybe you're still too young. Maybe it really doesn't hit until fifty-five."

Charles had started to laugh. "What?" said Ruth. "That was funny, what I said?" She was laughing herself, nervously craning her neck in an effort to make out his expression in the darkness.

"Yes it was funny," said Charles. "If you can think of life as a glide I congratulate you. I think of life as a plummet."

Charles's laughter brought on a coughing fit. When he'd gotten it under control they sat for a while in a comfortably despondent silence. Ruth was sober now, and very tired. The ordinary rules of social distance had reestablished themselves. She needed to return to a more conventional conversational footing. "I hear you're teaching a very interesting course," she said, glancing at him as if he were sitting to her left at a dinner party. "Sounds very literary."

"Ah," said Charles. "I just reach around and take books off my shelves more or less at random. I'm afraid I'm really not a trained philosopher. Not like your husband. I've done a good deal of reading and thinking, but not in any systematic kind of way."

"So you've done this before? This kind of teaching?"

"That and a number of other things. I worked in construction until I started sprouting hernias. I ran a bookstore. A few years ago I tried to set myself up as a kind of all-purpose consultant, working from home. I had no idea what I was doing, just imitating another layabout I know. Do I sound like a book jacket?"

"You left out lumberjack," said Ruth. "And stevedore. And short-order cook."

A pause followed, long enough to make Ruth begin to feel anxious. "A failed writer," Charles said at last, shooting her a quick apologetic smile. "That's really what I am."

"So am I! What do you write?"

"Poetry and plays. There was a time in the early eighties when my work got some attention. I had a couple of things produced off-Broadway. What do you write?"

"Short stories and novels. I haven't published recently. I had a kind of trilogy published ages ago." Charles Johns cocked an inquiring eyebrow.

"Getting Good," said Ruth. It had been years since she'd found an opportunity to tell someone, years since she'd felt this particular constriction around the heart.

"*Getting Good*? I know *Getting Good*. I can see it on the shelf."

"You've read it?" Ruth's hands flew to her cheeks. Involuntarily, she stood up.

"Not me. Ricia. It's one of her books. She's had it forever. I know she thinks well of it. I've never had a chance to look at it myself . . ."

The light went on over the back steps and Ben appeared. The party was over, had long been over. Ben was scanning the darkness, looking irritated. "Shall we go in?" Ruth said to Charles, who rose to his feet. She took the arm he offered. "Ben," she called out as they made their way across the hummocky yard, both stumbling a little. "You can't guess what Charles just told me!" The toad of the evening had burped up an emerald.

CHAPTER FOUR

You fat turd. The words were so much Ben's thought that for a moment he was honestly unsure whether or not he'd spoken them. Apparently he hadn't, because from her rocking chair across an expanse of sisal mat Roberta Mitten-Kurz was continuing to dispense paragraphs. "Of course we understand," she was saying, "that the relationship has to have been very special. Dolores was with the department for what—fifteen years?" As she spoke she was knitting something long and ciliated. She kept her eyes lowered and her big jowly chin tilted thoughtfully, as if modeling for Ben a recommended attitude of rueful detachment.

"Seventeen," he said.

"Seventeen. And we know that your relationship with her has been special as well. She's told us as much. We had to explain to her that while her loyalty is admirable, no department chair has an exclusive claim on any particular staff member."

"Ah, where . . . ?"

Mitten-Kurz's pause lasted a fraction of a second too long. Her eyes darted his way, then darted back. "She'll be joining us in sociology."

Of course.

"We've added several positions in the last few years. Two of the new people are doing ambitious quantitative studies. We've been limping along with one part-timer and one student assistant. It just hasn't been enough."

In its architectural bones, Mitten-Kurz's office was identical to every other on this corridor of the Lola administration building, but she had transformed it into a kind of jungle bower. Plants gathered thickly in the windows and crouched in every corner. She had seated Ben in a rocker opposite her own in a clearing defined by a circle of potted trees. A great fronded thing reared up behind him and over his head like a cobra; he found himself repeatedly twisting his neck to glance up at it. She kept at least two humidifiers going; the saturated air held a distinct compost smell and a hint of the urinous perfume of orchids. Big and Baby, Mitten-Kurz's two Weimaraners, lay heraldically at her feet.

"Now," she said, taking a punctuating sip of the pungent-smelling herbal tea she drank continually and never offered to visitors, "there's another more general matter I need to take up with you. I'm sure you're aware there's been a certain amount of talk among the other humanities departments, a perception that philosophy has been, historically, a bit of an outlier, a little less . . . accountable. We've heard that over the years. To be fair, it predated your chairmanship." She shot him a look over her half-glasses. "But I have to tell you, Ben, that lately we've been hearing it a lot. I have to tell you that philosophy is now the only humanities department that has yet to come into compliance with the SCAC guidelines. You've had plenty of time, Ben. Plenty of notice. We started sending out the materials last February."

Since when had she been using the royal we? Had she been doing it forever? Had he simply not noticed? "So that's why you're taking Dolores away?" he said.

Mitten-Kurz sighed and rolled her eyes. "Ben," she said. "Please." Now he was eleven and she was his long-suffering mother. Ben raised his own eyes and looked into hers. How small they were, he thought, punched into her face like raisins into dough. Abnormally small. Wickedly small. For a long moment, neither of them looked away. The dogs raised their heads and joined the contest, fixing Ben with their baleful yellow gaze. Mitten-Kurz was the first to let her eyes slide away, but even so, Ben hadn't won. He couldn't. Not in this Mitten-Kurz total environment, where Big and Baby and all the witnessing plants and even the antique brass samovar on the mantel were assembled against him.

"Ben," she said, "I'm sure you realize that the decision about Dolores Calderon had nothing to do with any . . . effort . . . to punish you. That's not what we're about. It's simply a matter of the efficient and equitable allocation of resources. You know," she went on, her tone suddenly confiding, "as a matter of fact it very likely would have happened soon anyway. We got a heads-up last April that Dr. Dreddle's employee-rotation policy would be going into effect in the next eighteen months."

Ben couldn't let this pass. "Employee rotation?" *Fat turd.*

"Yes, I know. Everybody had trouble getting their minds around it at first." (Everybody? This was the first Ben had heard of it.) "Dr. Dreddle comes to us with a doctorate from MIT *and* an MBA from the Wharton School of Management. He'll be giving us the benefit of some very new thinking. The idea behind ER is the same as the idea behind a lot of his initiatives. He says that a university—any institution, really, but *especially* a university—is like a circulatory system. The real danger is blockage. Institutions thrive on change. The mistake administrators make is to try to keep things frozen, keep change at bay."

Ben hadn't been there himself—he had his own policies and one of them was to duck out of any administration-sanctioned event where he wouldn't be missed—but it came back to him now that when Lee Wayne Dreddle, soon to be installed as fourteenth president of Lola, had been introduced to the university community by the provost last May in the Convocation Chapel, his first act had been to walk around the room throwing open all the windows. Apparently they had been painted shut until a few days before the event, when Dreddle's advance man called the dean, who urgently dispatched the Building and Grounds Department to pry them loose.

Outside the closed windows of Mitten-Kurz's office he could hear the lulling drone of multiple lawn mowers. B&G had been trimming and watering and pruning and planting frenetically in preparation for the ceremonies surrounding Dreddle's installation. Ben looked down on the shining tile of car roofs in the faculty parking lot and the jewel-bright lawn beyond it and beyond that the tall hedges that set the university off from the outer world of Spangler. He watched as a pair of long-legged girls in white shorts twinkled along a path under the live oaks, passing in and out of shadow and chattering soundlessly. He thought of Ecclesiastes:

What has been is what will be,
And what has been done is what will be done,
and there is nothing new under the sun.

Change is good. That old wheeze. He'd heard it first in high school, from a self-conscious young civics teacher named Wasserman who made a habit of twirling straight-backed chairs around and straddling them. Later he heard it from the resident adviser in his college dorm, who used it to justify moving him out of a single room when an alumnus who had just donated a skating rink to the university demanded it for his son. How many times had he corrected people who quoted Heraclitus as saying that you never step into the same river twice? (No, he'd told them. You never step into the same river *once*.) "Change is good" was the single most hackneyed notion he could think of. No, it was worse than hackneyed, worse even than false, because what could it mean? (Change is good? Any change? At the risk of belaboring the obvious, how could *that* be the case?) And yet decade after decade the phrase was rediscovered and repeated and made much of by people like Lee Wayne Dreddle and Roberta Mitten-Kurz, who understood the uses of meaninglessness.

Dolores was probably emptying out her desk right now. That was how they did things: endless committee creation, endless meetings, endless bureaucratic inaction, and then—suddenly and without warning and just when everyone was stuporous with boredom—they'd pounce. How would he manage? This news came just as he'd begun the difficult ascent of chapter seven. Now more than ever he needed his long mornings, his freedom of mind. If they'd waited even another six months he might have managed to scramble over the summit, with nothing but the easy downhill slope of eight in prospect.

". . . and we'll just take it from there," Mitten-Kurz was saying. Just what it was they'd take and from where they'd take it he had missed, but now she was stowing her knitting in a straw bag and rising ponderously to her feet. Evidently the interview was over. Ben stood. Big and Baby took this as their cue to spring up and escort him out of the jungle bower, one dog leaning into his thigh while the other kept him moving along smartly by using its snout as a rectal prod. Pausing at the door, Mitten-Kurz said, "So. Ben. We're on the same page now, are we?"

Same page? As he shook her big soft hand he did his best to produce a small civil smile, but he could feel that all he'd managed was a puzzled wince. "Oh wait," she said. "Hang on a minute. I have something for you to take to Ruth."

Ruth? She left him for a moment to the renewed attentions of Big and Baby and fetched something from her desk. "Here," she said, handing him an envelope. "I thought of Ruth after your lovely potluck last week. She and I had a very interesting talk."

Once out of the building Ben sat down on a bench in the breezeway and examined the envelope. Mitten-Kurz had hand-addressed it in flowing script. In the lower left corner she'd written "Courtesy of Ben," and underlined it emphatically. His teacher in fourth grade had done exactly the same when communicating with his mother. He and Ruth had never read each other's mail, but already he'd tucked a thumb under the flap and ripped the letter open. The bloated signature at the bottom of the page was the first thing he noticed. It was like a graffiti tag on a subway car, each character bellying belligerently into its neighbor. The letter read as follows:

Dear Ruth,

As you know, LDI is in the process of inaugurating a new president. Dr. Lee Wayne Dreddle comes to us with many exciting ideas. Very important among these is a rededicated commitment to community involvement. One of the Dreddle administration's most urgent priorities will be the crafting of a new mission statement for the university. Dr. Dreddle has charged us to identify community leaders in a variety of areas to serve on a number of mission-statement task forces. Each group will create its own mission-statement text, and Dr. Dreddle will draw from these to write the final statement.

When the task forces have completed their work, local artisans will stitch quotes from the texts onto fabric squares and fashion them into a colorful quilt, creating a work of art that will serve as a lasting tribute to the vibrant community from which LDI draws so many of its resources. The quilt will be framed and hung above the great hearth in the projected Sol and Lillian B. Katz Student Commons building, for which ground will be broken early next year.

As a prominent member of the Spangler writing community, you would be particularly well qualified to serve on the literary task force. Other task forces will be composed of musicians, painters, sculptors, potters, dancers, and multimedia and performance artists. Still others will represent the local educational, religious, legal, medical, and business communities. Please let us know if you're available to join us in this endeavor, which would require only a few hours of your time.

I send my best and warmest regards and thanks for your
recent hospitality.
     Cordially yours,
     Roberta Mitten-Kurz

Fat turd. Ben crumpled the letter in his fist. On his way across
the green he flipped it into one of the new oversize wire-mesh
trash cans the university had just purchased.

E ver since the night of the potluck dinner, Ruth had been
    waiting for a summons from Ricia Spottiswoode to lunch
or coffee. Or perhaps an invitation to an intimate dinner party:
that was her favorite among the possibilities she'd been imagin-
ing. Charles would cook, and there would be plenty of loosening
alcohol and the other couple would be publishing people from
New York, an agent and an editor. They wouldn't actually have
read *Getting Good*—Ruth liked to introduce a bit of the grit of
the plausible into her fantasies—but while Charles was busy in
the kitchen, Ricia would give a rapturous summary, perhaps even
take the book down from the shelf and read a few passages aloud.
The couple would strike Ruth as intimidating at first (especially
the woman, with her sleeveless black linen shift and Long Island–
lockjaw drawl), but soon enough Charles's deft pouring would
warm everyone up. The publishing couple would demand to know
how it was that a savvy pair like Ruth and Ben had come to rest in
this Texas exile, and Ruth would rise to a tenderly ironic defense
of Spangler, one which only a transplanted Easterner could give.
By the end of the evening she and the publishing couple would
be gathered by the door in a cozily intoxicated huddle, scribbling

down e-mail addresses and phone numbers. Goodbyes would not be spoken before a promise was extracted from Ruth to let the (the who? What would a couple like that be named? Kay Dworkin and Robert Glassell) the Dworkin-Glassells be the first to have a look at anything new she'd written since *Getting Good*.

She was carrying the manuscript of *Whole Lives Devoured* in a typing-paper box in her Guatemalan woven satchel. Foolish of her, no doubt, but what was the harm in being prepared? The box was sliding around inside the bag, its sharp corner bruising her thigh as she wandered, lost, through tiled underground corridors in the new Chemistry Building in search of the Sitwell Auditorium where Ricia Spottiswoode's introductory Q&A and signing was to be held.

She turned a corner into yet another stretch of corridor and found herself greeted by a three-quarter life-size cardboard cutout of Ricia as she appeared on the cover of *The Divining Rod*—the smiling Ricia of the leather mini and the bouncing curl—propped in the doorway to the auditorium. Claude Petrie, the owner and proprietor of Bagatelle Books, Spangler's only independent bookstore, had set up a table in the cave-like vestibule just inside. As she passed, Ruth gave him a quick cautious smile. She was afraid of this waspish and immaculate little man, the warmth of whose greeting was a sure gauge of one's standing in the Spangler arts and arts-philanthropy scene. He looked up and nodded faintly. To this she had fallen. Twenty years ago she'd have gotten the full treatment—the ecstatic wince, the out-flung arms, the double air kiss.

The first to arrive, she climbed the gently graduated steps to a seat in the next-to-last row, stowed her manuscript under her chair and sat down. Almost immediately, her thoughts ran off into a number of lightly monitored channels. She thought about the snub she'd just received from Claude Petrie, reminding herself that narcissistic wounds heal as readily as cuts in flesh and reflecting on how odd it was that she had come to realize this only a few years ago, and how the understanding itself tended to speed up the process, at least when the hurt was minor (as surely this one was). She thought about the nautilus shape of the auditorium, and that put her in mind of a book about the mathematical basis of the symmetry of natural forms she'd once paged through with Isaac in a used bookstore, close-up photographs of snowflakes and aerial views of deserts and mud slides. Where had they been? In Saratoga Springs. Ben had been giving a talk at Skidmore. When was that? At least ten years ago, because Isaac had been young enough to be led from one enlightening activity to another. Even at twelve he would still consent to look at a book with a parent, and in his absorption he would sometimes revert to the trust of infancy, leaning against her unconsciously as she turned the pages, allowing his hand to rest on hers. She could still retrieve the proprietor of that bookstore, an agelessly odd-looking woman wearing several sweaters over what looked like a dirndl, bald except for a feather of white hair growing out of the crown of her head. It was on that trip that Isaac threw a tantrum at breakfast in a coffee shop because, he insisted, the menus smelled bad.

She was thinking about how comfortable she felt sitting here alone in this still-dark, still-empty room. At a long stoplight Ben would swell with irritation, breathe harshly, drum his fingers on the steering wheel. He tended to be just as compulsively early to appointments as Ruth, but to him waiting was anathema while to her it was soothing, a natural condition. That was why she was chronically early. She liked to arrive ten or fifteen minutes before things began exactly because it gave her a chance to wait, to allow her thoughts to expand and fill unoccupied space. But now two boys and a tall girl had come trooping into the well of the auditorium, their shining hair lit by the overhead spots.

And a beat or two after their passage, Isaac followed. Or it was Isaac, but a clean Isaac wearing a sober dark suit. His hair was long, or at least his sideburns hung down in long curls. And he was wearing a wide-brimmed hat? No, that was not Isaac. That was a young Orthodox Jew. But in the fraction of a second the delusion lasted, the automatic pencil of her imagination had sketched in a vague and wildly hopeful explanatory scenario. Isaac had somehow pulled himself together, washed, bought new clothes, developed the interest in literature she had always hoped he would. He had gotten better. He had returned. That would account for the news he had to impart, for the mysterious appointment scheduled for next Monday.

After him, the deluge: a moment passed and suddenly, as if some seal had been broken, the auditorium proceeded to fill in less than two minutes. When the room had settled people were sitting in the aisles and standing in the entryway. It was the largest literary assembly Ruth had ever seen at Lola. The book editor of the *Spangler Advocate* was here, and a semi-famous transplanted poet and several of the glossy matrons who hosted the luncheons and galas that supported the arts in Spangler. A number of students were present—participants in writing workshops were often conscripted to attend these events—but they made up a smaller percentage of the audience than Ruth would have expected. She picked out a scattering of English Department faculty, mostly the younger people. Lee Odom, the department's elderly Faulknerian, was seated on the aisle near the door. He could be counted on to show up at every reading in Spangler, even ones held in far-flung suburban chain bookstores, scowling all the while. He had hooked his ivory-handled cane over the chairback in front of him and crossed his arms high over his chest. Everything in his attitude announced a grim determination to keep an open mind, and a concomitant preemptive exasperation.

The bulk of the crowd was made up of a constituency Ruth privately called the Women. This was a large, loosely affiliated group of readers, aspiring writers, book-club and workshop participants, mostly middle-aged. They shifted in tides from one reading or signing or charismatic writing teacher to another. Ruth had taught them in workshops offered by Lola's School of Continuing Education, but she had never managed to become one of the cult figures they followed, probably because her style was gentle and accommodating. They seemed to want harsh teachers, destructive critiques. Perhaps they also sensed the discrepancy between Ruth's encouraging manner and her private assessments of their work.

The Women came to reading and writing with an open and unappeasable hunger for Lessons Directly Applicable to Their Lives. When Ruth spoke, they listened eagerly, and when she failed to offer them what they sought their eyes went cloudy and they turned away. They gathered in force whenever a memoirist or a how-to-write author came through town. Once, five years ago, Bagatelle Books sent Ruth an announcement of a reading by an author whose name rang only the vaguest of bells. On the back of the card Claude Petrie had scrawled in green ink: "Ruth—you mustn't miss this!" Intrigued and flattered, she showed up, twenty minutes early as usual. Already, a number of the Women were circulating through the store, paging through quarterlies, hailing and embracing one another. A terrible suspicion was born in Ruth's mind, but she suppressed it until the place had grown so full she found herself forced to the back of the room and pushed up against the atlases and art books. The author arrived, flanked by her editor and publicist. Scrawny and pierced, white but wearing dreadlocks, she spoke hoarsely for a few minutes about the six-month anniversary of her sobriety and her recent acceptance of Jesus Christ as her personal savior, then sat down behind the counter to sign books. For the first time, Ruth saw how deeply she'd been demoted—not just a rank or two, but all the way to the bottom. Claude Petrie, who'd once held a book party in her honor, had lumped her in with the literary lumpenproletariat.

A few steps farther on, Ben turned back, fished the letter out of the trash basket, smoothed and refolded it, and tucked it into the breast pocket of his sports jacket.

Briefly, he cut diagonally across the green, but it was spongy from the aggressive watering of the last few days, so he returned to the sidewalk that led to the back portico of Horace Dees Hall. This had been a designated smoking area until last January, when the university senate established a new policy requiring smokers to move twenty-five feet away from all campus buildings. Today he couldn't help noticing that somebody was defying that edict. It was a woman—hard to guess her age—pacing agitatedly back and forth, talking on a cell phone, smoking away with abandon. She'd left a little trail of butts, in fact, behind her. She had a high, querulous, carrying voice and even at a distance he could catch particularly vehement phrases. "Don't give me that shit . . . That's old shit . . . Nobody's listening to that shit anymore, BJ . . ." Ben regularly heard foul language from students and colleagues. He used it himself, quite compulsively, but this was different. There was no irony in it, no distance. It was ugly, vulgar; for a moment it jarred him out of his preoccupied state. "Shit," as this woman spoke it, was no longer a reified linguistic placeholder: it was the stuff itself. He could actually smell it, as if someone had just dipped a finger in it and waved it under his nostrils.

Twenty minutes after the hour, Ricia Spottiswoode made a hurried entrance. Charles Johns was right behind her, moving faster than Ruth would have thought he could, carrying a small shopping bag of items which he efficiently unloaded onto the podium—a bottle of water, a packet of Kleenex, a number of smaller objects that Ruth couldn't make out. He reached over to lower the microphone and backed away to take a seat in the front row.

The acting English chair—the department was so contentious that Ruth couldn't remember a permanent one—gave a brief introduction. She was a tense, prim woman who always wore a triple strand of pearls. As she spoke, Ricia waited, poised like a Degas dancer in repose, head lowered, fingers loosely interwoven. She was wearing gladiator sandals and a very short gauzy dress in various shades of green with a ragged hemline. Ruth was reminded of the costumes for a production of Jean Giraudoux's *Ondine* that her progressive high school had put on in the late sixties. Her hair had been bundled loosely into a mesh snood. It wasn't easy to see her clearly from this distance—Ruth wished for a pair of opera glasses—but even so she was able to confirm that Ben had been telling the truth. Ricia was not beautiful: her lantern jaw disqualified her. But Ruth had known more than one case of a woman with a near-disfiguring physical flaw that had the paradoxical effect of making her exponentially more rather than less attractive to men.

Ricia made her opening remarks, something about the generous people here in Spangler and how touched she'd been by the reception she and Charles had received. What she said was conventional and unremarkable, but her soft voice had the effect of hushing the crowd and imposing a charmed intimacy. "We've just come from living in the Northeast," she went on, "in Providence, Rhode Island, and I can tell you that folks there aren't nearly so warm and welcoming as you are here." The audience rumbled contentedly at this. Over the years Ruth had noticed that many of the New York–based writers who came through town on publicity tours seemed to arrive with a ready-made Texas twang. The locals, unfailingly polite to a stranger's face, sniggered privately because these celebrities had gotten the accent wrong: it was the sound of the western part of the state they were mimicking. Ricia was the only literary visitor so far to have picked up the knack of producing the big round Spanglish "r," which one did by retracting the tongue and forming the shape of a rose with one's lips.

The interim chair sidled over and whispered something in Ricia's ear. "Oh yes," she said, clapping her hands together under her chin, "I forgot. Questions. Please."

Two dozen arms shot up. The chair pointed to a youngish woman who held up a copy of *The Divining Rod.* "Are you going to be signing these later?"

The chair leaned in once again to the microphone. "Ms. Spottiswoode will be signing for half an hour after this session out in the hall. You?" She gestured at another waving hand.

"I wanted to ask," called out a heavy woman wearing a turned-around Spangler Spitfires baseball cap, "what eventually happened to Danny?" Danny Dewitt was the molesting uncle in *I'm Nobody.*

"Not much, actually," said Ricia. "He did some community service. You see, everybody protected him. That's the way it works in small-town courthouses where everyone's in everyone else's pocket."

The audience reacted like a crowd of theatrical extras expressing outrage, muttering *rhubarb* and *garbage.*

As the din diminished, other hands shot up. Had Ricia considered filing a civil suit? Yes, but she'd decided against it. Did Ricia believe—this from a lecturer in early childhood education named Leah Lapin—that there was therapeutic value in writing a memoir? Had she found it healing to write *I'm Nobody*? Did she have anything to say about the uses of narrative in psychotherapy?

Ricia seemed to be listening intently. She waited for a beat before answering. "No," she said. "I don't know about narrative therapy. I assume that means telling stories about your life?" This response got one loud, barking-seal laugh from someone in the first row. Ricia paused again, for a good thirty seconds; by the time she spoke the audience was silent and riveted. "I can tell you that yes, I did find it therapeutic to write my memoir. But then I've found it therapeutic to write poems too, and plays and novels that never saw anything but the inside of a bureau drawer. I think writing is therapeutic in exactly the way that crocheting is therapeutic, or basket weaving, I suppose. That's the usual example. Or baking bread or throwing pots." She paused, turned, took a pull on her water bottle, returned to the microphone. Her voice,

Ruth noticed, had gained volume and taken on clarity. Ricia Spottiswoode was not at all, she realized, the person she'd been billed as. She was shrewd, thoughtful, grounded. The Ophelia act was a marketing strategy. "I guess what I think is that writing is therapeutic in the occupational therapy kind of way, not so much in the psychoanalytic way. Does that make sense?"

Crowds, Ruth had always believed, are stupid beasts, capable only of fawning or roaring, but Ricia seemed to have coaxed a new trick from this one. She could feel the audience considering Ricia's response: thought was passing over it like a breeze ruffling a lake. But in a moment it had forgotten, and a new field of hands sprang up. The chair moved to one corner of the stage and pointed toward the back of the room. Ruth turned to see that a boy with a gel-spiked forelock was standing in the aisle, grinning brilliantly and waving his arms as if signaling a plane onto a runway. "Benj Bradley?" he called out. "Ricia? We're all thrilled to have you here?"

Ruth had heard his name, or rather read it, in "Notes on New Faculty" in the *Lola Lantern*; he was a recently hired poet in the writing program. New, yes, but so young? She squinted to bring him into better focus. He was wearing flip-flops, for heaven's sake, and a sleeveless camouflage tank top and a pair of those grotesquely baggy cropped khakis that once would have betokened impotence and now meant—what? How old could he be? Twenty-two? Seventeen? Thirty? She could no longer judge the ages of the young. It was coming back to her now that this same Benj Bradley—this mall rat, this beardless ephebe—was the holder of the Belinda Peters Twombly Chair in Rhetoric and Poetic Composition.

Benj Bradley talked fast, bounced on the balls of his feet,

gulped frequently, ended every sentence with an interrogative lilt. "I've got a question? I've got a bunch of questions, actually? I'll limit myself to one?"

"That'd be good," Ricia said, flattening her voice just enough to let the audience know she was playing straight man to Benj Bradley's clown. Indulgent laughter followed, and Ruth was visited by the suspicion that these two actually knew each other. They all did, didn't they? But by the time Benj Bradley had opened his laptop and begun to read his prepared statement— it was more an extended disquisition than an inquiry—he was all gravity and earnestness. The words "trope" and "meme" and "precedent" were repeated several times: beyond this Ruth failed to register much. She was too inflamed with irritation at Benj Bradley's youth and calculated goofiness to follow him.

But what really agitated her was that suddenly she, Ruth, wanted to ask a question. The desire had come over her just as Benj Bradley was preparing to deliver his remarks. She recognized the feeling; in graduate school it used to overwhelm her like a wave of nausea. She hadn't spoken in public for many years, but now she was struggling to keep her arm from shooting into the air. She wanted—needed—to speak, but what to say? Something about memoir and therapy? Redundant: Ricia had already disposed of the subject. Truth in memoir? Too challenging, possibly insulting. Books that had influenced her? Leave that to the Women. Daily writing routine? That too. She hadn't read *The Divining Rod* and what could she say about *I'm Nobody*? There was the olive-green enamel watch, of course. That had left an impression. Might it form the nub of a question, an observation? She tried it out: Why was the olive-green enamel watch memorable? Because it carried the real emotional substance of the childhood that *I'm Nobody* was about, the lost childhood. It might seem incidental or peripheral, but wouldn't Ricia agree that the true heart of a memoir might be found in details like that? Don't memoirs in fact exist in order to frame living relics of memory like the olive-green enamel watch?

That might work, and it would give her more to go on than the wordless jaculatory impulse that used to shoot through her arm in graduate-school seminars. In those days she'd actually made a point of raising her hand before she had any idea what she was going to say. That was the risky pleasure of the thing: she put herself in a position where she was forced to improvise, and under the pressure of panic, ideas extruded themselves. She wouldn't try that now. She knew her limitations. She knew her motives as well. (The older she grew, the harder she found it to hide them from herself.) What moved her was a straightforwardly primitive desire for attention, for recognition, especially from Ricia.

And even more especially—she had to admit—from Charles. There he was in the front row, his pageboy glowing dully. How she longed to make him crane his neck and acknowledge her. She'd developed a small crush on him, the pleasant kind that marriage keeps in check. Nothing powerful, just a little polished stone she liked to finger. To date, she'd had no explicitly sexual fantasies about him, or rather she'd tried, but he was just too fat and it hadn't worked. But ever since the night of the potluck dinner, he'd been hovering benignly around her. His consoling spirit had stayed with her, accompanying her on her walks, at the bank, in the car. She thought about him as she lay drowsily in bed in the mornings, when Ben was already up and moving around downstairs. Charles is elemental, she said to herself. Charles is an earth father. She pictured him besporting himself in surf on some deserted beach, blowing like a zephyr, spouting like a whale.

More and more, these days, Ruth found that when she was thinking hard or retrieving a memory or lost in some fantasy, the channels to the outside world closed completely. Her ears sealed, her eyes glazed over; she simply didn't hear or see. (Was this dementia?) Apparently it had happened again just now. She had missed Ricia's reply to Benj Bradley—she could only hope it had been brief—because the sound that brought her back into the room was an explosion of laughter. Benj was clutching his chest as though he'd been shot. Ricia had crossed her arms over her bosom and was looking smugly delighted.

Ruth raised her hand, but the laughter had yet to die down. The chair, normally without humor, had covered her mouth with three fingers and was shaking delicately. Hoping to catch her eye, Ruth stood. The laughter faded; now the crowd was gathering itself, rustling and shifting and producing scattered coughs. Ruth sat down again. The chair looked out into the auditorium unseeingly. Ruth stood. The chair looked away. Ruth sat. The chair turned. Ruth stood once again. The chair saw her this time and pointed in her direction. "I was thinking . . ." Ruth began. All the heads in the auditorium turned toward her, like sunflowers toward the sun. (There was something about Ruth's voice that had this effect, some nakedness in its timbre, some wobble in its inflection.) "I was thinking . . ." she repeated, but now she saw that all the heads had swiveled once again. Some small disturbance was taking place in the upper right quadrant of the auditorium. It was Lee Odom, still seated but waving his cane aloft. The chair wheeled away from Ruth and pointed in his direction.

It took him a good fifteen seconds to struggle to his feet, supporting himself with his cane and the chairback in front of him. "*Miz* Spottiswoode," he began, puffing a little from the exertion. "Ah'd lahk to preface mah remahks bah say'n how much wih *pray*-shate y'all comin' down heah from those *civ*'lahzd pahts yawler ac*cus*tomed to . . ."

Ben found Dolores at her desk. She turned to smile up at him enigmatically, then returned to her task of wrapping family photographs in newspaper. He stood for a few moments looking over her shoulder. She used four sheets per picture, he noticed, and four pieces of tape, cut to a uniform length. If the job could be done more efficiently, he couldn't imagine how. But soon it began to seem odd to stand there kibitzing, as if watching her assemble a model airplane or dissect a small animal. "You heard?" he finally managed to say. Stupid. Of course she'd heard. She turned again and looked up at him with an expression of puzzled dismay that made him feel ashamed for having broached the subject. "When did you find out?" she asked.

"Just now. I just came from her office. When did you?"

"Last night. She called me at home. I tried to reach you this morning, but you'd already left."

Ben walked around the desk and sat down on the love seat facing it. This was where she put students taking retests, so that she could keep an eye on them, and where her friend Yvette Staples, the loud, hale South African secretary of the Classics Department, sat when she and Dolores ate their brown-bag lunches together. Ben himself had almost never sat here, in this small space between the great fan-shaped window and her desk. It was

Dolores's domain, and therefore inviolate. She kept her things here, such as they were—she was not one to clutter up her workspace. Only her photographs and her barely audible radio and a flourishing wandering Jew and a few paperbacks that she read on quiet summer afternoons. And on the side table an open box of Almond Roca, which she insisted had actual medicinal properties. These things and her other belongings had been packed away in two cardboard boxes, he saw. The few words they'd already exchanged had had the effect of blocking further talk. What could he say to Dolores? What could she say to him? She wouldn't be a party to angry words about Mitten-Kurz, and it was quite beyond him to tell her how much he'd miss her.

The photograph-wrapping was the final job, and she was coming to the end of it. He got up and backed away into his office. "I'll just . . ." he said. She nodded. He closed the door behind him, thought better of it, opened it a crack. Sitting at his desk, he flipped unseeingly through the day's mail. In a moment, Dolores was tapping on his door and then opening it, her usual practice. "Come," she said, with a small, uncharacteristically acid smile. "Come let me introduce you to my replacement." Ben followed her out into the hall. She was clicking along rapidly in her sensible heels, keeping a few feet ahead of him. As they entered the stairwell, Ben once again felt an impulse to say something, but the purposefully bobbing back of her head told him that the moment had passed.

As they descended the stairs, it occurred to him that this was the way he'd just come into the building. No, he thought. It can't be. But of course it was. The replacement to whom Dolores was about to introduce him was the woman he'd noticed only a few minutes earlier, the foul-mouthed portico-pacer. There she was, standing at the far end, still talking on her cell phone. For the moment, she seemed not to be smoking. Dolores paused at the glass door that led out to the portico. The woman's name, she told Ben in a discreet murmur, was Hayley Gamache. She was new to Lola this fall, recently arrived from Vermont. She had started in the registrar's office last week, but some kind of problem had come up.

At the sight of Ben and Dolores, Hayley Gamache raised a temporizing finger and went on with her conversation—presumably the same one she'd been conducting earlier—but now she'd lowered her voice to a raspy stage whisper. She'd cut out the expletives, and her tone had changed; now it was urgently sugary. "Mama's got to go now, honey. You take care. Love you, sweetheart. Mama's got to go right now, BJ. You be good. Bye now."

"Hayley," called out Dolores as they approached, "this is Professor Blau." She turned, and Ben had a quick impression of a puffy, faded blond prettiness. He had another impression as well—that this woman's face was somehow hard to see clearly, as though he were viewing it through a semitranslucent version of one of those quivering pixelated circles used to disguise identities on TV. Her age was hard to guess: somewhere between thirty-five and fifty. He hesitated, then extended his hand. "Dolores says you're new to Lola?"

"Sorry, Professor," said Hayley Gamache. "My kids are always calling me with one problem or another." She offered her hand— not her right hand, but her left, so that Ben was forced to awkwardly rotate his own. She squinted, as if trying to place him, and backed away several steps, still clinging to his hand. Suddenly he seemed to be playing the stolid male partner in some fantastical pas de deux. Releasing him, she twirled away and gazed up into the canopy of live oak branches that overhung the portico. "Is it always so hot this time of year?" she asked, fanning her neck with a vague hand. "The middle of September? In Swanton the nights are cool by now. Everybody's been so nice, but I just can't get used to it. I keep talcum powder in my purse and I'm dumping it down my front all day long."

As if to verify her claim, she opened the purse, which was white and overstuffed and shaped like a kidney bean, and dug out the can of talc. Confusingly, she handed it to Dolores. Evidently it was something else she was looking for, because she continued to root through the contents of the purse. "Here it is," she said. "This is my employment letter." She produced a much folded envelope. "They asked me to get the employer to sign it on the first day? Would you mind, before I forget?"

Ben ran his eyes over the letter. It was from Frank Buonafortuna, the president of an organization called Second Chance/New Start and it thanked him, the employer, for offering employment to someone who needed a break. It assured him that the vast majority of the people who passed through the program went on to become long-term, reliable employees. If there were any problems with this particular employee, he was to immediately contact Frank Buonafortuna's assistant, Alyssa Potter.

"There you go," said Hayley Gamache. "You can sign under the other signature. You could actually cross it out, I guess."

"You started in the registrar's office?"

"There was a gentleman there. It was a personality conflict. We couldn't be in the same room together."

Ben glanced at Dolores, whose expression was darkly noncommittal. He signed the letter. "Thank you *so* much, Professor," said Hayley, smiling now. "You will *not* regret it. I've had my problems, but that's why pencils have erasers." She took Dolores's arm, led her a few feet away, leaned in cheek to cheek, widened her eyes conspiratorially. "Can you direct me to the little girls' room?"

On her way from the Q&A to the parking lot, Ruth veered into the student store and bought a pack of cigarettes, which cost three times what they used to. She paid at the counter, walked away, realized she needed matches and returned. They no longer gave away matches, the pimply boy behind the register told her, so for another four dollars she bought a yellow butane lighter. She would face a dilemma later, when she discarded the partially smoked pack, because the lighter was really too expensive to throw away and she'd need to find a place to hide it from Ben. Maybe she could just leave it somewhere on campus, hoping a deserving young person might pick it up. She also bought a takeout cup of coffee as rent for one of the smoking-permitted tables in the courtyard outside the student center. She sat down and unloaded the box containing *Whole Lives Devoured* from the Guatemalan bag and opened it. She could leaf through the opening pages if she needed to look occupied.

In the old days she used to rip into a new pack of cigarettes like a lioness disemboweling a gazelle, but it had been so long now that she had to walk herself through the steps—pull the golden cord all the way around the four corners, remove the little cellophane hat, ease open the top of the box along the cardboard hinge, which tended to be stiff, loosen and lift away the protective square of silver foil. The actual lighting of the cigarette came easier; that series of steps was deeply encoded in her muscle memory.

She inhaled, and was shocked by the harm she felt it doing her—the searing of the long-healed tissues of her throat, the spasms of suppressed coughing that overcame her as she drew the smoke into her lungs. There was nothing of the effect she remembered so nostalgically, the instantly sharpened focus, the detachment that settled over her like a soft rain of tiny particles. The craving receptors in her brain had died at their posts; she'd have to work to re-addict herself. That would seem to be an argument against smoking another cigarette, but somehow she felt bound by some perverse sense of honor to try. The second was even less rewarding than the first; she stubbed it out almost immediately. It was a sad business when a person failed at backsliding. Was this another consequence of growing old—to no longer even want what was bad for her, or at least to feel herself so unequal to it that it was easier not to want it?

A party of students edged past her table. She looked up at them and down at her manuscript, running her eyes over the opening paragraph. She had reread these chapters so many times that a lacquer of familiarity had settled over them; even if the words seemed remote and drained of meaning, the writing usually seemed competent enough. But sometimes it was as if she'd caught a disastrous glimpse of herself in an unexpected mirror. This was just such a time. What could she have been thinking? What reader would get beyond the first three self-conscious sentences? Those sprung rhythms? That arch tone? Things got a little better in the second paragraph; the necessity for clear exposition saw to that. But not better enough, and then it got bad again, very bad, a few pages in. The question was, if she was able to see how bad it was, and determine where the worst badnesses were located, why did she feel powerless to revise it? It was as if too much time had passed and she'd forfeited the chance.

But here was Charles Johns, standing at her shoulder and asking to join her. "Please," she said, shifting her knees to let him by. He lowered himself carefully into a plastic lawn chair that she was surprised could accommodate him, or even bear his weight. She saw that he was looking at the mess she'd left on the table, the short butt and the long butt and the carnage of cellophane and foil and the still-full Styrofoam cup, marked by a scallop of slobber below the rim. "I was trying to start again," she said. "Can I offer you this lighter?" Wordlessly, Charles pocketed it. "And the rest of these?" Charles took the box of cigarettes. Ruth's relief and gratitude surprised her. "Thank you," she said. "The Q&A was a great success. I've never seen a crowd like that."

"I'm sorry you didn't get a chance to ask your question," said Charles. "She was dying on the vine toward the end. You might have revived her. She had to struggle to make it through the signing. Right now she's lying on the couch in her office with the lights off and a wet paper towel on her forehead."

"Oh dear," said Ruth. "I'd never have suspected for a moment. Everybody was absolutely"—Ruth had been about to say "eating out of her hand," but thought better of it—"enchanted."

Charles hoisted himself laboriously out of his chair into a semi-standing position so that he could dig into his pants pocket and produce the pack of cigarettes he'd just taken from Ruth. "Ah well," he said, lowering his eyes to light one, "she's always a consummate professional. What was it exactly you were going to say, before that old character interrupted you?"

"I'm not sure I can reproduce it. I kind of cobbled it up on the spot. I think I wanted to talk more than I actually had anything to say."

"Oh yes," said Charles. "That reminds me. She does indeed admire your book, very much. She's going to ask our house sitter to send it. She remembered a funny line from a scene at an academic convention, I can't recall it now. She quoted it verbatim. She has an extraordinary memory."

How he loves her, thought Ruth. How he loves to say "she."

"She very much wants to meet you," Charles went on. "I think we should arrange it. It would make a difference to her, to have someone to talk to. Someone other than me."

Would she, Ruth asked herself, want to be loved like that? Yes. No. Yes. No. She supposed she had been, but only by Isaac when he was very small, and of course that wasn't the same thing. And in fact it was she who had loved Isaac the way Charles loved Ricia, not the other way around. She found it hard to imagine Ben doting on her unqualifiedly. He was devoted to her, she knew, but attentiveness had never come naturally to him. From time to time he made gestures, but these self-conscious efforts quickly collapsed into facetiousness. Bringing her breakfast in bed on her birthday, he scuttled into the room like an officious waiter, bent deeply at the waist as he delivered the tray onto her lap, scuttled out again. And if she sulked—which she used to do quite regularly and now did less often—he got angry. "I do my best," he'd bark at her. "You know I care. You wouldn't want some guy fawning over you. You'd have nothing but contempt for someone like that." True, but if she'd sunk deep enough into her sulk she'd find herself once again entertaining an old and insidious line of argument: *I've never been loved enough.* And consequently she'd never been able either to command love or to accept it. Every serious fight she and Ben had ever had found its source in this idea, which was both right and dangerously wrongheaded.

She stole a quick look at Charles again, sitting in profile to her left. His belly, pressed into a great loaf by the confining chair, rose up to meet his chins. In this broad afternoon light his face was as mottled and weary as Rembrandt's in his late self-portraits. His nose was a dismaying sight. On his left temple she noticed a cluster of sebaceous keratoses, those odd "stuck-on" growths that appear overnight in late middle age. (Ruth had a number of them on her back.) The Charles of the other night, when she'd been drunk, had been a spirit. The Charles of this sober afternoon was an all-too-mortal man. Much as she found it consoling and diverting to entertain fantasies about him, she saw now he was no longer a suitable object for even the most qualified forms of idealization. Neither was she. If Charles looked meaty and old sitting here in this campus courtyard, where the starlings bounced from flagstone to flagstone, pecking at crumbs and quarreling in metallic voices, she could be sure that she also did not appear to her best advantage.

A shout and a shriek made them both look up. Some kind of wild horseplay was going on at the other end of the courtyard. Two boys were chasing a girl. She was running, dodging, laughing, grabbing plastic chairs, brandishing them like shields, hurling them at her pursuers. The boys worked as a team, one rushing, the other keeping a strategic distance. For a moment they had her trapped against a concrete-block wall. One of them confined her briefly between his spread hands, but she ducked free and darted out of the courtyard onto the green, both boys following.

Charles and Ruth turned to smile at each other. "What men or gods are these?" said Charles,

". . . What maidens loth?

What mad pursuit? What struggle to escape?

What pipes and timbrels? What wild ecstasy?"

He delivered the lines in a low, intimate burble, stifling an impending fit of coughing. The two of them sat companionably for a little while, their conversation having run aground. Charles looked at his watch and rose to his feet. "I must be on my way," he said, giving in to the cough and digging a handkerchief out of his pants pocket. "The beltway traffic gets untenable in exactly seventeen minutes." Ruth also rose, gathering her manuscript and returning it to its box. "What is that?" asked Charles.

"It's actually a manuscript," said Ruth, quite conscious of how much she had wanted him to notice and how full of dread she felt now that he had. "A partial manuscript. Work I did after *Getting Good*. I thought Ricia might . . . Actually I think I should work on it more before . . . It's really very . . ."

But Charles had lifted the box out of her arms and was walking away. "Thanks!" she called out. "Thank you, Charles! Thanks so much!"

CHAPTER FIVE

B en was third in line if you didn't count the motorized-cart brigade. Tara D'Alainville of French and Fred Barber of physics were first and second, respectively, and Liz Portnoy of chemistry, standing directly behind Ben, was fourth. He'd been up since five thirty this morning, trying to get in his three hours of writing, and counted himself lucky to be surrounded by introverts.

Marcy Bainbridge, who worked in the dean's office, had shepherded the faculty into a long snaking line in the provost's rotunda, which backed onto the platform where the new president's installation was about to held. She and her assistant had been trotting up and down, checking to see that everyone was appropriately rigged out and wearing their mortarboards at the right angle, and now Marcy had dashed over to the sound system and inserted *Twentieth-Century Organ Fireworks* into the CD player.

The line shuffled forward a few feet and bumbled to a stop because the third of the five motorized carts that led the procession had stalled. (This was the first time they'd been used: at commencement two years earlier an elderly participant had lost her balance and tumbled off the stage. The lawsuit was settled out of court, but over the last summer the university purchased a dozen of these carts and issued a directive requiring anyone over seventy-five to ride in them whenever a raised platform needed to be negotiated.)

"Give me a hand with this wheelchair," Marcy Bainbridge called to her assistant. "It won't move."

"It's not a wheelchair," said the motorized cart's occupant. "It's a motorized cart."

"Do you think you could get off for a second, sir? We may need to turn it over."

The occupant, whom Ben recognized as C. Trevor Dixon, long retired after a distinguished career in mechanical engineering, climbed down ably, knelt on one knee, lifted the cart a little and peered at its undercarriage. "The emergency brake's engaged," he said. "See the little green lever? That'll release it."

Once again the procession began to move. Following his colleagues in their rustling gowns Ben felt a familiar prickling behind his eyes. It happened every time, a Pavlovian response to wearing the ancient robes of his profession and walking to the slow beat of solemn music and feeling himself the object of respectful attention from what the dean would have called the university community. Ruth had noticed his rapid blinking at more than one commencement, and mentioned it to him—quite tenderly, in truth—and he'd been acutely embarrassed.

The faculty was seated in a C-shaped formation surrounding the speaker's podium. Ben found himself in the front row on the left side, with a comprehensive view of the audience and the speaker's platform. He needed only to turn his head unobtrusively to see which of his colleagues had obeyed the provost's summons. The administration had applied heavy pressure, going so far as to send out an e-mail "reminding" the faculty that a documented medical excuse would be expected from anyone not attending the installation. Apparently it had worked: all the chairs were full. Even Charles Johns and Ricia Spottiswoode were here, wearing bachelor's robes. Why? For them there was no penalty in skipping this event. Perhaps because Ricia knew how fetching her red curls would look spilling out from under a mortarboard.

It was a few minutes after ten and the temperature was already in the low nineties. The faculty was comfortable enough, kept cool by a forced-air system under the platform floorboards, but in the audience people were fanning themselves with programs and opening umbrellas against the sun. Howling babies were being removed to the shade of the library archway. Ben spotted Dolores, far in the back with her husband, and picked out a number of last year's students. There was the reference librarian he liked, the one with the limp, and the very tiny woman who worked in the back room in personnel. And there, in the third row, wearing sunglasses and an enormous black straw hat, was Ruth.

What was she doing here? She hadn't mentioned any interest in the installation. Of course they hadn't spoken much since the night of the potluck. Probably she was hoping to encounter Ricia and Charles. Where had that hat come from? He'd never seen it, and it was too big to hide. It was the kind you put on the ground and danced around, not the kind you actually wore, especially if people were sitting behind you. Where, for that matter, did she get all those long black shapeless bedouin dresses, those odd-smelling folkloric vests, those great cowbell necklaces that would have looked more plausible under glass in a museum display case than hanging from the neck of a living woman, those earlobe-stretching earrings that dangled to her collarbones. Actually he knew quite well where she got them: from expensive online import stores. He'd seen the credit card statements. The question was why? Why would Ruth want to look this way? There was something self-mummifying about this late-life taste for barbaric splendor. These days she was beginning to look—it pained him to admit—like photographs he'd seen of the sculptor Louise Nevelson, or even Isak Dinesen in her syphilitic later years, except that Dinesen looked grim and ill, while Ruth continued to look girlish and vulnerable, if only to him. When Isaac was small she'd worn jeans and T-shirts, like any other young mother. Her hair was reddish brown then, and he'd nagged her to grow it. Now it was gray and long—though she rarely wore it down—and he wished she'd cut it, or at least color it, as every other woman her age seemed to these days.

A lanky, broad-shouldered girl in stiletto heels and what Ben felt sure must be an inappropriately short white sequined dress came clattering up the plywood steps of the platform to the microphone, urged on by whoops and cheers from a claque of students in the audience. She ducked her head, flipped her blond hair out of her eyes, and proceeded to perform an a cappella rendering of "Amazing Grace" in a wobbling contralto. Two signers stood on either end of the stage, gesturing energetically. Ben checked his program to find the singer's name. She was Hannah Whatley, a sophomore from Greenwich, Connecticut. What would a girl from Greenwich, Connecticut, make of the idea of salvation by grace? And how, for that matter, did American Sign Language designate the word "wretch"?

Hannah Whatley left the stage to enthusiastic applause. The provost came to the microphone. "Welcome ladies and gentlemen. Welcome, faculty. I want to thank each and every one of you for coming out on this very warm day to help us welcome Dr. Lee Wayne Dreddle." He turned to nod to a giant young man seated in the inner ring of chairs arranged around the podium, not a person Ben would have taken for a college president.

The provost continued: "Dr. Dreddle comes to us from the State University of Wisconsin, where he served as provost. Prior to that he was dean of the Business School at Land O'Lakes University in Waldorf, Michigan, with a joint appointment in the Untapped Human Potential Faculty Working Group. Professor Dreddle's research and teaching interests include the application of behavioral psychology in the classroom and the boardroom, the management of change, and the development of motivational techniques in academic and corporate settings. He holds a BA with highest honors from the University of Pennsylvania, a doctorate from MIT, and an MBA from the Wharton School of Management. He is the author of six books and numerous articles . . ."

Lee Wayne Dreddle's spread knees pushed aside the folds of his academic gown; his too-small mortarboard sat precariously on his oversize head. Ben had noticed him on his way in and wondered idly if he was some kind of bouncer, hired by the provost to keep fractious faculty members in line. Over the years he'd come to accept the new breed of college president, chosen more for fund-raising prowess than for intellectual distinction. Lola's last one had been a red-faced, hail-fellow-well-met type who'd presided over a radical expansion of the student body and the construction of a new gym and a new complex of science buildings. He was a vulgarian, but a plausible one, human-sized and appropriately middle-aged. What was Ben to make of this brute who sat flung back in his seat between the director of the board of trustees and the dean of the Medical School, looking like nothing so much as a ballplayer sprawled on the bullpen bench, waiting for the coach's signal?

Selecting a college president had been a long and difficult process, the provost was telling the audience. The effort had begun two years ago with the naming of the members of the search committee. That committee did their work almost too well. They searched high and low and in the end they managed to dig up a bumper crop of seventeen candidates. (The provost had a background in agricultural science.) Of those seventeen, eight were weeded out and nine were brought to campus for further interviews. The three finalists returned to campus twice again and talked to everybody from the board of trustees to the student oversight committee to the line cooks in the cafeteria. The final decision was an agonizing one, but the seed had been planted and he felt quite confident that in spite of the many impressive accomplishments of the two who in the end, and with some regrets, had been culled, they'd gotten the pick of the litter.

"And so," concluded the provost, "all that remains is for all of us to give the biggest warmest welcome we can to Lee Wayne Dreddle, the fourteenth president of the Lola Dees Institute!" Lee Wayne Dreddle bounced lightly to his feet and jogged to the podium. Or moon-jogged, rather; the podium was only a few yards away.

"Hey," he said to the audience, "mind if I take this off?" He removed his mortarboard, revealing a head of expertly barbered dark hair with a vivid splatter of white right above the fontanel. "That's better." With these few words, several things about him fell into place. His high, husky voice would have a strong appeal to women, Ben felt sure. And his smile was dazzling, a big gleaming wraparound that instantly relaxed and stimulated the audience. Only a moment ago it had responded obligingly to the provost's prompting, but now spontaneous applause was breaking out. Students whistled and stomped; soon people were rising to their feet.

"Hey," said Lee Wayne Dreddle, raising a constraining hand. "Hey. Hey. Hey." The audience grew calm. "I'm going to make just a few remarks today," he began. "I won't keep you long because I know it's hot." He produced and put on a pair of reading glasses. (Ben revised his age upward, from thirty-eight to forty-two.) "I'll begin by sharing an insight from the sage Hillel: 'If I am not for myself . . .' "

Oh no, thought Ben. Not that.

" '. . . then who will be for me? And if I am only for myself, what am I? And if not now, when?' "

Ben had heard these words a hundred times at convocations and commencements, never without irritation. It wasn't Hillel's fault, of course. He couldn't have meant to endorse the contemporary pop-psychology notion that putting oneself first is always healthy and that self-love is required to be lovable, but no present-day listener could hear this quote differently. And if the first clause was taken this way, then the second could only be understood as a mild corrective to what otherwise would be an injunction to rampant selfishness. As for the puzzling addendum,

"And if not now, when?": either that was a non sequitur or something was missing.

Having invoked Hillel, Dreddle launched into his address. It didn't take long for Ben to recognize it as a familiar amalgam of bottom-line crassness:

> "Our continued success in attracting support from granting institutions and friends of the university depends on satisfying our clients. And who are our clients? Our students!"

and communitarian pap:

> "While we must keep the financial health of the institution foremost in our thoughts, we must never forget our mission to foster community, the immediate community here at LDI, the wider community of Spangler, and the biggest community of all—the earth, our home."

These were the conceptual poles of the written part of Dreddle's speech, which he read aloud a little haltingly, stumbling over an occasional polysyllabic word like a mildly dyslexic teenager. After a few minutes he abandoned his prepared remarks and embarked on a series of anecdotes about his early experiences as a college football player and his later adventures as a fund-raiser.

What was Ruth making of Dreddle? Ben saw she'd taken off her sunglasses. She could never keep glasses on for long because her nasal bridge was low and they tended to slide down, especially when her face was sweaty as it was now, so sweaty that her chalky foundation makeup had melted off, and her raccoon eyeliner too. She was looking up at Dreddle, who was telling a story about being so intimidated by a potential donor, a wealthy Nob Hill art collector, that in the end he forgot to make his pitch and left empty-handed. He was an engaging raconteur, adroit at balancing triumphalism with self-deprecation. No wonder the search committee had chosen him: he'd been born to schmooze, born to attend galas and cocktail parties, born to move in on some mark, to throw an arm around his shoulder and lead him off into the shadows, spinning a narrative web all the while. Ruth was listening with a small smile playing around the twitchy muscles of her mouth. Without the mask of makeup, her reactions were readable—amusement, skepticism, consternation, wary delight. Ben looked at Ruth every day, of course, but it had been a very long time since he'd watched her. How sad she is, he thought. Often unhappy, sometimes diverted from her unhappiness, always sad.

The audience was sitting in full sun now. The ambulance parked around the corner on the access road hadn't been called upon yet, but an elderly man had been escorted into the shade by two ushers. Dreddle put on his reading glasses again and returned to his text, leafing through it quickly. It was the peroration he was looking for, and when he found it he looked up and gave the audience another of his patented grins.

One thing he couldn't say, he read, was that he hoped to turn LDI into a world-class university, because it already was a world-class institution. His predecessors had seen to that. Instead, he wanted to ask everyone, faculty, staff, students, administration, to give more . . .

". . . just a little more. To make the move from 100 percent to 110 percent. To come up with innovative ways to identify and solve problems, to study harder, to learn more, to keep the physical plant of this great university in the best possible condition, to prepare and serve healthy food so that the students in our charge can give their best, every day . . ."

Here he turned to face the faculty.

". . . to find ways to motivate students, to make them care, to sharpen their intellectual curiosity, to engage in the passionate pursuit of research, to roll back the frontiers of knowledge . . ."

Ben twisted his head to look back at his colleagues. Who among them, he asked himself, was actually engaged in rolling back the frontiers of knowledge? Many of the scientists were, he supposed. At least they were continually hustling for grant money. But had even the most productive of his colleagues in the humanities rolled back those frontiers as much as a millimeter? The irony was that despite the claims of trendy people in English and anthropology and the language departments, it was only the driest of the traditional scholars—the painstaking collectors of textual correspondences, for example—who made advancements, and those were immeasurably small, a snail's kind of progress. The rest of them, Ben included, were like carp in an ancient mossy pool. Some were great and some were small, but all of them swam in circles and that was as it should be.

Dreddle had read his concluding remarks and now he was releasing the audience, making brushing motions with his hands. "Get out of here," he shouted over departing cheers and whoops. "Get out of the sun. Back over there in the reception tent. Get yourselves hydrated."

Waiting his turn as the faculty unwound itself and filed back into the provost's rotunda, Ben watched Ruth edge her way down a row of seats. He waved, but her view of him was blocked by the brim of her hat. He called to her—he couldn't bring himself to shout—but she failed to respond. Why was he so anxious? It wasn't as if he'd never see her again. She was on her way home, probably, or perhaps to the reception. Even so, if he'd been twenty years younger, or even ten, he'd have made the easy four-foot jump off the platform—some of his younger colleagues were doing that even now—and caught up with her.

On his way to the reception he stopped at the office to exchange his gown for the blazer he'd dropped off earlier. It was still locked, as it had been before the installation, but now the work-study student was sitting, or rather squatting, on the floor just outside the door, her long arms wrapped around her knees. "Rhoda," he said. "Sorry you had to wait. Dolores is no longer with us. She's over in sociology now."

"Oh no," said Rhoda. She was a senior who had won a prize last spring for a superior honors project paper. "Since when?"

"Since yesterday," said Ben, unlocking the door and flipping on the overhead lights.

"Why?" said Rhoda. She turned to look Ben in the eye, confident that any question she asked was a reasonable one and would be answered reasonably. Rhoda reminded him of a girl he'd known in his youth, a self-possessed countercultural type who cycled everywhere and grew her own herbs and kept a hand-bound journal. She too had been a squatter, not a sitter. He'd been involved with her on and off for a few years, a necessarily tentative business because this girl—Naomi, her name had been—was so coolly independent. Then came Ruth, whose insecurity and moral glamour offered more opportunity for adhesion.

What would a life with Naomi have been like? She wouldn't have been interested in marriage, he supposed, but absent Ruth they might have fallen into some kind of domestic partnership— living in a solar-powered cabin in British Columbia, perhaps. Raising goats? Making cheese? Starting a cottage industry? At twenty-four he'd been in graduate school, not yet firmly bitten by academic ambition, still plastic enough to have actually embarked on some kind of "alternative" life if events had moved him in that direction. At sixty his sense of himself was so rigidly set that he found it difficult even to envision having led a life other than the one he actually had. That was the thing about aging, or rather that was *one* of the things about aging. It wasn't only that he couldn't—or didn't wish to—imagine the future: he also couldn't imagine the past.

"I don't really know why," he said. "The word just came down." That was telling her more than he should, but her quick comprehending nod reassured him. "You'll meet her replacement when she gets in." (And where was Hayley? She'd been late already when he came by earlier.) "There's a pile of copying Dolores left you on the shelf over there." And there were a number of things she'd left for Hayley as well, three of them urgent. The registrar should be prodded to change a number of inappropriate room assignments. The paperwork for medical insurance for the new crop of graduate students needed to be taken care of. She should call the bookstore about the texts for 201, the Historical Survey, which hadn't yet arrived.

Rhoda set about her copying with her usual efficiency. Letting himself into his own office, Ben saw that the red light on the desk phone was blinking. He hung up his robe and sat down to listen to the messages. The first was from Hayley, as were the three that followed.

"Professor Blau? Hayley here. Hayley Gamache. Hope you're having a good day. Sorry to say I'll be a little delayed. I've got a bit of a situation here and I've got to deal with it before . . ." Here came a pause, followed by a thud and a muffled shout, followed by another silence, this one longer and more absolute, followed by a faint click.

"Professor Blau? Hayley again. Sorry we got cut off. I'm taking care of things just as fast as I can and I assure you . . ." Silence. "Just a moment, Professor. I'm asking for your patience. Just bear with me . . ." Silence. More silence. Click.

"Professor Blau? I'm on the freeway now? I'm just coming to the exit? I think it's the right exit? Twenty-three? I'm coming from the south? Is that right? You've got to get over so fast. Man oh man. Hold on a minute. Stay with me . . ." Ben heard the faint squeal of tires, scattered car horns, a sharp intake of breath and then more softly, as if at a little distance, "Oh my God. Some guy just dumped a mattress . . . A burning mattress . . ." Soft giggle. Click.

"Professor Blau? I'm at . . . I'm at Bellevista and Frontenard. Do you know where that is? I think I'm lost. I guess I could get back on the freeway but I'm not sure whether I got off too early or too late. Hang on a minute. I'm going to . . ."

A series of muted flutters and bumps followed, as of a cell phone tumbling to the carpeted floor of a car, and for the next few minutes Hayley's travels were documented only by obscure whooshes and creaks and changes in the background noise of the engine. Then the car radio was turned on, tuned to the eighties station. Ben heard the last chorus of "I'm All Out of Love" followed by a bellowing ad for a car dealership he happened to know was not far from the freeway exit Hayley had just taken and then "The Tide Is High" by Blondie, which he remembered from his academic gypsy days, when he commuted every week between three universities in western and central Massachusetts. Not a bad song. Evidently Hayley liked it too, because she turned up the volume and sang along lustily.

> The tide is high but I'm holding on.
> I'm gonna be your number one,
> *Nahm*ber waaa-hun . . .

He found Ruth sitting hatless and alone near the open flap in the air-conditioned tent, drinking something swarming with green flecks. "Mint julep?" he asked as he worked his way around the table toward her. Or rather shouted: the acoustics in here were like the Marabar caves.

"Mojito."

He sat down. "What's a mojito?"

"It's like a mint julep, but it's made with rum."

"What happened to the hat?"

"I left it in the car," said Ruth, giving him a quick warning glance. She had reapplied her makeup, or some of it.

"What are you doing here?" he asked.

"I can't be here? Why shouldn't I be here?"

Ben reached over and took her hand. "I meant to say I'm glad to see you." And in fact he was. "How about we drop it?" he added.

She turned away for a moment, no doubt to hide whatever calculations her face might betray. But her hand remained in place under his and that gave him hope that they might skip the actual playing out of the fight that always started with the move Ben had just made—the no-fault peace offer—and continued with Ruth refusing it and demanding an apology and Ben countering with a threat that his proposal wouldn't stand much longer and Ruth stipulating that an apology was necessary if he wanted to demonstrate that he'd taken responsibility for whatever he'd said or done and Ben provocatively insisting that he didn't think that what he'd said or done was wrong and therefore he couldn't apologize and that the best they could do was to agree to disagree, and so on. This was one of the secondary fights that often followed a major, primary fight, and it was a standard item in their repertoire. Ben always thought of the old joke about the joke convention, where everyone knows the jokes so well that all a joke-teller has to do is shout out a number: Eighty-four! After thirty years of marriage, he and Ruth had learned their fights by heart; to enact them had begun to seem less and less necessary. This might be wisdom of a sort, he supposed. Or maybe just exhaustion. Not that it always stopped them.

He stood and extended his arm to Ruth, who rose to her feet rather hesitantly and took it. Together they embarked on a counterclockwise tour of the reception. Right away it was clear that the Dreddle administration was not afraid of a little expense. This wasn't the usual food-service spread—grapes and one-inch squares of cheese and one jug each of respectably cheap red and white wine. This was the top-of-the-line level of catering, heretofore reserved for donor and alumni dinners and the president's suite in the football stadium. Nor was the food laid out prosaically in aluminum bins on steam tables, as had always been the case even at the annual chair-holders' gala. Stations had been set up around the tent serving carved meats and smoked salmon, customized omelets, sushi, artisanal cheeses, elaborate desserts. Waiters—real ones, not undergraduates—circulated, some offering hors d'oeuvres, some flutes of champagne and mojitos. Ben took Ruth's arm and spoke loudly into her left ear, the one without a minimal hearing loss. "So is this an improvement?" he asked. "Is this maybe not quite so boring?"

Ruth shrugged and smiled. Ben stopped a waiter. "Can I get a beer?" he asked. The waiter smiled apologetically, took a deep breath. "We have Fat Tire, sir. We have Redhook Ale. We have Anchor Steam. We have Guinness. We have Sam Adams. We have—" "Anything," said Ben, "a beer. Just a beer." Tall, sardonic Josh Margolis from political science clamped a hand on his shoulder and shouted into his ear, "A beer? Just a beer? Can't you outgrow your proletarian tastes? It's a new era. Try a mojito. It's Dreddle's favorite drink. No? How about you, Ruth?" Ruth needed no persuasion to try another. "So," said Margolis, "are we ready for enhanced leadership?" Margolis was barely forty, ambitious, served on multiple committees. It was rumored that he let the provost win at tennis. On the other hand, he was the only academic Ben knew who had spent a year at the Kennedy School at Harvard without incurring a swollen head. This, and his habit of making undercutting remarks out of the side of his mouth, inclined Ben to like him.

Ruth was tugging at his sleeve. They moved on, fording their way through the growing crowd. Here was the elegant basketball coach, surrounded by a coterie of well-heeled black Spanglerites. His last few seasons had been lackluster, and everyone said his days were numbered. And there, sitting a little glumly at a table with his handsome worn-out-looking wife and five small children, all of them addressing large pieces of cake with plastic forks, was the new, very Christian football coach, whose last season had been such a surprising success that it was said perhaps he really did have a special relationship with the Almighty. And there was Lee Wayne Dreddle himself in mid-anecdote, surrounded by an element Ben had never seen at a university function before, at least in such numbers. These were Spangler society people, florid oilmen and their sleekly muscled wives, all of whom seemed to have been retrofitted with impossibly slender and bosomy eighteen-year-old torsos.

And here, veering unexpectedly into their path, was Roberta Mitten-Kurz and her husband. "Ah, Ruth," said Mitten-Kurz, pointedly ignoring Ben, "just the woman I was looking for. I've been waiting for your call. I'm hoping so much you'll say yes."

"Ah, what?" said Ruth, cocking her head. "Say yes to what?"

"Didn't Ben tell you?" No need for Mitten-Kurz to shout; her stentorian voice was easily audible. "Didn't he give you the letter?"

"Sorry," said Ben, addressing Ruth but allowing his guilty gaze to slide in Mitten-Kurz's direction. "I meant to. I guess I left it in my other jacket. The pocket."

"That was really unfortunate," said Mitten-Kurz, glaring at Ben. "There was a time-sensitive element to that letter. If you have a moment now, Ruth, I can explain." She took Ruth's arm and pulled her aside, leaving Ben with a look a mother might give the molester of her child as he was led from the courtroom in shackles.

Bobby Mitten-Kurz was a retired high-school-ring salesman, an amiable fellow about a third the size of his wife. Ben knew him a little from the locker room at the gym, where he played racquetball and Bobby used the cardiovascular equipment. Outside that sweaty fraternal context—Ben could bring to mind an image of Bobby's sizable manhood, startling because he was otherwise so physically unimpressive—the two of them had little in common. "Still working out?" he asked.

"Not like I was working out a few years ago," said Bobby ruefully. "I was a true believer for a while. Now I've kind of let it slide." He patted his small potbelly deploringly. "You still play racquetball?"

"Not much," said Ben. "I got lazy too, I guess." The two of them stood silently, each smiling tenderly at his shoes, until the waiter approaching with Ben's beer offered a distraction. "Whew," Ben said, taking a long draw on the bottle. "I've been waiting for this. I'm not a champagne drinker. Not a mojito drinker either." Bobby nodded noncommittally. More silence. "Do anything exciting this summer?" Ben hazarded.

"As a matter of fact we did," said Bobby, looking up and smiling shyly. "We took a trip to Nova Scotia. We're celebrating our fortieth."

"Hey," said Ben. "Fortieth. That's something. Congratulations. Nova Scotia's beautiful, I hear. I've never been, myself." The image of Bobby's member returned to him, unsummoned this time, closer up and exponentially more vivid. It was followed by a rapid interior slide show of childishly dirty pictures, all variations on the theme of small creatures copulating in surprising ways with much larger ones. He shook his head and it passed. Dolores had told him, he remembered now, that the Mitten-Kurzes were a particularly devoted couple.

A hand fell on his shoulder. "Ben," said Alfred Jovanovich of political science. "Can you come over here for a minute? We've got a little dispute and we need an ethicist to settle it."

It just hit me like a bolt from the blue after our . . . talk . . . at your potluck the other night, how absolutely perfect you'd be," said Mitten-Kurz. "Considering your special expertise."

"I'm a little embarrassed about that," said Ruth. "I think I came on kind of strong."

"Ah no no no no *no* no no," said Mitten-Kurz. "Don't apologize. You're a woman who's got a lot to say, Ruth. Perhaps you haven't been afforded enough opportunities to say it." She shot a dark look in Ben's direction. "We'd like to help however we can."

"Well, thank you," said Ruth. "I'll certainly try. When is this meeting?"

"This coming Monday, I'm afraid. I know it's terribly short notice. I do wish you'd seen the letter. I'm sure I've left out some details in all this noise and crush."

"I have an appointment in the afternoon."

"Ah, well it's in the *morn*ing," said Mitten-Kurz. "Perfect! So you'll come?"

"I'll try," said Ruth once again, intending to do no such thing.

"I'm so pleased," said Mitten-Kurz. She was wearing a long

pale-green-and-salmon satin kimono over a matching pair of wide-legged pants and cowl-necked tunic. Where did she find these clothes, in size twenty-eight or whatever? "I'll e-mail the details, care of Ben. You'll have to excuse me now. I see Bobby's been abandoned." She squeezed Ruth's hand and began to move away. "Oh by the way," she called back over her shoulder. "Would you have any interest in helping out with the phones for the WNNP fund-raiser? I could see if I could get you in."

"Thanks," Ruth shouted. "That's nice of you. Let me think about it." Mitten-Kurz's eyebrows rose and quivered. A place on the local NPR affiliate's on-air fund-raising phone bank was a plum. Faculty wives waited years for it. Ruth had never even sent in a contribution, though several times she'd intended to.

Apparently Ben had moved on. Ruth struck out on a diagonal across the tent, hoping to find him or to spot Charles and Ricia. Lee Wayne Dreddle was still in place, she saw, still surrounded by a tight cordon of society people, the men guffawing at the punch line of some story, the women doing their best to modify the frozen smiles in which multiple surgical procedures had fixed their faces. In photographs in the *Advocate* they looked normal enough, if a little blurry and blank, but in person some of them were quite monstrous—noses shrunken or collapsed, cheekbone implants gone lopsided, lips half inverted by swelling, brows paralyzed by Botox, eyes darting like desperate fish.

A waiter appeared. Ruth took another mojito and soldiered on. A second waiter offered a tray of hors d'oeuvres. She stopped and considered, chose a fardel of grilled asparagus wrapped in prosciutto and a cocoon of puff pastry stuffed with something she couldn't identify. These items and the drink and the requisite napkins were more than she could manage without a surface to put them on, so she sat down at a table populated by three elderly women, refugees from the ceaseless flux and yammer of the reception, and a text-messaging adolescent girl. The grill marks on the asparagus were purely cosmetic, she discovered; it was quite raw and too fibrous to chew. The puff pastry was stuffed with something fishy and salty and creamy she'd have spat out into the sink if she'd been at home. Under what she took to be the censorious gaze of one of the three elderly women she made a neat pile of her semi-masticated leavings on a napkin and wrapped that up in another napkin and the whole thing in yet another napkin and twisted all the ends together to create something like a grimly utilitarian party-favor bag. Just as she was about to rise and look for a trash basket, Fran Tevis sat down next to her.

Fran was a potter and jewelry maker, married to a historian. She was the mother of Isaac's last recorded friend and, truth to tell, she'd been Ruth's last friend as well. It was a measure, she realized, of just how malcontented and misanthropic she'd grown in recent years that Fran was the only person she'd encountered at this gathering she was glad to see, though she'd certainly have taken evasive action if she'd seen Fran first. They embraced, separated, took long assessing arm's-length looks at each other, impulsively embraced again.

"I *thought* that was you, Ruth," said Fran, who after eight or nine years was still exactly herself, still small and keenly focused and warm, though her curly hair had gone gray. Ruth had always gravitated toward people like Fran, take-charge extroverts who earned her gratitude by cutting through her shyness and passivity. Fran's son Malcolm had been in Isaac's sixth-grade class. The two of them were placed in the same advanced section of math. Actually Malcolm took advanced everything and Isaac was assigned to the B group in all subjects but math and was removed from the classroom three times a week for remedial reading. At any rate, they were inseparable for an academic year. They lolled around in each other's rooms playing video games, pitched a tent in the backyard on warm autumn nights. When Ruth drove Isaac to his various appointments, Malcolm came along and did his homework in waiting rooms, and then she picked them up and drove them to novel destinations like the rink, the miniature golf course, the movie theater, the soft-serve ice-cream stand.

How wonderfully ordinary it was to see the boys climb off the school bus together, deep in talk, to hear snorts of preadolescent laughter as she walked down the hall past Isaac's room. Ruth even found a mildly pornographic flip-book, the kind of thing that passes from hand to hand in the schoolyard, under his bed. No clinician had prescribed the friendship between Isaac and Malcolm, no committee had recommended it. It had simply happened, like rain falling on parched ground, and she and Ben stood at the sink with their backs turned, hardly able to breathe for delight and gratitude as the boys ate macaroni and cheese at the kitchen table. (Ben whispered, "See? What did I tell you?") As it happened, Malcolm was a nice boy, but he needn't have been. What mattered to Ruth and Ben was only that he was entirely normal, if a little undersized and newt-like. For one charmed school year he made their lives normal too.

It wasn't that they expected the friendship to last forever, they assured each other as they lay in bed conducting one of their endless discussions of Isaac's development. The point was that Isaac had showed himself capable of friendship, and surely that meant he'd find other friends. That was what they told themselves when Malcolm grew two inches over the summer and joined the swim team. Soon it became clear that he was hovering on the periphery of the popular group and that the price of full admittance was abandonment of Isaac. In spite of all the strategizing Ruth and Fran did on their morning walks, there was no way to save the friendship, and of course that was the end of the friendship between Ruth and Fran as well.

"How's Malcolm?" she asked now. It was inevitable that they'd talk about the boys: she might as well seize whatever preemptive advantage she could.

"Ah," said Fran, hesitating for a telltale moment. "We worry. He's been out of law school two years now and he hasn't even begun to settle down."

"What's he doing?"

"He's in D.C., clerking for a judge."

A Supreme Court justice, no doubt.

"We keep hoping he'll find someone," Fran went on. "He was actually engaged to the sweetest girl for a while and all of a sudden she was gone. We'd gotten close and then she was out of our lives and there was nothing I could do. I'd started having fantasies about grandchildren. It's so frustrating when you have no influence . . ." Here she trailed off, and the two of them sat in silence.

"So what do you think of all this?" Fran waved a vague hand at the reception. "Have you ever seen so many worked-over women? What do you think of all these money people? What do you think this means for Lola?"

"I don't know," said Ruth. She did know, actually, and under other circumstances she might have gone on at some length about it, but now she was fixed on getting the painful part of this conversation over. "Oh look," said Fran. "There's Cindy Deaver. She's gotten so heavy. Do you know her?"

Ruth didn't.

"Tell me," said Fran after a long moment, placing a warm hand on Ruth's. "How is Isaac?"

Isaac is a filthy street person. Isaac never graduated high school, never went to college, never had a job. We haven't seen him in years, haven't heard from him since he mailed us his tooth and it's Malcolm's fault for deserting him. No, it's *your* fault. "Isaac's at loose ends," Ruth said, slowly withdrawing her hand. "He's unemployed at the moment."

"Living at home?"

"No."

"Well, that's a mercy!" said Fran. Both of them smiled conventionally at this entirely conventional gambit. "These kids," Fran added, shaking her head and looking down at her folded hands on the table. Ruth could see that she was weighing the merits of pushing her inquiry further, considering the angles like a cat planning a leap onto a kitchen counter. A furrowing of her brow told Ruth she was moving into position now, preparing to spring. "Well well Fran," Ruth said, rising to her feet and extending her arms. "It's been so good to see you. I was thinking you're just about the only person here I'd have wanted to see." Fran stood and they embraced. Each swore to call the other, to find a day to meet for lunch and catch up.

Ruth plunged back into the reception, cutting a new diagonal through the crowd. Ah, there was Ben, only a few yards to her right, talking to a fuzzy-haired woman in leggings and a sleeveless tunic. A particularly dense clot of people blocked her way to him, all of them howling with laughter and evidently drunk enough not to mind or even notice when she put her head down and swam her way through, parting the human tide with her arms.

"But don't you think there has to be some spirit or influence or *some*thing? Do you think the universe just *happened*? Do you think it's just by *chance* we're here?" Apparently this woman was oblivious to Ruth's arrival. Ben, as always, failed to introduce her, though he shot her a quick look of entreaty. This was all too familiar a situation; once again he'd been trapped by an interlocutor in whom some lever had been pulled or button pushed the moment he mentioned that he taught philosophy.

"Many people," he was saying, "certainly do believe there's something. It's just that as philosophers we have to ask *why* we believe that." Ruth took his arm. "I think we should get *go*ing," she shouted in the general direction of his ear. "I think I left something in the *oven*." The woman continued to tip her rapt face up into Ben's. He was riveted like a mongoose caught in the gaze of a python, beyond any help Ruth could offer.

Just out of Ruth's reach a waiter was threading his way through the crowd with a tray of mojitos. A fourth? she asked herself. Why not? Why ever not? They seemed weak enough, and her capacity seemed to have grown fairly limitless in recent weeks. She followed him, but he kept a few feet ahead, his hips twitching as he slalomed around human impediments. Just as she had gotten within tapping distance of his shoulder she saw that Barbara and Noah and Joel and Ariel Bachman were bearing down upon her. They'd all joined hands to form a human chain and Ariel was crying out, "I think I see him! I think I see Daddy!" Ruth dodged quickly to the left, then to the right, escaping the Bachmans, but losing the waiter.

It was time to get out of this tent, she decided, and she struck out for the square of light that was the only means of ingress and egress. It seemed very far, but a general exodus had begun and soon enough she was flushed from the tent in a wave of others, everyone blinking and squinting in the hazy brightness of an ordinary Friday afternoon. For a moment she stood uncertainly while the crowd eddied around her. Should she wait for Ben? Go to his office? Drive home? But there, standing under the brick arch of the library colonnade, looking pale and vulnerable and seminude in this broad light, was Ricia Spottiswoode. She was wearing a tiny skirt and a skimpy flesh-colored leotard festooned with shreds of multicolored fabric. On either side of her were two of the oldest and mossiest members of the Lola board of trustees, both of them evidently fascinated by her and both deep in their cups. The tableau reminded Ruth of something. What was it? Oh yes! *Susannah and the Elders.*

As she approached, she saw that one of these old sports had moved behind Ricia and had actually laid his hands on her bare shoulders. Ruth felt a small shock of maternal indignation: how dare he! But now Charles appeared. He must have been hovering nearby. The trustee was leaning in so that his withered lips were moving a quarter of an inch away from Ricia's pearly ear. "I got to ask you, honey," he was croaking. "You say you a *mem*wa-ist. Now dunnat make you a *nah*sussist?"

Charles moved in closer. "Look who's here, Ricia," he announced in his deepest, most carrying voice. "It's Ruth Blau. Finally the two of you meet."

"Ah," said Ricia, her face lighting up with what even Ruth could see was genuine interest. She shrugged off the hands of the trustee and moved toward Ruth, extending her own hand. "I've been looking forward to this. I read your trilogy years ago and now I'm having the pleasure of reading your new novel. I was hoping we might get together soon and talk."

CHAPTER SIX

It was Daphne Porter's house, of course. Ruth had been here twice before, once for a meeting of a book club out of which she immediately dropped and once for an impromptu craft fair where she bought a pair of earrings that never hung straight and a jar of apple butter because it seemed rude to leave empty-handed. And during the years when she still attended such events, she'd run into Daphne and her husband, Sidney, at concerts and art-show openings and readings.

Now she was here for the Monday morning meeting of the dean's mission statement group. She was ten minutes early, so she parked and sat in the car. This was a part of town she liked, with narrow streets and mature trees and casually maintained yards. She felt more at home here than in her own neighborhood, where standards of upkeep were so high she feared one day she'd find a signed petition in her mailbox. Through a bay window she could see Daphne moving about in the dining room, setting the table.

Daphne—here she was now, gliding out onto the porch carrying an old-fashioned galvanized aluminum watering can—was a few years older than Ruth. She was also taller. She wore her long gray hair in a chignon, like Ruth, but more loosely and more becomingly, and she dressed like Ruth too, but somehow more convincingly. Not that she was imitating Ruth: it was quite the other way around. The effect that Daphne achieved effortlessly was exactly the one that Ruth repeatedly shot for and nearly always missed.

She watched as Daphne strode from pot to pot, watering her collection of thriving plants with an unself-conscious, unhurried grace, even now when people were due to arrive at her house at any moment. In the same situation Ruth would be dashing around distractedly, replacing the TV-guide supplement from the *Spangler Advocate* and the dog-eared collection of thrillers Ben had left on the coffee table with a display of recent issues of *Salmagundi* and *The New York Review of Books* and tossing stained throw pillows into the hall closet, all the while marking in her mind how much this behavior was at variance with her carefully cultivated sense of herself as a person who rose above appearances. And by the time guests arrived this cognitive dissonance would be buzzing and clanging so loudly inside her head that her social timing would be thrown off and things would go rapidly from bad to worse, especially if it was late enough in the day for alcohol to be served.

Daphne had never been a friend; she was too much all of a piece for Ruth to feel any real kinship with her. But neither was she a nemesis like Barbara Bachman or any number of others. Ruth liked and admired her for her simple warmth and authentic tranquillity. Of course she also envied her, for many things—for just about everything, in fact, except for Sidney, a pipe-smoking Spenser scholar with a reputation for grabbiness in elevators. She envied Daphne her beauty, which grew more austere and wintry with the years. She envied her her house, which was a commodious, slightly worn wooden cape set far back from the street. She envied all its comfortably bohemian furnishings. She envied the semi-wild garden where Daphne grew herbs and vegetables and heirloom roses. She envied her her three grown daughters, all willowy like their mother, all devoted to her and to one another, all quietly successful in their various careers. Two of them had already produced five grandchildren. (No doubt the count had gone up since last she'd seen Daphne: she'd have to brace herself for hearing that this morning, and prepare to deliver congratulations.)

But what she envied Daphne most was the way she seemed to fully inhabit her own life. Ruth knew what it was to do that for short periods of time. A shift in the light, a change in the angle from which she surveyed her surroundings and suddenly she'd find herself on the inside, for the moment at least. But what would it be like, she asked herself as she watched Daphne shake out an area rug over the porch railing, to live there all the time? Unimaginable, especially for Ruth, who had never been inside for long and had lately taken up more or less permanent residence outside, like a feral cat.

But now Daphne had caught sight of her and was headed down the porch steps in her direction. Ruth rolled down the car window. "Ruth," said Daphne, leaning in to kiss her cheek. "What are you doing watching me from the car? Please come in the house and have some coffee. I made a pineapple upside-down cake."

"It wasn't quite time," said Ruth. "I didn't want to get in the way."

"I'd have given you a job to do," said Daphne, ushering her through the door and seating her at the table, which was covered with a blue-and-white batik tablecloth and set with an attractively eclectic array of Daphne's hand-thrown plates and mugs. In the center was a great crackled-enamel vase erupting with zinnias and marigolds from the garden.

"Can I do anything now?" Ruth asked.

"Nothing. It's too late. You missed your chance," said Daphne, disappearing into the kitchen and reappearing with the cake, which she set on the table in front of Ruth. "Oh my," said Ruth. "My mother used to make upside-down cakes, but this is like a Byzantine mosaic." And it was.

As Daphne filled her mug with coffee, Ruth looked around. High ceilings, wide shining floorboards, Oriental rugs, books behind glass. She'd always taken Daphne's house as a standing rebuke to her own, the more so because like hers, the furnishings and atmosphere harked back to graduate-school days. But while Ruth and Ben's house was aboriginal, with its chipped saucers and lumpy futons, Sidney and Daphne's was a lovingly cared-for historical preserve. Usually the contrast caused her active pain, but today she found herself happy to be here. For once in her life, admiration had trumped envy. Her eye was pleased wherever it wandered and the temperature was tolerable enough this morning for the air-conditioning to be turned off and the windows opened. Surely that too had something to do with this sensation of well-being and expansiveness.

"Who all is coming to this?" she asked as Daphne headed back into the kitchen. "I only got the word about it last Friday." But apparently Daphne hadn't heard her, because she called out, "How's Isaac?" over her shoulder as she disappeared through the door.

As Daphne rustled in the kitchen, Ruth considered her options. Could she pretend she hadn't heard? Daphne would only repeat the question. Mutter something evasive? Somehow she didn't want to do that, not this morning. The backward and sideways moves both seemed blocked. Why not go forward?

"He's not good," she called back.

"Not good?" said Daphne, returning to sit down kitty-corner to Ruth with her own mug of coffee.

Ruth hesitated. Another decision point. Why not ask? Daphne was the right person, neither friend nor enemy, and she knew everyone.

"Daphne," she said, "tell me something. Do you know Eusebio Martinez?"

"No," said Daphne. "I don't think I do. Who is he?"

"He's Isaac's therapist. We're supposed to talk to him this afternoon." Daphne looked faintly puzzled, ready to hear more.

"When was the last time you saw Isaac?" Ruth asked. "When was the last time we talked about him?"

"Oh I think five, six years ago? He was just finishing high school?"

"He never finished. He never went to college. He's homeless. We haven't seen him in two years."

A moment of shocked silence. "Oh," said Daphne. "I'm so sorry. You must have been beside yourself."

Beside myself, thought Ruth. That's it exactly. I've been beside myself. "To tell you the truth I don't think about it that much," she said. "I put it in a box. Ben does too, even more than me. But Isaac keeps on with this Martinez. We're going to his office this afternoon. He says Isaac's going to be there."

"Well that's good isn't it?" Daphne's voice broke into a warble on the word "good."

"He was supposed to be there once before and he wasn't. We're not getting our hopes up. Actually we think he may be part of the problem. This therapist might, I mean. He just called us up out of the blue when Isaac left home. He seems to have taken over. Everything has to go through him, even the money we send Isaac every month."

"The *money*?" said Daphne, rising to her feet and padding into the kitchen and returning with paper and a pencil. "I wonder who might know this man. Would you mind if I asked around?"

"Please," said Ruth. "Please do."

"What's the name again?"

"Eusebio," said Ruth. "E U S E B I O. Eusebio Martinez."

A stiff rap at the front door startled them both. Ruth turned to see that a small-headed elongated shadow was swaying behind the leaded glass. It was Tony Del Angelo, the playwright. Of course!

When Ben reached the office at ten thirty he found it once again locked and dark, but when he opened the door and turned on the light he saw that Hayley had been here, probably on Friday after he'd gone to the reception. She had transformed her workstation into fairyland. Fairy posters had been tacked to every wall. There was a fairy with a fishing rod perched on the tip of a crescent moon, angling for smiling stars. There was a gathering of fairies lounging and preening on the branches of a decayed tree. There was a gothic fairy in a dark cape riding on the back of a wolf. There was an infantine fairy conversing with a frog on a lily pad and a redheaded fairy executing a semipornographic squat on the lid of a jack-o'-lantern. This last one reminded him uncomfortably of Ricia Spottiswoode.

A collection of ceramic fairy figurines was displayed on a mirrored tray on the desk. Others were lined up along the shelf where Dolores once kept her radio and her paperbacks and her box of Almond Roca. The standard Lola computer screensaver—the university logo superimposed over a soft-focus avenue of live oaks— had been replaced by a blowup of Tinker Bell trailing magic dust. There was a company of plastic fairies with sequined bodices and tiny gauze skirts suspended from the ceiling on strands of thread, all twirling in the breeze from the air conditioner. There was a fairy coffee mug holding pencils fitted with fairy erasers.

What there wasn't, Ben determined after a quick inspection of the desk and its environs, was the pile of work Dolores had left for Hayley. It wasn't on the fairy-occupied shelf or on the computer stand. It wasn't in any of the desk drawers. Ah, here it was, along with Friday's mail, on top of the cabinet by the window where Dolores kept computer paper and toner. The mail consisted of the usual publishers' brochures and conference announcements and a postcard from Bruce and Sissy Federman in Majorca, showing an assortment of tapas displayed on a red tablecloth. "Off the beaten track in Cala Figuera," Federman had scrawled diagonally. The pile of work appeared untouched, still bound by a stout rubber band and tagged with a yellow sticky marked "Urgent." Nothing looked too pressing. But no, here was a thick interoffice packet from the dean. Opening it, he found a stack of impenetrable SCAC material, tabulations and graphs printed in pink or green or yellow (one of his rules of thumb was that anything in color could safely be ignored), copies of letters to the dean from various state officials, congratulating her on Lola's high levels of compliance with the program directives—the kind of stuff he'd been tossing into the recycling box for a year now. But the cover letter, he saw from a quick perusal, was important. The dean was giving the faculty notice that the SCAC inspectors were expected on campus some day next week. (That meant *this* week, he realized.) They'd be talking to faculty in the halls, interviewing students, dropping in unannounced on classes. He found a sticky, a highly visible pink one, wrote out "Please Alert Faculty, Very Important" and left the letter on Hayley's desk, right in the center of the blotter where she couldn't fail to notice it.

He retreated to the door of his office, turned, and took in the fairy display once again. Call Dolores. That was the thing to do. Ask if there was any way to fire an employee. He couldn't remember a precedent, but there had to be one. He thought of Mitten-Kurz and how he'd like to walk over to her office right now and knock over some of her plants. Yes. And then he'd take that forty-pound sack of fertilizer she kept propped up in the corner and upend it over her desk.

But here was Hayley now, arriving for work at—what was it?—ten thirty-three. He'd made up his mind to confront her about her lateness, but one look at her silenced him. She was flushed, unwell. Her eyes were red-rimmed and swollen. She had the look of someone who'd spent a sleepless night, the look of someone so distraught she hardly knew where she was. He saw that this was not the moment to say anything about lateness or to demand she take down the fairy display or to chide her for the work she'd left undone. "Are you . . . ?" he began, but she had turned her back to him and was closing the door. She did this deliberately and theatrically, using both hands and throwing her back into it, as if simultaneously closing this particular door and pantomiming the closing of an imaginary door. Turning back to face him she said, "May I have a word with you?" in a dangerously flat monotone.

"Of course," said Ben.

"A *private* word?" said Hayley. "In your *office*?"

"Certainly." Ben led the way. There was nobody else around, so any word she had with him would be private by definition, but never mind; there was no reason not to oblige. He ushered her into the office, sat down behind his desk, gestured at a chair. Hayley shook her head. She stood in front of the desk, head lowered, hands twisting. "A problem?" he asked. "Something I can help you with?"

Hayley's lower lip was quivering. Tears were leaking from her eyes. "Everything all right?" Ben asked stupidly, standing up to push the Kleenex box in her direction. She examined it blankly, as if it were a brick or a loaf of bread, then seemed to recognize it. She took a tissue, wadded it tightly in her fist. "She is the snippiest, rudest . . ." She was weeping openly now. Tears were actually popping from the corners of her eyes. Projectile weeping; Isaac used to do that. "She has no regard," she wailed. "She has no respect."

Her daughter? Who was this? "Who is this?" Ben asked.

"*Rho*da." She exhaled the word in a voiceless whisper.

Rhoda? The very reasonable Rhoda? The steady and efficient work-study student Rhoda? What on earth could Rhoda have done or said to cause this reaction? "Why don't you sit down," he said. "Hayley," he added, remembering the seminar on employee relations he'd been forced to attend when he took over the chairmanship. Use the employee's name, the facilitator kept saying. "Why don't you tell me exactly what happened?"

To his surprise, Hayley sat. "She crossed a line," she said. "She overstepped her boundaries."

"How so?"

Hayley paused, twisting the tissue in her hands. "She tried to tell me what to do."

"What exactly did she tell you?"

"She told me all *kinds* of things. She told me where the bunch of stuff what's her name left me was. She showed me where the *supplies* are kept. She showed me where the list of phone numbers what's her name kept Scotch-taped to the inside of the desk drawer were. She tried to tell me how to operate the copier. She's not my boss. I'm *her* boss. She can't boss me around."

"Do you know how to work the copier?" Ben asked. "Hayley."

"Not exactly, no," said Hayley. "But that's not the point. I'm the one who's supposed to be in charge. I don't need somebody telling me what to do."

"Is it possible that Rhoda was just trying to be helpful? Might this all be a misunderstanding?"

Hayley's face darkened. She stared furiously at her hands. "She thinks I'm lower than her," she said. "She thinks I'm dirt."

She pronounced this last word in a startling low rasp, as if some demon that had been struggling to take over her personality had at last succeeded.

"Why would she think that?" Now Ben was a nondirective psychiatric social worker.

"Because she comes from money and I don't. Because she's got an education."

For the first time this morning, she looked him in the eye, and with an expression of satisfaction. By playing this trump card, she had cut off every possible honest response. He wanted to let her know that Rhoda came from a small town in South Dakota, not from money, and that she was working her way through school (three jobs). But a bald correction would bring to the surface what he couldn't say: that Rhoda came from the working poor, while Hayley was . . . But that was the thing about people like Hayley (he'd known a few, never one so extreme). When dealing with these interpersonal terrorists, every response had to be calculated; spontaneity was always a mistake. He was doing his best to radiate calm, to compose his features into an expression of judicious sympathy, but his mind was racing. What to say?

"Rhoda is very shy." He'd guessed this would appeal to Hayley's sentimentality, but it was a desperate gambit, far off the mark. "She is not shy," said Hayley, and she was right. Rhoda was not shy. Score one for her.

"Reserved. It doesn't matter. What matters is that you two women" (she brightened a little at this) "come to terms. She's a very efficient worker. Try to give her a chance." He paused for a moment, and now it came to him—an inspiration. "You need to look at Rhoda as a *resource.*"

Watching Hayley react to this was like watching one of those sped-up botanical growth sequences from the Disney movies of his youth. Her scowl unfurled and became something like puzzlement and that in turn gave way to a look of dawning comprehension. "A resource," she said. "I suppose if I assert my authority—"

"You don't need to assert your authority. You just need to remember that you *have* authority."

Now she was smiling tearily, wiping her eyes with the tattered tissue she'd been clutching, straightening up in her seat and adjusting the hem of her skirt. "Thank you for that, Professor," she said. "I like the way you listen." He got to his feet and walked to the door. Hayley wasn't quite ready to accept the prompt. "Professor," she said, still seated. "If that doesn't work . . . if I still have trouble . . ."

"I'll have a word with her," he said, or rather whispered. The transformation was complete. He was all breathy mandarin discretion. When he'd arrived at the office this morning his integrity had been more or less intact. Five minutes alone in a room with Hayley and he'd become a creature of oleaginous insincerity, like Charles Boyer in *Gaslight*.

"Thank you," she said, at last getting to her feet. "Thank you for understanding. I think maybe I overreacted. It's been a difficult time. My kids are having a very rough adjustment."

Ben was nodding, smiling, ushering her out. At the threshold she paused. "Tell me, Professor," she said. "What do you think of my fairies?"

Community, Ruth was thinking as she contemplated the eight people sitting around Daphne Porter's table, is always an appealing notion in the abstract. It's the members of a community who make it problematic.

Ruth knew all the members of this one, in some cases mostly by reputation, in other cases directly. She knew that every one of them knew every other one and she knew as well that everyone here was genuinely dismayed to see everyone else. (The only exception was Daphne, who liked everyone and whom everyone liked.) Furthermore, she knew that everyone *knew* that everyone felt this way about everyone else. She'd watched as the assembled eyes slid in the direction of the door at each knock of arrival, and she'd monitored the inadequately suppressed sighs, the curled lips, the dropped glances when Daphne announced the newcomer. Once the group was assembled she looked around the table, watching as each member registered the totality of the Tapestry Task Force Mission Statement Working Group. Oh no, every one of them was thinking. Not this bunch.

But what could they—what could she—have been expecting? That the dean had somehow uncovered a new and uncontaminated cache of writers who'd been living and working in Spangler in fruitful obscurity? And what was she, Ruth, doing here? Had she forgotten the reasons she'd dropped out of the MFA program three years ago—the tachycardia-inducing tension in the hallways, the grim rivalry of the workshops? All she could think was that when she'd taken her coffee out to the screened-in porch this morning the world had smelled of the changing season and she'd thought: Maybe I'll just take a chance. Otherwise I'll spend the time jittering about the appointment with Martinez. I can wear the embroidered *thob* I ordered off eBay and the new amber beads.

Considering the degree of unanimity in this room—here were

seven people who shared a single thought—it seemed a painful irony that nobody could turn to anyone else for confirmation or support or even for an exchange of meaningful glances. In the absence of (nearly) all lateral connection, the only relationship that brought the members of this community together was the acceptance, even if reluctant and only for the moment, of the idea that this *was* a community. Was it? If so, it was a community in the paradoxically pure way that the "Chelsea sadomasochistic community"—she'd come across this phrase in *The Village Voice* twenty-five years ago—was a community. Ruth thought of the Ik, the displaced nomadic tribe about whose members Lewis Thomas wrote: "They breed without love, and they defecate on one another's doorsteps."

Not that there was any lack of history here. If anything, there was too much. To catalog the rivalries, grudges, betrayals, lapsed friendships, divorces, feuds, and physical assaults that had severed past connections between the people in this room would require the kind of mind that finds histories of the Balkans comprehensible.

Tony Del Angelo, the playwright, and Mary McGonnigle, the children's book author, for example, had been lovers during most of the years of their marriages to other people. After a number of public scenes and much therapy, both marriages dissolved. Almost immediately after they moved in together Tony threw Mary down the back stairs of their newly purchased condominium. She left him and he was dropped from the Lola English faculty, where he'd been teaching workshops as a charismatic adjunct.

If the Tony and Mary story was the most dramatic, there were others that matched it in rancor. Devorah Grandin, sitting to Ruth's right, and Celia Sapowitz, who had declined a place at the table and seated herself on a ladder-back chair against the far wall, were longtime antagonists, both products of the writing program where Ruth had also briefly been a student. Both had had stories short-listed in the same best-of anthology, and both had been acolytes of the same famous novelist writing-teacher, who made the mistake of agreeing to blurb both women's first novels, which came out simultaneously. Celia's blurb contained the word "brilliant" while Devorah's book was described as "deeply engaging." When Devorah fell into an agitated depression the famous novelist nominated her for a Pushcart, but this attempt to soothe had the perverse effect of rekindling her resentment of Celia. If their mutual mentor thought so well of her writing, she told anyone who would listen, that could only mean that Celia had won the warmer of the two book endorsements through a deliberate campaign of flattery and the use of sexual wiles. She was a kind of animosity hub, this Devorah: she also carried on active feuds with two of the other writers present this morning, for reasons Ruth had either never known or forgotten.

Ruth herself disliked everyone here on general principles, except for Daphne, and assumed they disliked her in return, but she had no particular history of trouble with any of them. No, that wasn't true. Liz Tortuga, an old student of hers from a Lola extension workshop, was glaring at her from across the table. She'd forgotten that she'd offended Liz by making an ill-considered crack about how she had yet to meet an intelligent member of Mensa. Some people never let anything go, she was thinking, but she was also thinking what a pleasant novelty it was to be the least angry person (except for Daphne) in the room—the one in whose mouth, comparatively speaking, butter wouldn't melt.

But wait. What was Liz doing here? She was no writer. She had published a few sentimental pieces in the "Readers Have Their Say" column in the *Advocate* Sunday supplement—a Mother's Day reminiscence, a tribute to a dog she'd had to put down. That was it: no books, no prizes, no stories in serious journals. And the dean had appointed *her*? Could it be because Liz and her husband regularly played bridge with the Mitten-Kurzes? That might not be so bad if Ruth herself hadn't so obviously been an afterthought.

Ah, she said to herself. Now I'm thinking like a writer.

Daphne had cajoled Celia into joining the group at the table and now she was pouring coffee and serving the upside-down cake. All the women praised it, but the two men present, Tony Del Angelo and Gideon Calloway, were engaged in a staring contest and let theirs go uneaten. Gideon was a West Indian poet who had briefly been married to Mary after the back-stairs incident. He and Tony were regulars at Bad to the Bone, where in their younger days they had a history of brawling.

"Wasn't it lucky for us," said Daphne, reseating herself and offering a bright general smile, "that Gary took a turn east? I really shouldn't say that," she amended. "It wasn't so lucky for the people in Louisiana."

"Denise was the one that made landfall in Louisiana," said Sophie Drucker, an elderly know-it-all who carried a grouse stick to outdoor events. She had published a fictionalized life of Anne Boleyn a few years before Ruth's trilogy came out, but somehow her book stayed fresh in local memory while Ruth's work remained as forgotten as a mass grave in the Siberian hinterlands. "Gary went to Florida and turned into a rainmaker."

"We've gotten off easy this season," said Daphne. "I hope the stores will have supplies on hand if the next one—what's her name, Heather—hits."

"Remember Lisa?" said Liz. This was the first time anyone but Daphne had addressed the group in general. Everyone but Ruth remembered Lisa, a monstrous Category Four that struck in the late seventies before she and Ben and Isaac had arrived. To bring up Lisa at any Spangler gathering was to cue a storm of anecdotes—how the bayous overflowed and how great eighteen-wheelers floated beneath the freeway overpasses like Matchbox toys, how the patients in the oncology unit at Five Timbers had to be airlifted from the roof, how the city smelled like worms for months after the waters receded. Three or four of the assembled task-force members drew breath to tell their own, but then they remembered where they were and who they were among and fell awkwardly silent.

"I suppose we should get to our agenda," said Daphne. "Celia has been designated our rapporteur. Didn't the dean give you some materials to distribute, Celia?"

Celia passed around the pastel packets. "Why don't you just read this first few pages aloud to us, Celia," said Daphne. "The 'charging instructions'? And then perhaps the sample statements?"

Celia sighed heavily and cleared her throat. "Thank you for your service to the Lola Dees Institute and to the community of Spangler, Texas. As an appointed member of a TTFMSWG you are tasked to consider the enclosed first draft of the proposed amended mission statement submitted for the approval of Dr. Lee Wayne Dreddle by the board of regents. Your group should work toward arriving collaboratively at your own version of the statement, bringing to bear the particular gifts and aptitudes of the community to which you belong, reflecting the unique perspec-

tive or perspectives of that community, and using your statement
to advocate for its needs, requirements and visions . . ."

She went on, reading in a flat mumble like a police officer
Mirandizing a suspect. Ruth looked at her fellow task-forcers, all
apparently as absent to the moment as she. The staring contest
between the two men continued as a standoff, but now Gideon
had colonized a portion of the table with his elbows and was leaning forward with a menacing smirk. Sophie was peering up with
an appraiser's interest at three brass Moroccan lanterns Daphne
had installed over the table. Mary had her purse open in her lap
below the level of the tabletop and was stealthily sorting through
a stack of receipts. Devorah was sitting with arms locked under
her bosom, breathing noisily through her nose.

Only Daphne was listening, reposed and alert, her head
slightly tilted, like a cat attending to a rustling in the bushes. This
must have been the way, Ruth was thinking, that she listened to
her three daughters, photographs of whom were displayed in silver frames on a silver tray on the teak sideboard, along with other
family pictures. She turned to look at them more carefully. There
was Pru, the eldest, in hiking shorts, heavy pack on her back,
turning to smile down at the photographer from the rocky summit of a wooded trail. Here was Sarah as an eight- or nine-year-
old in a Halloween witch costume, and a very tall and slightly
awkward Ellie at a school dance in a floral empire-waisted dress
that looked like an altered version of something Daphne might
have worn in the late sixties. The grandchildren were shown at
various ages and in various attitudes. Here was Daphne with a
newborn in her arms, a Madonna once removed. Her beauty,
Ruth was thinking, was of the kind that seemed to have a moral

dimension, or perhaps even a moral origin—as if a lifetime of loving thoughts had purified her face from within. But no, Ruth remembered. That was not possible.

"...to serve and stimulate society..." Celia was reading. "...to promote cross-cultural competencies..."

If Daphne had a green thumb for gardening and child-rearing, Ruth supposed that she, Ruth, had a black one, a puckered thing that blighted everything she touched. And yet even this familiar line of thinking failed, somehow, to depress her this morning. Instead, watching Daphne, she felt—was this another odd trick of her aging brain?—that Daphne's beauties and virtues had somehow rubbed off on her a little, as if the ability to admire had in some primitive and magical way become the power to appropriate.

But something was happening. Celia was no longer reading and Devorah had turned a dark and mottled shade of red. She was shaking her head violently and Daphne was looking alarmed. In near unison, Devorah was saying, "I'm sorry. I'm just not comfortable," and Celia was saying, "Oh for Christ's sake, Devorah, come off it," and Tony Del Angelo, having broken eye contact with Gideon Calloway, was jumping to his feet and shouting, "Hey! Hey! *People!* Can we get a little perspective here?"

So I guess it was a waste of your time," Ben was saying. He'd been about to say "your valuable time" but his internal censor, ever vigilant these days, stepped in. He was mildly irritated that all weekend Ruth had refused to listen to his arguments in favor of attending the dean's task-force meeting—made entirely in the interests of her well-being and against his natural inclination to oppose anything Mitten-Kurz had proposed—and then turned around this morning and decided to go. But this was not the moment to provoke a squabble. They were on their way to Eusebio Martinez's office and in a moment he was going to have to maneuver around a line-straddling rattletrap pickup truck in order to get into the lane for the exit. If that was the right exit. He wasn't sure. Martinez's old office had been five minutes from the Lola campus on a verdant street in the Museum District. His new office was in a remote part of town near the secondary airport. (Ben wondered: How on earth did Isaac make his way there? By bus? Did Martinez pick him up? Did he make house calls at the dumpster behind the Cosmos Coffeehouse?)

"It wasn't entirely a waste of time. I talked to Daphne before it got started and I asked her if she knows Martinez and she said—"

"Quiet a minute," said Ben. "I need to concentrate." He'd swung drastically to the right to give the wobbling pickup the widest possible berth, but the driver took that as his cue to step on the accelerator and to weave even more wildly, forcing Ben to veer into the breakdown lane. The exit was fast approaching. "Is that the exit we want? Should I take it? I think I've *got* to take it."

"I don't know," said Ruth, her hand flying to her throat. "How should I know?"

He took it. It was wrong. Something about the angle of the exit ramp told him so. "Oh no," he said. "Oh *no*! I think this is wrong. I know this is wrong. Is this wrong? Does this look wrong to you?"

"It looks like every other exit," said Ruth. And it did. In view was a stretch of access road lined by car dealerships, fringed blue banners flapping in the wind above them.

"Where's the map?"

Ruth rummaged in the glove compartment. Sliding his eyes in her direction as he pulled off the ramp onto the access road, he watched as she flipped through a stack of maps, eliminating Southwestern United States, Oregon, the five boroughs of New York City, Minneapolis. "We want the central Spangler one?" said Ruth.

"Yes."

"I think I left it in the other car," she said in a small voice. For what seemed a long while they followed the access road, Ben shaking his head bitterly and muttering under his breath. "We're going to be late, Ruth. We're going to miss him because he won't wait. We'll get there right after he's gone and we won't see him again for another two years."

"We've got plenty of time," said Ruth. "You allowed an insane amount of time." It was true. They had fifty minutes, but in Spangler it was always possible to get lost for hours. "If you take a map out of this car and put it in the other car then we don't *have* the map anymore," he said. "Ruth."

"We have it. We have it in *my* car," she said. "Oh wait. Here it is." She pulled the map out of the side pocket. Glancing at her face in profile, Ben could have sworn he detected the ghost of a smirk.

Making a jolting right turn into a weedy pothole-strewn parking lot in back of a wholesale nut distributor, Ben parked and spread the map out over the steering wheel, running his finger along the torturous route he'd have to take: back to 201 via 115 in the other direction (how he hated to retrace his steps), then north to the Bojangles exit, then west on Cotton for 4.5 miles and right on Mary Humphries Boulevard. They had time, but only just enough.

They followed the numbers on Mary Humphries for block after block, both reflecting with a kind of bleak wonderment on how far Martinez seemed to have fallen. This was the part of town the locals called the Wild Wild West; stretches of litter-sprinkled pastureland alternated with patches of tentative settlement—storefront Pentecostal churches, auto body shops, cantinas with crudely hand-lettered signs. They might have been somewhere in the Philippines, Ben was thinking, someplace hot and green and underdeveloped and perhaps outside the reach of the law. At last they pulled into a tiny mall and parked directly in front of a one-story brick building with burglar bars on its windows. He would have found it hard to believe that this was the right address if it hadn't been for the late-model smoke-gray Mercedes parked next to them. They were thirty minutes early.

"I don't think we should wait in the car," said Ruth. "If Isaac comes along he might just turn around and go back."

"How's he going to come along?" said Ben. "That's what I don't get. How's he going to find his way out here?"

"Maybe he's in there already," said Ruth, though she didn't believe that was likely.

To the right of Martinez's building was an outlet store selling sheepskin car-seat covers. To the left was Paperback Exchange, evidently closed, possibly defunct. A few storefronts down was a small Mexican restaurant, empty at this time of day, but open. Ruth ordered a bowl of menudo, Ben the combination platter—a burrito, two tacos, rice and beans, pico de gallo, guacamole. They ate for a while in silence, looking through the smeared window at the empty parking lot and the road beyond it, where cars passed by at a rate of perhaps one every thirty seconds. Ben got up and rummaged through the bin holding free flyers and newsletters and returned with a copy of the *Spangler Shopper*. "Do you mind?" he said. His reading at the table had always been a bone of contention between them. She shook her head: forbear, she told herself. Let him run his eyes over print if he finds it comforting. After a moment she said, "Hey. That's in Spanish."

"I read a little Spanish," said Ben. "You knew that." He pushed aside a basket of tortilla chips and a jar of pickled nopals to make more room for the paper and returned to his perusal of yard-sale listings and his steady, systematic mastication. Ruth was struggling with a growing sense of irritation. She couldn't help finding it a little unseemly that he would choose to eat a great pile of lunch like that under these circumstances. There had always been something about watching his eyes follow newsprint as his fork conveyed food into his mouth that raised her blood pressure.

She looked around. In the rear it was dark and chairs were piled on tables. The only illumination in the room was natural light from the windows, though she could see orange-and-yellow paper garlands hung in scallops over the service counter in back. Their waiter sat a few tables over, looking through what she took to be the classifieds.

"Ben," she said. "Do you think he'll be there?"

Ben looked up thoughtfully, as if he'd just now been working this out for himself. "On the one hand," he said, "it would be odd if he weren't. Martinez must have gone to some trouble to make arrangements to get him out here. Why would he do that if he didn't think he could produce him? On the other hand . . ." He gave an eloquently skeptical shrug.

"Why would he move his office out here?"

"Rents have gone up in the Museum District," said Ben.

"But here?" She threw out an arm to indicate the restaurant, the empty parking lot, the pocked road with its weedy verge, the low-rider car just now cruising by with all its windows rolled down. The waiter turned to look at her. For a moment she saw herself as he must have seen her: a kind of Margaret Dumont figure, tall and peremptory and ridiculous, with sweeping gestures.

Another shrug. Ben checked his watch, stood, dug out his wallet, and counted dollars for a tip. Ruth looked at her own watch: two fifty-seven. She got to her feet, then sat down again, abruptly. The waiter looked her way again, but Ben was turning toward the door and hadn't noticed. She was awash in a sudden debilitating panic, as if she'd just this minute remembered an exam for which she had no time to cram. For the first time she realized how unprepared for this encounter she was. Ben's air of methodical calm—now he was pausing at the door to refold and replace the Spanish edition of the *Spangler Shopper*—irritated her to the point of fury.

Why hadn't they talked about this? The two of them had always been compulsive hashers and rehashers. Never was a scab allowed to form over a dispute; never was a topic left unaired. They had always discussed everything, exhaustively and exhaustingly, particularly Isaac. They used to confer about him daily, sometimes hourly, but in recent months—years?—a kind of gentle taboo had settled down around the subject.

Ben had been the first to shy away from talk of Isaac—that stoical shrug of his had been a recent development. But she had followed his lead quite willingly. The truth was that Ben had quite naturally begun to give up hope, to turn his attention elsewhere, and so, a little later, had she. Neither wished to be caught at it, or to catch the other. Their silence was an unspoken collusive agreement that allowed them both to forget.

He wasn't here. Ruth knew it even as they walked down the long, dim, carpeted hall, which smelled as hollow as the inside of a tennis ball, and passed what seemed to be the only other occupied office in the building, some kind of import/export enterprise. A handwritten note had been tacked to the door, instructing FedEx to bring packages in through the back. She knew it as they were buzzed into the waiting room, half the size of the old one, windowless and low-ceilinged.

Isaac wasn't in evidence in the sanctum of Martinez's office, or at least she failed to hear his voice or catch any glimpse of him over Martinez's shoulder as he leaned through the door and apologized for keeping them waiting. "I'm just now trying to reach the person who does my conveyances for me," he stage-whispered, holding a cell phone a few inches away from his ear. "Please make yourselves comfortable. I'll be with you momentarily."

It wasn't easy to make oneself comfortable in this waiting room, where the outsize, dramatic furnishings of the Museum District office had been uneasily warehoused. The orange leather couch was too long to fit anywhere except diagonally, and the basalt-cube coffee table was separated from the flamboyantly winged side chairs by so little space that they'd had to sidle their way into their seats. And in spite of the acoustic-tiled ceiling and the whirrings of a number of white-noise machines, they could hear every word Martinez spoke.

"What is it that I pay you for?" he was declaiming from behind the office door. "I ask only that you pick up the client at the designated place at the designated time!" Ruth and Ben glanced at each other. "We might as well just leave," said Ben. "That's all for our benefit. There's probably nobody on the other end."

"But why?" Ruth whispered. "What on earth would be the point?"

"To keep the payments coming," said Ben. "What do you think?" Now he was on his feet, edging his way sideways in the direction of Martinez's sanctum, which had suddenly gone silent. The door opened. "Please," said Martinez, tucking his chin into his collar like a butler ushering in a duke and duchess, "Professor and Mrs. Blau, come in. I must apologize that there is nobody to greet you. This is only a temporary state of affairs."

The inner office was as austere as the waiting room was over-stuffed—furnished with only a utilitarian metal desk and chair, a foam-rubber couch, and a pair of straight-back chairs. Boxes of files were piled against the far wall, and a single window looked out on yet another parcel of flat Spangler grassland that Ruth found it hard to believe had any more monetary value than a stack of old *National Geographics*. Martinez was wearing a starched white oxford-cloth shirt, cuffed blue jeans with an ironed-in crease, and oxblood loafers polished to a high sheen. His hair, which used to sweep luxuriantly over one eye, had been buzzed into a field of dark stubble in the currently fashionable manner. His chin was all the tinier for it, his damp, rosy lower lip the more pendulous. He looked, Ruth realized, exactly like the waiter in the restaurant a few doors down. A lunatic conjecture formed itself in her mind: Could he be moonlighting? Dashing back and forth between his office and the restaurant via some underground tunnel?

They all sat down. "I'm afraid once again I must ask for your patience," said Martinez. "Apparently Isaac was not found at the collection point. The driver was a few moments late. He's presently circling the area, looking for him. You and Mrs. Blau are free to wait if you wish. Or leave, if that's your preference."

Ben looked at Ruth. Ruth shook her head. Martinez nodded fatalistically. "Much patience is required when dealing with a child like Isaac," he said. "One must roll with the punches."

"I must say I wonder," said Ben after a moment, "why you didn't make sure you had him here before the appointment. We wondered the same thing last time."

"That effort was made," said Martinez. "The arrangement had been that Isaac would wait for the driver earlier today, and when he was not there I managed to track him down by phone and make an arrangement for a later time. Isaac is a severely decompensated young man. One can't assume that a resolution taken one moment will hold until the next."

"If you can reach him," said Ben, "then why can't you tell us where he is?"

"Professor Blau, we've been over this before. Several times, I think. If Isaac does not wish to hear from you, I cannot in good conscience let you know."

Ben turned to Ruth and shrugged a particularly bleak and weary shrug. Ruth realized who it was he'd been reminding her of; his late father, of course. He'd been a shrugger as well, and also a sigher. When Ruth first met him he had just been diagnosed with a sluggish prostate cancer and his doctors had advised a policy of "watchful waiting."

Having apparently read Ben's shrug as final, Martinez stood. "One more thing," said Ben, keeping his seat, "I don't believe we've ever gotten an itemized statement from you. We have no way of knowing how our payments are used."

"I will be pleased to send statements," said Martinez, sitting down and scribbling a note and swiveling in his chair to leave it on his desk. "May I ask you to leave a payment now? I believe one is due. I'll have to ask for an additional one hundred and fifty dollars, to meet the requirements of a changed circumstance in Isaac's life."

"Which you won't tell us about," said Ben.

"Which I cannot," said Martinez.

Ben reached into his jacket pocket, produced his checkbook, balanced it on his knee, and wrote out a check. "I'd like to assure you," said Martinez, receiving and pocketing it and rising once again to his feet, "that although I have made inevitable errors of judgment in my treatment of Isaac, I have always dealt with you in good faith. I hope you will believe this. I hope you can find it comforting to know at least that through me provisions have been made for him."

"I really don't know what to believe," said Ben, standing. At the doorway Martinez extended his hand. Ben shook it. Ruth made deliberate eye contact with Martinez and offered him her hand as well—somehow it was important to her that she be recognized at least once during this transaction. She applied as much pressure as she could to the handshake; in response his hand wilted. She dropped it and followed Ben as he turned sideways and renegotiated the narrow space between chairs and coffee table—not an easy thing to do while retaining one's dignity.

"One thing," Martinez called as they were out the door. "Just one thing before you go. I am under an obligation to respect Isaac's privacy, but I can tell you one thing. He is a young man capable of surprising. Isaac will surprise you."

CHAPTER SEVEN

⁓

Never?" said Ben.

"Never," said Dolores.

They were meeting for lunch in a back booth in the Student Union snack bar. Dolores had brought hers in a brown-paper sack—an egg salad sandwich wrapped in wax paper and a Granny Smith apple, which she adroitly peeled and quartered with a small knife, also imported from home. Ben was eating a cheeseburger and fries and drinking a Coke. The patty was thin but fatty and flavorful, in the atavistic Texas style. The Coke was heavy with syrup, like an old-fashioned fountain drink. Only the fries were generic.

"Really, never?"

"Not that I can remember."

"So I'm stuck with her," said Ben. If Lola had an institutional memory, Dolores contained it. "Forever," he added.

Dolores tapped at her lips with her napkin and raised a finger. While she discreetly transferred a bite of sandwich from the front to the back of her mouth, Ben looked around at this small, low-ceilinged rotunda which smelled faintly of grease and disinfectant and burnt coffee, and out the multipaned curved picture window at the flagstone patio and the massed azalea bushes beyond it, which had been used as a backdrop for nearly every bridal photo that appeared in the *Spangler Advocate*. The Student Union had been constructed in the year of Ben's birth and it made him sad to know that it was slated for demolition in the spring. It was too small, too modest, too worn, not consonant with Lee Wayne Dreddle's grandiose vision of the university, and so this nice old yellow-brick building, still serviceable, where generations of Lola students had joked and studied and courted, would be razed and replaced by an off-kilter postmodern confection twice its size with a floor-through "great room" arranged around a coffeehouse with Wi-Fi and a performance stage and a food court featuring tapioca drinks, whatever those were, and ethnic "street food" concessions.

Ben felt comfortable here. The Student Union building carried associations for him, as did Dolores, sitting there refolding the wax paper in which her sandwich had been wrapped—planning to reuse it for tomorrow's lunch, he felt sure. Why would the Dreddle administration tear down a perfectly good building? Why would they take away a perfectly good secretary? How cozy she is, he was thinking, sitting here in the booth with her ubiquitous raincoat draped over her shoulders. How economical and precise her words are, how unmistakably directed *to* him, in contrast to Hayley's, which were directed *at* him and could be understood only as behavioral artifacts—meaningless, gestural, hysterical. He was feeling particularly Manichean this afternoon; he found himself picturing Dolores and Hayley as a pair of cosmic goddesses filling both halves of the sky, like those two Hindu ones whose names escaped him. Dolores was Order, a stern matron in flowing robes. Hayley was Chaos, a many-armed whirling blur.

"How's it going over there?" he asked. "Are you settling in?" Ben meant the Sociology Department—the Land of Many Hugs, as he called it privately. Hard to envision brisk Dolores among those mournful women in long skirts and trailing scarves, moving languidly from office to office, stopping in the halls to embrace, rubbing one another's backs consolingly.

Ben could see a struggle in her face, but the habit of discretion was too strong. "I'm getting used to it. The work is much the same."

He'd put her on the spot, as he often seemed to do. The penalty for that was a period of awkward silence. "You could always *talk* to Hayley," Dolores finally said. "You could suggest she might be happier in some other department, or one of the administrative offices. But then she's been moved once already, hasn't she? From personnel?"

"That's right," said Ben. "The personality conflict." The two of them sat glumly for a moment as a quartet of giggling girls piled into the booth behind them.

Dolores brightened. "Things have a way of working out," she said. "If one party is unhappy, the other is often unhappy too. People can't be fired, but they can quit."

"That's the thing," said Ben. "She's not unhappy. She's happy. She tells me so all the time. She comes in two hours late and before I can say a thing she jumps in and tells me how much she loves this job and how I'm the best boss she ever had and how she's so grateful to be working here and not at all those other offices where she was mistreated and abused. Have you seen the fairies?"

"I've heard about them," said Dolores. The quick glance she gave him told Ben that everyone else had too. People were probably in and out all day to gawk at them. He wouldn't know, keeping his office door closed as he did. "Have you asked her to take them down?"

Here was the rub. "She has . . ." he began. Telling Dolores this was a bit of a risk. Even if she understood, she might lose whatever respect she had for him. "She has an odd effect on me," he continued. "I keep trying to talk to her. She doesn't do any work. None at all. Rhoda and I do everything. I've given up my writing because I have to come in at eight so someone is answering the phone at least part of the time. And once she arrives she leaves the office twelve times before lunch to go down to the pavilion and smoke—she isn't even supposed to smoke there, but it's actually a relief because all day long she's having loud wrangles with her kids on the phone."

"Yes," said Dolores. "I didn't like to mention it, but one of the girls from the audiovisual lab said something. She said they could hear her all the way down the hall. And her . . . language."

"Yesterday a student was taking a makeup test in her office and he actually knocked on my door to complain that he couldn't concentrate. I keep making up my mind to confront her but just as I get ready to open my mouth she comes at me from some new angle and she always manages to throw off my timing. And then the moment is lost . . ."

All through this recitation Ben sensed rather than saw that

Dolores was listening intently. For some reason his attention had fixed itself not on her eyes but on her disproportionately large and knobby wrists, one laid across the other on the table. For the first time, he noticed that she wore a man's watch with a wide flexible steel band, very loose. Was it her husband's? Did she suffer from arthritis? How little he knew about her, but somehow those wrists and that watch seemed to embody exactly what it was that he was learning. In the last few weeks he had begun to see her for who she was, to appreciate not only her discretion and efficiency but also her sympathy, her shrewd emotional realism, her rigorous judgment. Looking at her now he understood why it was he'd always seen her as belonging to his mother's generation rather than his own. It was because he felt unequal to the challenge implicit in her virtuousness ("Be like me"). As a moral philosopher he dealt in the idea of virtue. For him it had become an abstract notion, a matter of categories and competing claims, but Dolores reminded him that virtues reside only in human behavior and that human behavior finds expression only through the movements of living human tissue. Virtues, he was thinking, are not airy things. They're meaty.

When she spoke, it was in a newly low and urgent voice, like a doctor alerted to action by the recognition of textbook symptoms. "I know these people," she said. "They grow and spread like that weed—what's it called?"

"Kudzu."

"Kudzu. Soon they cover everything. You must cut her back. You must correct her."

"I'll do my best," said Ben.

"When?" said Dolores. "When will you do your best?" In

her vehemence she had evidently forgotten the distance between them. She was catechizing him, and he welcomed it.

"The next time. The next time there's a reason."

Dolores interrupted. "No no," she said. "Not the next time. You must do it today. Do it now."

Ruth typed in "Eusebio Martinez." The result was 34,000 hits. She added an ampersand and the word "psychotherapy." This narrowed the field to 270, but she found no recognizable correspondences. She tried once again, adding "Spangler Texas" to the other two terms. Two hits, one a duplication, but here was the first clear mention of the Eusebio Martinez she had in mind. The linked Web page listed Martinez as one of a number of local psychotherapists, giving his old Museum District address and phone number. She paused for a moment, deleted "Spangler Texas" and typed in "Mexico City." Forty-nine items appeared, all in Spanish. The third linked to a newspaper article entitled "The Rescuer of the Zona Rosa," with a photograph showing a younger and chubbier Eusebio Martinez in a neon-yellow polo shirt standing in a rubble-strewn lot with his arms draped around the shoulders of two very dark adolescent boys, both smiling beatifically. The Google translation was literal and contained unprocessed Spanish words here and there, like olive pits in a jar of tapenade. The first lines of the piece read "Eusebio Martinez is a therapist with a Program for Young to have flown their homes and homeless youth." Farther down the page she found another photograph. This time Martinez was shown in the same yellow polo shirt hovering over another group of adolescents, four boys and two girls, all of them small and dark, with aquiline Indian features, sitting around a card table in what looked like a very low-ceilinged basement. "Dr. Eusebio Martinez shares a time with children of the street who have gathered in a one-time disco where he has provided a warm meal."

Ruth printed the article and took it out to her chaise on the porch. "Dr. Martinez has also been able to conduct a practice of psychotherapy in the States," she read. "Here he has recovered sufficient revenues to support his good deeds in Mexico City, but in the States he has not neglected his work with homeless and troubled youth." On the last page of the article she found the following quote from Martinez: "I find a large sympathy for the adolescent because he is sometimes not so pleasant and not any longer loved by adults. I have made it the work of my life to help him."

She got up and fetched the phone, but just as she was sitting down to call Ben at his office to let him know what she had discovered, it startled her by ringing. Answering, she heard her own "Hello" as elderly and confused, inflected by a wondering mistrust. "Ruth?" said a young and silvery female voice. "Ricia. Ricia Spottiswoode. Do you happen to have a little time this afternoon? In the next hour, actually? I have some time and I'm ready to talk about your manuscript . . ."

Now. Do it now. Ben was taking the back stairs because the elevator doors faced the Philosophy Department's offices and even if Hayley wasn't actually on the elevator, as she almost always seemed to be, she could see the elevator doors opening and closing from her desk and that would deprive him of the element of surprise. This time he'd be upon her before she knew it. No premonitory throat clearing, no anxious glance to give the game away. He'd walk down the hall, taking care to keep well over to the right where his approach would be invisible to her, and then he'd come bursting into the office like a one-man SWAT team, talking so fast and seamlessly that she'd have no chance to draw breath to argue or interrupt. He'd startle her out of the cover of whatever persona she might choose to adapt—the martyred mother, the chipper Girl Friday from a forties movie, the muttering mental patient with the paranoid sidelong squint. He'd jolt her out of whatever martial-arts move she might come up with to throw him off-balance and use his psychic weight against him. What was that quote? One of those touchstones that people his age half remembered from high-school English. "There is a tide in the affairs of men, which, taken at the flood, leads on to . . ." Leads on to what? He couldn't recall. Some kind of good result. Was it Tennyson? No. It was Shakespeare, of course. *Julius Caesar.*

The hall was clotted with buzzing dyads and triads at this hour, graduate students and young faculty who had finished eating their brown-bag lunches in the seminar room and were lingering in conversation for a moment before making their way toward classrooms and the library. Threading his way through these schmoozers, Ben picked up the subtle but unmistakable impression that eyes were rapidly swiveling in his direction and just as rapidly swiveling away, that conversations ceased at his approach and resumed in the wake of his passage. Ted Danziger and Josh Margolis were lounging against a wall, deep in shoptalk. Josh waved him over, but he demurred with a quick smile and an apologetic wave. He would not allow his momentum to be broken. Out of the corner of his eye he saw Ted rise onto his toes and make small fluttering motions with his fingers.

Here was the office door looming ahead and now he'd walked through it, and here, veering into his surprised view, was Hayley sitting at her glorified desk, eating a slice of pizza. She'd never taken her lunch in the office before. "Hayley," he said. She smiled warmly.

"Ben," she answered. After less than a week she was using his first name. Another thing not to let pass. "Hayley," he said, taking care to keep his voice deep and even, "I'd prefer that you call me Professor Blau."

"Oh," said Hayley, holding the drooping slice in midair. "I thought it was OK. I thought I heard Sylvia in art history call her boss Dennis."

"That's their arrangement," said Ben. "I have different expectations."

Hayley carefully laid the pizza slice on a paper plate. "So it's not one way or another," she said, a considering frown creasing her forehead. "There's no hard-and-fast rule. It's different in different offices."

"Exactly," said Ben.

"And you'd feel more comfortable if I called you Professor Blau."

"Yes I would."

"Rhoda calls you Professor Blau."

"Yes she does."

"Well thank you," said Hayley. "Thank you, Professor. This is how I learn."

"You're welcome," said Ben. Out of habit he walked into his own office and closed the door behind him. No no, wrong. He wasn't done yet with Hayley. He'd hardly begun. He paused for a moment so as not to seem like a vaudevillian blundering in and out of a broom closet. "Hayley," he said, returning to stand over her at her desk. She had finished the slice of pizza and was tipping the crusts into the garbage. "Yes, Professor Blau?"

"I'd like to have a word with you. Is this a good time?" Ben was uncomfortably conscious of a need to stoop slightly to keep his head from brushing up against the tiny sharp plastic feet of the fairies dangling from the ceiling—there were even more of them now than there had been a few days ago—but to withdraw from the fairy-occupied zone would take him out of conversational range. Now Hayley was opening a package of hand wipes. "Certainly," she said. "This is a dandy time, actually," she added brightly.

"A number of problems have been presenting themselves," Ben began. "I need to let you know about them so that we can, you can . . . address them." The systematic wiping of each of her fingers seemed to be occupying the better part of Hayley's attention, but she had reserved enough to continue meeting his gaze. She was nodding energetically, as if to encourage a faltering petitioner. "Good," she said. "I can certainly see that. You need to let me know. Keep the lines—"

"The lateness," Ben interjected. "That's probably the most serious problem. You see, when you're not in the office in the mornings, in the early mornings, that means that Rhoda and I, or Rhoda or I, or Rhoda and/or I, have to come in to answer the phones, and that's not always convenient." No, no, he thought. Leave convenience out of it. That's not the point. "And even if it were convenient, I'd still expect you to get in on time, regardless."

"On time," said Hayley, nodding steadily. "Regardless."

"And I mean exactly on time."

The nodding continued, but a look of puzzlement or distraction had stolen over her features. It was as if she had suddenly become aware of some deep internal rumbling or leaking sensation, some painless but disconcerting symptom. Or as if she had just remembered an appointment.

"You need to plan your life around your duties here at school. Sometimes I get the feeling it's the other way around for you and your work here gets sandwiched in around those other demands—your kids, your other . . . concerns. We all have those outside . . . preoccupations, and it's not always easy to keep them on the periphery and keep the work at the center—"

"You know," said Hayley. She leaned forward abruptly and a sudden warm delight flooded her face. "I've been meaning to tell you, Professor Blau. You were so right about Rhoda. I don't know why I won't let people help me. With me it's always, 'Let me do it for myself! Let me figure it out!' " To illustrate her point she took off her watch and dangled it in front of her eyes, her brows contracted in mock-simian curiosity. "With me it's like, what *is* this thing? Let me take it apart and see how it's made. Let me figure out how it works. No no, don't show me!"

"Hayley," said Ben. "We need to get back to what we—"

"I could have saved myself a lot of time and trouble if I hadn't been so stubborn. Rhoda knows her way around. She's a resource, like you said."

"We need to—"

"And then I finally give her a chance and you know what I find out? She's a doll. An absolute doll. I couldn't have been more wrong about her. She and I were talking the other day and I've learned so much about her. Did she tell you about her dad?"

"No," said Ben, instantly regretting it. "But that's not what we were—"

"He's a paraplegic," said Hayley. "He's a Vietnam vet and he stepped on a land mine and he lost both his legs from the knees down. He drives a special van with hand controls and the whole family goes camping all over the country. Did she tell you about her sister?"

Now she had truly derailed the discussion. Behind his eyes Ben saw a club car lying on its side in a ditch in mountainous terrain, smoke rising, wheels revolving. What was needed here was something dramatic, a sudden move that would throw her off her game as she'd thrown him off his. He turned abruptly on his heel and walked back into his office, stopping at the door. "Hayley," he said, "please come in."

Hayley rose hesitantly to her feet, her face registering curiosity and suspicion.

"Come in," said Ben. "Please."

Like a doe drawn out of the woods by a salt lick, Hayley approached.

"Take a seat," said Ben, standing aside and ushering her into the room. She sat. Ben propped himself against his desk. Now he had seized the advantage. "I don't want to talk about Rhoda," he said. "I don't want to talk about anything but the problems that have come up with your work here. That's our agenda, and I'm going to make sure we stick to it. The lateness is only one issue. There are others and one of them is this business of you going downstairs all the time. Going out to the pavilion—and by the way I'm not sure if you know, but smoking isn't allowed out there. It used to be, but now you have to go clear across the green, all the way to that big live oak." His arm, he realized, had risen up from his shoulder of its own accord and was flapping in the direction he was describing.

"Anyway, I have no intention of being . . . punitive . . . about your private habits. I've never been one of those neo-prohibitionists." (Why couldn't he stop qualifying, conceding, digressing, justifying himself? It was as if some insanely reasonable dybbuk had seized control of his brain.) "I'm quite willing to make accommodations," he went on. (But he was doing it again, wasn't he?) "The bottom line is that you're going to have to limit your breaks to two or three a day. Let's make it three. No more."

Hayley had raised an anxious finger. "I'm sorry," she said, her voice a squeak. "I don't mean to interrupt but before we go any further I have to let you know I'm expecting somebody at one. I told them I'd be at my desk. Do you think we could . . . ? So I could see them when they . . . ?"

Ben moved to the door, swung it open, returned to his post at his desk. "So, three breaks a day. And you'll take them when your work schedule permits, not just anytime you feel like it. Are we on the same page?" Hayley was nodding, but her nods were small and staccato, as if generated by a new internal rhythm, and her eyes had gone cloudy with thought. It seemed that something was happening inside her, some development, some process, something that would emerge of its own accord. "You know, Professor," she said. "Isn't it amazing the way somebody will say something exactly when you're ready to hear it and not a minute before? Do you know what I mean?"

Ben made a noise.

"What you just said, about smoking? Well, that was one of those times. Just these past few weeks, since I've been working here at Lola, I've been thinking really hard about quitting. It helps that practically nobody else smokes because everybody's so educated. There are so many reasons . . ." She spread out the fingers of one hand and bent each one vehemently with the index finger of the other as she enumerated the disadvantages of smoking. "It's not good for my health . . . it's disgusting . . . it's bad for my kids to be around . . . it's expensive . . . it makes my clothes smell." She'd run out of fingers. "Professor," she said, allowing her hands to fall heavily into her lap, "I'm sick of it. I've had enough. I think I'm ready to quit. I needed one good push and you gave it to me and I can't tell you how grateful I am." She raised her eyes to his and just as he'd feared, they were wet, shining with tears.

And then she was on her feet, waving and halloing in the direction of the open office door, her face blooming with welcome. A student and an older man with a Mennonite beard had come trooping into the outer office, the latter shouldering what looked like photographic equipment. "Will you excuse me, Professor? It's the *Lola Lantern*. They're here to do a story about my fairies."

Ruth was waiting for Ricia in the Cosmos Club, a Museum District coffeehouse. She had already run her eyes over the local alternative newspaper, from the front-page exposé of the indiscriminate use of nitrous oxide by local pediatric dentists through an omnibus review of Spangler's new crop of Malaysian restaurants to the advertisements for Thai masseuses in the back pages. A copy of the manuscript of *Whole Lives Devoured* was parked by her chair in the Guatemalan bag. The thought of taking it out and looking it over filled her with dread. It might as well have been a packet of X-rays she was transporting to a consultation with an oncologist.

She was drinking plain hot tea, sitting in one of two sagging armchairs on an elevated wooden platform in the center of the room. This area was a kind of reading nook, defined by two free-standing bookcases. Later it would become a stage for the proprietor, a stringy ex-con in sky-blue clogs who perched on a wooden stool with his guitar and picked out embellished versions of "The Girl from Ipanema" and "Blowin' in the Wind" for the wine-drinking crowd that began to trickle in after four o'clock. Ruth felt awkward and exposed, an object of speculation for the early-afternoon clientele sitting in booths around the room. She must look, she thought, like a dowager queen preparing to grant an audience. She'd have felt more comfortable at a booth or a table, but the only one available was by a window and she knew she'd be distracted, scanning the rear parking lot for signs of Isaac, who sometimes spent his nights there in a colony of homeless men—or so she'd imagined, though her only evidence was that once she'd seen a pair of derelicts emerge from the wooded area behind the Dumpster, one carrying a duffel bag, the other zipping up his fly.

In one quadrant of her mind she was ruminating over the information she'd uncovered about Eusebio Martinez, trying to settle on an attitude to take about it. If the article she'd found on Google was to be believed, it seemed unlikely that Martinez was taking advantage of her and Ben. Or if he was it was in an entirely well-meaning and forgivable spirit. Even if he'd been squeezing them for funds to support his charitable enterprise in Mexico City, he no longer seemed to be a person capable of holding Isaac captive. It now appeared that it was Isaac who had chosen not to see them, just as Martinez had said. Whether that was good or bad news she hadn't yet decided.

But here was Ricia, standing in line at the counter. Ruth simply hadn't picked her out from the others. She looked anonymous this afternoon, small and ordinary, like any number of the young and youngish women waiting to order and receive their frothy coffee drinks, each of which seemed to take at least three minutes to assemble. She was wearing a backpack; no doubt the manuscript was in there. Her copper-penny curls were dully translucent under the track lighting, and for the first time it occurred to Ruth that their color might not be natural, that they might be dyed and need recoloring.

Ruth lifted a tentative hand in greeting. No reaction; Ricia seemed to be making a point of looking away. She'd been brisk and noncommittal on the phone. That needn't be taken as a bad sign, Ruth reminded herself. It could just as easily portend a happy outcome. How many times had she kept her own expression scrupulously neutral when she first sat down with a promising student, the better to offer the gift of relief when she pronounced a positive judgment? And when she had bad news to deliver, didn't she prattle on evasively about this and that until she could no longer postpone the process of lowering herself into her critique by degrees?

But even if Ricia didn't approve of her work, would that really matter very much? In recent years she had come to think of herself as a tube. Good or bad, experiences loomed into view. Good or bad, they passed through her and out the other end. The future was food, the past was the fungible product of its metabolic processing. There was nothing, it seemed, she couldn't digest. Well, there was something, but it wasn't likely to come along for a while. Or was it?

Ricia had made her way to the front of the line where she was paying, Ruth could see now, for a bottle of water. No coffee drink meant no delay, no grace period, and Ruth was suddenly quite overwhelmingly anxious. Her fingers had gone cold and her heart was fluttering in her throat. This panic was nothing new. It came over her every time some verdict was about to be delivered, and its intensity bore no necessary relation to the importance of what was to be disclosed. It would pass, but she did wish she'd remembered to bring something to read, something impressive to hide behind, like the new translation of *Swann's Way* Ben had picked up at a used bookstore on his last trip to Toronto. Ricia was paying for her bottle of water and now she was walking toward Ruth, her expression unreadable. She shrugged off her backpack and settled herself into the other armchair. How tiny she looked in it, like Alice after she'd drunk the potion.

"I didn't like it," she said.

"You didn't like the novel?" Ruth asked, stupidly.

"I didn't."

"Ah," said Ruth. "You didn't like it." To disguise the idiocy of this reiteration she tilted her head and squinted, as if to subject Ricia's pronouncement to careful consideration. After a moment she raised her eyes and said, "Why?"

"It disappointed me. It struck me as an attempt to write your first book over again. Your first books. At first I thought you'd meant it to be a sequel to the trilogy and I thought: A sequel to a trilogy? That's got to be a letdown for your readers. Then I thought, no, you couldn't have intended that. You didn't, did you?"

"No," said Ruth.

"It was certainly funny in places. I laughed. But somehow I

got the sense *you* weren't amused. You wrote it—what?—twenty years after the trilogy?"

"Yes," said Ruth, though it had been more like twenty-two.

"Excuse me for this. It didn't strike me as the book of somebody twenty years older. Or twenty years wiser. That wouldn't be a problem if you really still were that twenty-years-ago self, or even if you weren't but you managed to pass yourself off successfully as that person. But there's a new element in the new book. There's a depth in it that speaks of sadness. More than sadness: a deep melancholy. But it's in there without recognizing itself, if that makes sense. It's hiding behind the laugh lines. It throws off your timing, your comic timing. Funny writers aren't usually happy people, but there's a threshold past which you can't be comic anymore. If you're that sad, then your business is with sadness, not comedy. The book is hobbled. The whole book has a limp."

The two of them sat in silence for a moment. Ruth turned away and ducked her head so that Ricia could not see her expression, a very complicated and inward-turned smile—a smirk. "I hope I haven't been too harsh," said Ricia. "Ruth?"

"Excuse me," said Ruth. "I need the . . ." She heaved herself up from her armchair, stepped down from the wooden platform with an exaggerated gingerliness that drew glances from the coffee drinkers, and made her way around a collection of tables and past the counter and down a dim hallway to the women's room, which was kept dark by the ecology-conscious management. She fumbled for the light switch. There she was, peering into her own pouchy eyes in the mirror over the sink. The walls in here had been painted with a wraparound mural of an underwater scene in shades of green and blue. Under the fluorescent light these piscine colors made Ruth herself look like a great flounder, nosing up against the glass wall of an aquarium. She backed away, lowered the open toilet seat cover, sat down.

The reaction she'd fled to the bathroom to conceal seemed to have dried up the moment she got behind a closed door. What she felt now was nothing like the gut-punched breathlessness she'd felt out there. She felt acutely self-conscious but mobilized and composed, ready to make a plan. The first order of business was to get herself out of the bathroom and past Ricia and into her car with as little loss of face as possible. To that end she stood up and reexamined herself in the mirror. Her hair needed attention. She took it down, brushed it out energetically, put it up again with pins and a barrette. She applied fresh lipstick. Once she got home she could allow herself to react to Ricia's critique. (But would she? It had been years since she'd felt much of anything but anger and embarrassment. Was that a condition subject to change, or would she plod through the rest of her days like an ancient dry-eyed tortoise?)

But now she heard a small noise, a kind of soft scrabbling. A mouse? One of those mouse-sized roaches that roamed freely in Spangler? She looked down at her feet. Nothing but gritty black-and-white tile and shreds of toilet paper.

"Ruth?"

"Just a minute," said Ruth. "I'll be out in a minute."

"I'm so sorry," Ricia whispered urgently through the door. "That must have come out sounding brutal. I got it backward. I meant to tell you . . . May I come in?"

"I'll be out in a minute," Ruth repeated. Somehow it seemed unthinkable to open the door and confront Ricia, standing out there in the hall. She needed to be driven back into the main room of the coffeehouse, so that Ruth would have room to maneuver around her. "I'll be out in a minute," she said for the third time. "I'll join you out there."

Had she locked the door? Before she could reach it Ricia pushed her way in and closed it behind her. Inappropriately, Ruth giggled. What was this, high school? Whispering in the girls' room? Some obscure territorial imperative made her back away from Ricia and sit down again on the toilet. "Oh Ruth," said Ricia. "I've upset you. I'm so sorry. I got it backward. You understand, don't you, that what I was saying comes from a fan? That's why I felt free to be so blunt. I would never talk this way to a writer I didn't respect. A writer I didn't look up to."

"Oh, please," said Ruth.

"No, I do," said Ricia. "You can't for a minute think I consider myself . . . I've found a popular vein, that's all, and my publisher has a genius for marketing. You're something else. You're a real writer. I hope to be one myself some day. When I tell you I didn't like your book, I'm speaking as a reader, not as a critic."

Ricia was squatting at Ruth's feet now, looking up imploringly. How clear her eyes are, thought Ruth irrelevantly. How clear her skin. No tweezing the upper lip for her. Looking down at the wedge of light that was Ricia's face, she saw that she'd been wrong. Ricia *was* beautiful. She understood better the doggedness of Charles's devotion. The thing she'd learned about youthful beauty, now that she was no longer young, was that it inspires not just lust but love. The hem of Ricia's flounced peasant skirt was spread out on the filthy bathroom floor. "You probably don't want to do that," Ruth pointed out. "It's not very clean."

"Oh, I don't care," said Ricia, glancing down scornfully. "I

just want to get it across to you how much I admire your work
and how much . . . sympathy I have for whatever the circumstance was—"

Evidently some busybody had put her in the picture. "Who
told you?" Ruth asked, her voice sharper than she'd intended.

"Ah," said Ricia, pausing for a moment as if to consider and
override a qualm. "It was someone in the department."

"Who?"

"Ellen Treacher."

The timid interim chair with the three strands of pearls who'd
turned down Ruth's applications for part-time teaching for the
past five years. "I hate her," said Ruth. "She's such a vicious little
conciliator." All of a sudden she was feeling quite pleasantly reckless.

"I hate her too," said Ricia, throwing back her head and fling-
ing her arms wide. "I hate the whole department. I hate the whole
university. That's an exaggeration. I like the kids. I like some of
the faculty. Actually, I don't hate anyone. It's just that everyone's
so cautious and pussyfooting around and there's all this Byzantine backstory I can't begin to know about and I'm always having
to pull my punches. That's part of the reason I was so rude with
you. I've been so frustrated and for once I thought I could be
candid. I was so relieved to be talking to a real writer, not some
academic playing at being one. One thing I've learned in the last
few weeks is that I'm not cut out to teach in a university."

Ruth nodded. "I've never for a moment felt I belonged," she
said. "But it's my home. All my life academia has been home
for me. I wouldn't know where else to go. I feel like an egg that
hatched in the wrong nest. I feel like one of those birds that rides
around on the backs of hippopotamuses."

Ricia sank into a lotus position, tucking her skirt in around her knees. "Sometimes I think we're in some new dark age where everything is being sucked back into the universities, the way everything was sucked back into the monasteries in the twelfth century, or whenever it was." She seemed content to let this speculation hang in the air. The two of them sat for a moment in a silence that had begun to feel companionable.

"What exactly did she tell you?" Ruth said.

"She said you have a problem with your son. She said he has—how did she put it?—mental-health issues. She said he moved out and now he's homeless. How old is he?"

"He's twenty-four. Would you like to see a picture?" She reached into her bag and extracted her wallet. "He's three here. Three and a half."

"Oh my," said Ricia. She held the tiny curled snapshot on the flattened palm of her hand, like an archaeologist examining a newly unearthed coin. "Such a lovely boy. So solemn. I see your husband around his mouth. Around the eyes he's all you."

Ricia returned the photograph. Ruth put it away. Tears were welling now. "You say he's twenty-four," said Ricia.

Ruth nodded.

Ricia said, "I hope this doesn't offend you, but the first thing that pops into my mind is that he isn't dead. I'm sorry. What I mean to say is that it's not *as if* he's dead. I mean he's homeless, not dead. Maybe it's my blue-collar background, but these academic families put so much stock in their children's success. If they don't turn out to be lawyers it's as if they'd died. Of course the parents would never admit it . . ."

Ruth sat quietly for a moment, trying to absorb this new idea. *He's not dead.* It struck her as a kind of Zen koan, a deceptively

simple observation that somehow presents a challenge to comprehension.

"I mean," said Ricia, "please tell me if I'm treading on thin
ice here, but it seems to me the real problem with him—what is
his name?"

"Isaac."

"The hardest time with Isaac must have been when he was
living at home. He's grown now. He's an adult."

"I suppose so," said Ruth. This had seemed a small point, an
obstructive technicality. "He doesn't want anything to do with
us. Somebody's been looking after him, in a minimal kind of way,
but we haven't been able to help. Except with money."

"Is he a danger to himself or others?"

"No. Not really."

"So what can you do?"

"Nothing. Wait."

"You could write."

"I've been *stuck*," said Ruth.

"Yes," said Ricia. "That's it exactly. *Whole Lives Devoured* is a
very *stuck* book."

"Stuck," said Ruth again, as if puzzled by the word. The two
of them sat in silence. Unaccountably, Ruth's shoulders began to
shake. Ricia looked up at her with concern, leaned forward to lay
a hand on her wrist. But Ruth wasn't weeping; she was laughing.
This had happened several times before, most memorably when
she was pregnant, during a Lamaze class. Eventually the instructor asked Ben to escort her out to the hall. These fits were caused,
Ruth believed, by a kind of neuronal storm, itself the result of a
collision of two emotional fronts. Given the right conditions, al-

most anything could set them off. The present episode had been occasioned by the newly alien word "stuck," which had gotten caught somehow in the craw of her mind.

"Hey," said Ricia, drawing away a little. "Ruth. Ruth? Are you all right?"

"Stuck!" gasped Ruth. Ricia continued to stare at her, but now the corners of her mouth were quivering. She paused, gazed off into the middle distance. Nodding faintly, like a dancer picking up the beat, she produced a few forced exhalations and then she was laughing too, artificially at first, but soon enough genuinely and contagiously. As if following some choreographic signal, Ruth and Ricia staggered to their feet and flung themselves around the narrow high-ceilinged bathroom, wheeling in circles and caroming off walls, trying desperately to expend the energy of the convulsion. At last breathlessness forced them into opposite corners to rest. Ricia was limber enough to slide to the floor with her legs extended straight in front of her. Ruth contented herself with leaning her cheek against the stucco-painted wall. After a moment's restorative panting they glanced at each other and burst into wild laughter once again.

Gradually, the spasms subsided. They were breathing more normally, starting to regain composure, but then their eyes happened to meet once more. "Stuck," said Ruth, widening her eyes and mouthing the word voicelessly. "Stuck!" shrieked Ricia, pounding her fists against the wall. Now they were howling in unison, quite out of control. A quick hard rap on the door startled them into quivering silence. "Excuse me," said a male voice. "Ned here." Ned was the proprietor. "I'm going to have to ask you to break it up in there. Only one customer at a time in the restrooms."

"Yes sir," said Ricia. She'd clapped a hand over her mouth and turned her back to Ruth, who was standing over the sink splashing cold water on her face.

"Take your time," said Ned. "We just can't have—"

"Sorry," Ricia called out. She sounded snide and facetious behind the muffling hand and that was almost enough to start the cycle again. They waited, frozen, until the danger had passed.

"You go first," Ruth whispered to Ricia. "Give me a minute."

"Just one thing," said Ricia. Her hand was on the doorknob as she glanced back at Ruth. Her face was pale and drawn, her eyes rimmed with red, for all the world as though she'd been weeping. "Tell me quick. Is there anything else you're working on?"

"I started a series of sketches. They're very patchy. Just little vignettes."

"If I were you I'd put the novel aside. Put it away. Go back to those sketches and see where they take you. Or start something new. It doesn't matter. Just sit down. Just write."

W hen is a life not worth living?" Ben asked. This was the fourth meeting of Philosophy 101 and he was doing his best to stimulate discussion.

Four hands shot up in front, but Ben looked past them. He was pitching this question to the great middle, and he was willing to wait for a response. He had learned, over the years, to fight down panic in the face of silence. He had also learned to use his gaze to challenge and he did this now, trawling systematically along the rows for a tug of response.

This was an unusually sludgy group; he'd never known that

question not to snag at least a few beyond the front row. But today even the pink-haired *compañero,* on whom he'd relied heavily
during the past week's class discussions, was looking away. Just as
Ben was about to give the nod to one of the eager beavers in front
he noticed movement in the back, a stirring among the jocks. At
first he thought it was a twitch or a squirm that had caught his
eye—the athletes were often restless in repose—but no, it was a
hand, unmistakably raised and signifying a desire to speak. It belonged to Benson Boland, the 290-pound offensive lineman from
Emir, Texas. Just this morning Ben had been reading about him
in the *Lantern.* "See this guy?" he'd said to Ruth, calling her over
to look at a crouching Benson Boland, snarling for the camera in
the *Lantern*'s sports pages. "He's in my 101."

"Ah, Benson," said Ben. "When do *you* think a life is no longer worth living?"

"When you're really really old," was Benson's reply, "and
there's nothing worth living for."

Heads turned in front and hands shot up in the middle rows,
but Ben was too grateful to Benson for breaking the silence to
throw him to the dogs immediately. "Benson has a point," he said,
backing up a few steps and allowing his voice to swell. "I think
there's a general consensus that there's something about growing
old that sometimes makes life less worth living. But what is it exactly? It can't just be the number of years you've lived, can it?"

Another silence, but this time Ben could hear gears working
inside it. "What is it about growing old?" he asked once again.

"Older people get . . . conditions," said a girl in the third row
who had never spoken before.

"What kind of conditions?" asked Ben.

"Chronic diseases," said someone.

"Hearing loss," said someone else. "Vision loss. Tooth loss." A few students giggled.

"Is life worth living with a chronic disease?" asked Ben. "Is it worth living with cancer? Is it worth living with heart disease?"

"It depends," said the never-before-heard-from girl.

"Is it worth living with chronic pain?"

"It depends," said someone else. "If the pain is too bad—"

"So there's a point past which pain makes a life not worth living," said Ben. "We can agree on that. Is life worth living when you're blind or deaf?"

"It depends."

"Depends on what?" asked Ben.

"Your attitude."

"What does your attitude depend on?"

Ben folded his arms and leaned back against the desk as the class considered; this was the position he assumed during his Socratic anglings. He maintained it until a solitary hand went up. "There in back," he called out, pointing to Sirlancelot Mims, the promising cornerback from Shreveport, Louisiana.

"My grandmother's got cataracts," said Sirlancelot. "She can hardly see. She walks with a cane. Her feet swell up and she has to wrap her legs in Ace bandages. I think she's got cancer too. At least she used to have it."

Ben saw where this was going. "So what is your grandmother's attitude toward these conditions, Sir . . . ah . . . lancelot?"

"She's got a real good attitude. She's in the kitchen cooking all day, and she goes to church every week. She's learning to read her Bible in Braille. She raised the grandchildren and now she's taking care of the great-grandchildren—"

"Ah," said Ben. "She takes care of the children. Is that important?" The class murmured its assent. Many hands went up, among them this time the pink-haired *compañero*'s. "Leslie," he said. "Why is that important?"

"It's a change in the relationship between the past and the future," began Leslie Bogdanovich, whose gender remained stubbornly undivinable. Leslie had already emerged as the best student in the class, with an express-track mind that tended to speed past the local stops. For the benefit of those less quick to connect the concrete and the abstract, Ben jumped in. "Is there a future for Sirlancelot's grandmother?"

"Not so much," said a muffled voice from somewhere in the third row. The class laughed. Sirlancelot glowered.

"Not . . . so . . . much," Ben repeated soberly, appropriating the allusion and turning it to pedagogical uses. "If we interpret 'future' as Sirlancelot's grandmother's *personal* future, that's almost certainly true. What other kinds of future might we have, besides a purely personal future?"

"Something that continues after we're gone," said a girl in the front row. "Something we're doing or making or working on that will survive us."

"Like Sirlancelot's grandmother's grandchildren?" asked Ben, turning to write PLANS AND PROJECTS in large block letters on the blackboard. "I guess that has to mean Sirlancelot himself. He's his grandmother's project, isn't he? One of them, anyway." Ben smiled in Sirlancelot's direction. Heads turned toward the back and a murmur arose. Sirlancelot continued to sit stoically, arms crossed over his chest.

"I was just reading a book about Freud's last days," Leslie Bogdanovich remarked conversationally. He or she—just now Ben had an intimation it was the latter—did this sometimes, addressing Ben as if the rest of the class were not present. Meanwhile, the back row was seething with movement; Sirlancelot's teammates were leaning over to poke and jab at him and thrust their mugging faces into his. "The Nazis were after him and he was dying of jaw cancer and up until the very end he was working on *Moses and Monotheism* . . ."

But now it seemed that Rhoda had materialized. In her soundless way she had entered the classroom and was standing at Ben's side and murmuring, "Something's happening. I think you'd better come." Her manner told him that this was not a moment to ask questions. "Sit tight," he called over his shoulder as he followed her out the door. "I'm not dismissing class. You might get a jump on Thursday's reading."

Rhoda was moving down the hall at an alarming clip. Was it a bomb threat? Someone threatening suicide? One of Hayley's ex-husbands roaming the corridors with an AK-47? "What's going on?" he whispered as he speed-walked alongside her—though there was no reason, he supposed, to lower his voice.

"It's Charles Johns," she said. "In the seminar room. He's shouting."

Shouting? For that she'd pulled him out of class? The seminar room was down the hall from the Philosophy Department offices and already Ben had learned to tune out the chants and booms and incantations that emanated from Charles Johns's Ecstasy seminar. This shouting was probably just the audio of some shaman whipping himself into a frenzy. Rhoda was five feet ahead of him now. Turning back, she said, "*Really* shouting." As he followed her into the stairwell, Ben heard it for himself. It was Charles all right, using the full theatrical range of his voice, sliding it up and down the scale, bellowing like an ogre, shrieking like a panther. And then it came to him. The SCAC inspectors. He'd completely forgotten. Or rather he'd left it to Hayley, which was the same thing. He bolted rudely past Rhoda and sprinted up the stairs.

A small crowd of students and a few faculty members had gathered around the door of the seminar room. They were an odd lot, he noticed through the veil of his distraction—tall, short, tall, short. "All of you, get back to your classes," said Ben. They moved several yards down the hall. "Go on," he said. They retreated into the stairwell. "You go too," he said to Rhoda, who had just caught up with him. She stood her ground. "Go now," he said, "if you want to be helpful." Her eyebrows registered surprise—he'd never spoken to her like this—but still she declined to budge. He took her by the shoulders, spun her around, gave her a gentle push. He was surprised at himself, but the authority that had descended upon him seemed to require that he do this. Rhoda was so unprepared to be manhandled that she stumbled a little, then moved away with an offended backward glance. No doubt he'd hear about this later; touching a student was a violation of university policy.

Having emptied the hallway, he opened the door and walked into the seminar room, where all was ominously quiet and had been, Ben realized, for some moments. Charles had the SCAC inspector backed up against a wall. Not a wall, actually, but a bank of windows. The inspector was a slender, balding man in his late thirties or early forties, several inches shorter than Charles and perhaps a hundred and thirty pounds lighter. His clipboard, its pages curled and sprawling, lay upside down on the floor next to an overturned chair. Charles had pressed himself against the inspector engulfingly, his chin jutting into the space between his rapidly blinking eyes.

"Charles," said Ben. "Hang on a minute. Let him go. This is my fault. I should have let you know. Let me explain."

"This person," said Charles, addressing Ben but continuing to speak into the inspector's forehead in a deep hum that seemed intended not only to intimidate but to lull, "this person invaded my classroom. He walked in during the break and sat down *there*"— he jabbed a finger at the seminar table, as if the inspector's violation had forever contaminated it—"and made free to ask my students a number of idiotic questions. He never explained. He never apologized. I asked him to leave several times. He simply ignored me. Did he not?" He turned for confirmation to the students watching this scene from the far end of the table, horror and delight flickering across their faces. They nodded in unison.

"I should have let you know," said Ben. "He's here from the state. It's all OK. It's all legitimate."

"It's not legitimate," said Charles, swinging his alarmingly reddened face around to glare at Ben. "And so much the worse if he's from the state. I won't have my class disrupted." With that, he took the inspector by the shoulders and rotated him, much as Ben had done to Rhoda (but not so gently), locked one arm under his chin and the other under his ribs, and frog-marched him across the room and out the door. Ben followed at a distance as this man-and-a-half made its staggering humping progress down the hall. Much of the time, the inspector was walking—albeit under compulsion—but for seconds at a stretch his feet were in the air and he was kicking like a toddler. The crowd Ben had dispersed earlier had reassembled to watch. Stationed in the doorway of the Philosophy Department, the *Lola Lantern* photographer was taking pictures, flashbulbs popping at stroboscopic speed. Behind the photographer's shoulder, well back in the office, Ben caught a glimpse of Hayley's frightened face.

A few yards short of the stairs, Charles stopped for a moment, as if to consider his options. With an air of disgusted weariness, he let go of the inspector, who slid to the floor in limp folds. As Charles stalked back into the classroom, the inspector got to his knees and then, rather jerkily, to his feet. He shook his head to clear it, ran his hands over his torso diagnostically. Ben approached, calling out apologies, but the inspector raised a hand to stay him. He'd pulled a cell phone from his pocket, and as he hobbled away in the direction of the men's room Ben could see that he was making a call.

CHAPTER EIGHT

⟍⟍

You have 6 new messages:

From: President Lee Wayne Dreddle
To: bblau@lola.edu
Subject: Yesterday's Incident

TO ALL MEMBERS OF THE LDI COMMUNITY: It has come to my attention that an incident occurred yesterday afternoon in Horace Dees Hall involving a part-time, temporary member of the LDI Philosophy Department and a campus visitor. While the details have yet to be fully sorted out, eyewitness accounts indicate that a physical assault of some kind took place. In a meeting early this morning with the university attorney it was determined that the faculty member will be terminated immediately. Other action may be taken as well. I will keep you updated.

This incident, unfortunate though it was, affords us an important teaching moment. It brings home the urgent need to place security at the very top of our agenda. Students need to know that they are safe. Faculty/staff need to know that they can go about their important work in an atmosphere of peace and security. Parents need to know that the beloved children they have entrusted to our care will meet with no harm. To this end, the provost and I will appoint a study committee to consider what measures can be put in place to assure student and faculty/staff safety in the future. Other institutions have recently installed university-wide e-mail and cell-phone alert systems. This is only one of many ideas that will be evaluated for its appropriateness to the LOLA community's needs. Another measure we plan to look at from a feasibility point of view is the campus-wide distribution of individual pocket or purse panic buttons, connected to GPS technology in the Campus Security Office.

In closing, I want to offer a personal expression of concern and caring to each and every member of the LOLA community and to remind you that my door is always open.

With warmest personal regards,
Lee Wayne Dreddle

From: Roberta Mitten-Kurz
To: bblau@lola.edu
Subject: See me

I need to speak to you as soon as possible. Please give Marcy a call when you get in this morning.

From: Donald Wertz
To: bblau@lola.edu
cc: rmitten-kurz@lola.edu, lwdreddle@lola.edu
Subject: transfer credits for Jade Wertz

Dear Prof. Blau,

I'm writing to let you know that my daughter Jade has been unable to get help from your office in her efforts to document transfer credits. She gave the form to your secretary on the first day of classes and has yet to get it back. She tells me that she has come by the department on several occasions to find nobody there. When she calls she gets a recording, and when she leaves messages, they go unreturned.

I understand that standards tend to be less stringent in an academic department than in the offices of a law practice, but I can tell you that any secretary who was chronically absent from her desk and neglected to return calls would not last long here at Wertz, Faust and Blasingame.

I would very much appreciate your expedited attention in the matter of Jade Wertz's transfer credits.

Sincerely,

Donald Wertz

From: Stuart Dilbert
To: bblau@lola.edu
Subject: none

A week ago I complained to the department secretary that the registrar has placed my 105 HistSurv, with an enrollment of 78, in HD317, which seats thirty. Students are sitting on the floor. I've tried to complain directly to the registrar, but as you know, this is a quixotic undertaking.

In past semesters I've counted on Dolores to apply steady pressure on the registrar. The current incumbent seems to have done nothing at all, which is odd because apparently she has plenty of time on her hands. I see her smoking cigarettes out on the Bledwell Pavilion several times a day.

From: Campus Security
To: bblau@lola.edu
Subject: 1992 Oldsmobile parked in fire lane

Dear Dr. Blau,

Over the past ten days, a 1992 Oldsmobile, gold in

color, has been parked consistently athwart the fire lane in the West Oak faculty/staff lot. A number of citations have been placed on the vehicle's windshield, but as yet this office has not received any response and the violations have continued.

The vehicle's owner or driver has been observed entering your building. She is identified as a Caucasian woman in her early to middle forties with blond hair. If this individual works in your office, or in any other office you know of, please contact us immediately. Parking in a fire lane constitutes a fire hazard, and if this infraction is repeated, we will have no choice but to tow and impound the vehicle in question.

Sincerely,

Bettina Podler

Campus Security Liaison

From: Frank Buonafortuna

To: bblau@lola.edu

Subject: follow-up questionnaire

Dear Employer,

Frequent and regular follow-ups are an integral component of our program here at Second Chance/New Start. Click on the attachment to find a short questionnaire that will help us to initiate an ongoing evaluation of the performance of Hayley Gamache, a diplomate of our pro-

gram who was hired at your firm or place of business on
September 14. Please take a moment to fill it out.

    With Best Regards,
    Frank Buonafortuna

As he turned away from the computer screen to call the dean's
office Ben saw that the message light on the phone was blinking. He blinked back at it for a moment before deciding it could
be safely ignored—it was almost certainly Hayley's daily trouble
report and first estimate of arrival time. He dialed the dean's extension and Marcy Bainbridge picked up on the first ring. Ordi-
narily he found her fire-glazed cheeriness bracing—he knew she
viewed her boss with considerable irony—but this morning her
chipper "Dean's Office" jarred him deeply.

    "Marcy," he said, "is she in?"

    "Oh," said Marcy, "Ben." The hush in her voice alarmed him.
"She certainly is. She's in there waiting for you."

    "Coming now," said Ben.

    "Good luck," said Marcy.

    Just as he was rising from his desk, his computer trilled to an-
nounce the arrival of another e-mail. Sitting down, he clicked on
a link, forwarded by Rhoda, that led him to a YouTube video entitled "Prof Goes Nuts." At first he could make out only a conge-
ries of moving shadows, but soon enough he understood that he
was looking at a murky cell-phone documentation of the SCAC
inspector's eviction from Charles Johns's classroom. The ten- or
fifteen-second sequence was repeated a number of times, sometimes at normal speed, sometimes—to undeniably comic effect—

greatly accelerated. The video was accompanied by a grinding rap soundtrack with a taunting female obbligato snaking around the bass line. Each time Charles and the inspector were shown clearing the seminar-room doorway, Ben's startled face loomed into view.

After a few minutes the screen went blank; the audio hissed and hummed. Then the scene shifted to the steps of the Student Union building, where the cell-phone documentarian was recording the reactions of student witnesses. The first to be interviewed were a pair of female students. "I don't know," said one. "It made me uncomfortable when the guy just walked in there. We've got privacy rights, don't we? But the professor didn't have to have a complete meltdown like that. I didn't think he was setting a good example." "Yeah," said the second girl, "talk about anger management! He looked like he was about to stroke out."

The interviewer moved on to two males who'd been quivering impatiently in the background. "Man, he went *off* on that dude," said one. "It was *awe*some!" said the other, his head bobbing in frenetic agreement. "He ran that pencilneck out on a rail."

The proverbial blank white page, Ruth was thinking, could hardly be more daunting than an empty computer screen. You looked *at* the page but *into* the screen, that deep-blue domain with its illusion of gelatinous depth that made her think of the farthest reaches of deep space. Not the deep space of the mind but the deep space of space, where there was no oxygen and a dead astronaut who'd come untethered from a space station could go spinning head over heels for all eternity . . .

Just write.

She got up from her desk and gathered all the loose papers in her study and placed them in file folders and stood them in the file holder Ben had given her in one of his periodic attempts to help her get organized. Then she moved to the downstairs half bath where she scrubbed the sink with Ajax and French-braided portions of her hair. After that she spent some minutes in the kitchen stuffing handfuls of dry cereal into her mouth as she waited for water to heat up for Postum, a suitably pointless beverage to which she was reverting only because she'd drunk it during what had seemed at the time like a fruitful writing period several years ago.

Just write.

But not about the dead astronaut. That's the kind of thing a stoned sophomore up against a deadline would write. Do an exercise, one of those exercises she made her students do when she'd run out of ways to fill time in a workshop. Do the automatic-writing thing. Ten minutes of continuous action of the fingers on the keyboard. Doesn't matter what, she'd told them. Write the same word over and over if you must. Prime the pump. Send the bucket down, haul the bucket up.

She checked the clock. Ten twenty-seven, a discouragingly indefinite starting point. Better wait for the half hour. She took three minutes to check the headlines on the CNN Web site, half hoping to find that six bombs had gone off simultaneously in the holds of six planes flying over the Atlantic. Not that she required anything as calamitous as that—just some piece of breaking news lurid and large-scale enough to serve as an occasion for amazed procrastination. When the page opened she saw that the lead story was the approach of Hurricane Heather, just as it had been for the past three days. Her heart rose momentarily when she saw how much larger the whirling blender-blade had grown and how much progress it had made across the Gulf of Mexico, but then she noticed that the wide pink wedge radiating out from it had shifted disappointingly to the east. HEATHER HOPS? was the headline. "According to Spangler meteorologist Roush Spanier, Spangler and the east Texas coast will likely be spared Heather's worst. 'We can't be 100 percent sure, but this morning nearly all our models are telling us Heather will come right up to our front door and then do a dogleg and pay the folks in western Louisiana a visit.' "

Ten thirty. Back to the blue screen. Just write. Just write. Just write. About what? About what? About a man getting on a bus somewhere in the Midwest, a lean graying man in a cheap Windbreaker who's been forced to leave the family farm to get a job in Omaha and as he settles into his seat he's thinking about his widowed mother, or maybe it's his wife, and the cows in the barn and the chickens in the—what do you call it? The henhouse.

The henhouse. Why was it that under the pressure of this exercise, which should have squeezed something authentic out of her, she'd come up with a subject she knew nothing about, an alien style that couldn't be further from her own—as if she were channeling some hack? And how was she to perform the required dredging of her memory and imagination? It wasn't as if she kept an actual tool in her mind she could use to do the job, and of course there was no excavation site in there either, only slimy furrowed tissue.

Glancing at the clock she saw that less than a minute had elapsed, and she'd spent thirty seconds of it with her fingers suspended over the keyboard. No, automatic writing wouldn't do. She got up, walked around the room twice, returned to her chair, fell into it heavily. What to do? Where to find distraction? Google. She'd Google herself, a practice she found both tempting and dread-provoking and usually indulged in only when she'd had a number of drinks. But this morning despair had made her reckless and recklessness had numbed her: Why should she care how many hits she had? Her books, after all, had been published long before the advent of the Internet; that was always a face-saving thing to remember. Today the count was 1,052 for Ruth's name alone—most of these hits, of course, had reference to other Ruth Blaus, many of them highly accomplished—and 97 for her name paired with *Getting Good*. The last count, if she remembered correctly, and she did, had been 1,081 and 351, respectively, and the time before that the numbers had been higher still.

Her Google flame had been flickering for years and now it was sputtering. It was an oddly luxurious sensation, watching herself disappear. Even so, she scrolled down through the pages, looking for something new, some mention, perhaps, of her name in a retrospective consideration of academic comedies, something on the order of "And who could forget *Getting Good*, Ruth Blau's sparkling contribution to the genre?" Or even a citation in a doctoral dissertation: that would be better than nothing. But what she found—what she'd known all along she'd find—was only page after page of used- and rare-book listings and a few familiar gum wads of acknowledgment she'd already chewed flavorless.

Back to the blue screen. Back to the mug of luke-cool Postum. Just write, just write, just write, just write. "Just write," Ruth said aloud, her own voice startling her.

· · ·

Once again he was seated in the jungle bower, once again breathing the mist of four humidifiers, once again subject to the steady gaze of four golden canine eyes.

"It's probably just as well you kept your distance when Charles Johns was acting out," Mitten-Kurz was saying. "Another chair might have seen a way to take charge, but all things considered it was the right decision. We can't have you jeopardizing your safety. As it happens, the SCAC inspector doesn't appear to have been seriously injured. We can be thankful for that. He does have some pain in his ribs. His neck is discolored. They e-mailed documentation this morning." She produced a photograph from a manila folder on her chair-side table: the inspector's shirt had been unbuttoned, exposing his puny sternum and his radically craned neck, on which Ben could make out faint purple imprints of two of Charles's meaty fingers. "We're still not quite out of the woods," Mitten-Kurz went on. "It's possible he may have internal injuries. He's scheduled for an MRI this afternoon."

"Good," said Ben. "I mean I hope he's OK."

"As I say, we can't fault you for hanging back. What concerns us is that you put the university at risk for a lawsuit by letting him leave without medical attention."

"I tried," said Ben. "He refused."

"And you further complicated the situation by allowing a student to make the cell-phone video we've woken up this morning to find all over the Internet. Dr. Dreddle's particularly concerned about it. It opens us up to media scrutiny."

"I saw it," he said. "Pretty funny, I thought." He'd been staring down at his folded hands, but now he raised his eyes and gave Mitten-Kurz a look of bland defiance.

He'd broken the civility barrier, and the glint in her eye told him she was ready for it. As if slapping a trump card down on the table, she arched her eyebrows and said, "We've also had a report that you touched a female student inappropriately."

More than anything else he'd done yesterday, the possible repercussions of this act had worried him. It was also the only act he felt proud of (Dolores would have endorsed it, he felt sure, though she might have advised against it on prudential grounds). He was disappointed to hear that Rhoda had betrayed him; he'd thought she was more sensible than that. "I was trying to get her out of harm's way," he said. "She complained?"

"Ah," said Mitten-Kurz. "It wasn't a complaint, properly speaking. It was a report from someone on the scene."

Oh. If that was all she had on him, he could get up and leave right now. "So," he said, rising to his feet, "are we done? I have a lot to see to this morning."

The dogs lifted their heads. "We're not done, Ben. There's more we need to discuss. Please sit down." Ben remained standing, arms crossed over his chest.

Mitten-Kurz paused for a moment, a little rattled by this refusal, then gave a quick hard nod. "The last time we spoke I told you we'd been getting"—she paused to find the right phrase—"a slow drip of negative feedback about the department. Now, more recently, I'm afraid I have to tell you we've been getting multiple, *multiple* complaints. Are you aware that your graduate students have been without medical coverage for the past two weeks? The paperwork simply hasn't been filed. We have a prominent local lawyer telling us his daughter can't get help from your office. Dr. Dreddle has asked us to red-flag that one—he's very concerned. We have classrooms mismatched with student rosters. They're standing in the doorway, Ben. They're sitting on the floor. Why hasn't your office gotten back to the registrar? We're getting calls from parents. They want to know what they're paying tuition for. Security is complaining about repeated parking violations—"

"Hayley—" Ben blurted out, instantly regretting it.

"Never mind Hayley. You're the one in charge. If Hayley's not doing her job, you need to get after her. You need to correct her."

Advantage, Mitten-Kurz. That was just the word Dolores had used, though she could hardly have known it. He felt himself teetering slightly; it was as if the autonomic brain mechanism that normally held him upright had failed, and the only way to keep from falling down was to dispatch a continuous stream of conscious messages to the muscles of his thighs and calves. One of the dogs, he noticed, was going into "pointer" position—slowly rising on its haunches and crooking a paw, as if Ben were a buckshot-riddled pigeon plummeting from the sky.

He sat. Mitten-Kurz made a sound like air escaping from a sofa cushion and gave him a cajoling smile. "We're of an age, aren't we Ben?" she said. "We both remember 'the buck stops here.' "

The dog that had identified him as prey sank slowly to the floor. Mitten-Kurz redistributed her bulk in her chair, wincing a little as she did so. Just now Ben noticed that she wore a white sock and an open-toed canvas shoe on one foot, and kept it propped on a low footstool. Broken toe? Bunion surgery? Gout? It served to remind him that Mitten-Kurz was human, evidence to the contrary notwithstanding. She had a life, an assiduously cultivated life. She had her devoted Bobby; they had their famous weekly bridge game with potluck hors d'oeuvres. If Ben leaned a little to one side he could see around the potted sago palm to the cluster of silver-framed photographs on her desk: nieces and nephews (presumably), the young Bobby and Bertie on their wedding day. She'd been slender and handsome then; Ben was almost touched to see that what was now a frizz of gray was once dark and straight and glossy. The dogs were shown posed in front of the tidy bungalow with elaborately landscaped grounds where the Mitten-Kurzes had lived since anyone could remember. And there was the present-day Mitten-Kurz at some kind of administrative reception, leaning into one side of Lee Wayne Dreddle as Marcy Bainbridge leaned into the other. Dreddle had draped his arms around the shoulders of both women. Marcy was smiling her blazing smile for the camera, but Mitten-Kurz had rotated her face to gaze up adoringly into Dreddle's; in the penumbra of his masculinity she was suddenly and poignantly feminine.

Yes, Ben and Mitten-Kurz were of an age, and for that reason alone he should try to remember their common humanity. She'd wanted what she'd gotten—her cozy domestic life and her small domain of petty power near the administrative heart of the university—with an intensity he could understand. He could understand how she guarded it and sought to enlarge it. He did the same every day when he closed the door of his study and banged away on whatever manuscript he had in progress. Perhaps her childlessness had been a grief to her, as his child had been to him. Perhaps the two of them both compensated for these disappointments by turning their attention to work. At any rate, they were old enough to feel their mortality, and her afflicted foot was a memento mori, a reminder of how short a time they both had to enjoy the estates they'd made in the world. For that alone he could summon, and briefly maintain, a large vague sensation of fellow feeling. Or at least he could until he looked up again into her piggy little eyes.

"So," she went on, waxing expansive, "the last time you sat in that chair we spoke about the Philosophy Department's attitude. I continue to see that as the real problem. It's not just you; it's a historical thing, an institutional thing. It's a *cultural* thing, really. As far back as I can remember, there's been a kind of arrogance in that department, a refusal to join in the common project of the university. I hardly need to bring up specific instances. I'm sure you know what I'm talking about."

Ben did. He could match her example for example. There was the department's general refusal to cross-list courses with other departments, and the possibly impolitic use of the phrase "quality control" as justification on one occasion. He was proud of that. There was the business of the rejection of the sociology chair's proposal of a joint colloquium on Strategies for Implementing Social Change on the grounds that any philosophical contribution to such a discussion should enter in at a level more foundational than implementational. There was the department's infamous neglect of its collegial duties. Ben was not proud of that, but he couldn't help finding it amusing that the only member to serve on a university committee last year was Stuart Dilbert, who drove the Parking Committee wild with his insistent demands that the university produce a justification for charging any parking fees at all.

Yes, Mitten-Kurz was right, the Philosophy Department had a culture, a culture of fogginess and cerebral distance, of lofty, puzzled indifference to the bureaucratic intrigues and power machinations that convulsed the administration and many of the other departments. He and Bruce Federman were reasonably alert and grounded, but most of the others were throwbacks to a time when the world viewed academia as a preserve for the gently befuddled.

Not that all philosophy departments were like his. He knew from the yearly meetings of the American Philosophical Association that these days most in his profession were indistinguishable from those in any other. They were accomplished networkers; they knew how to initiate, maintain, and break off conversations; how to order from a complex menu; how to send a fax or summon a cab. Thirty years ago the attendees were an unhygienic herd of tweedy bumblers; swollen gums were in evidence then, and dandruff. Riding an elevator with a crowd of philosophers was an experience that engaged all the senses. These days many were as kempt and suave and "professional" as their counterparts at the MLA, and the ones who weren't seemed to have made a conscious decision not to be. They had what their predecessors lacked, a sense of themselves as seen from the outside.

Mitten-Kurz was winding up for the pitch. "In most ways you've been a fairly competent chair, Ben. In spite of the recent difficulties I'm not particularly concerned about the day-to-day workings of the department. It's the larger thing that has me troubled, the vision thing, if you will . . ." She shifted her weight in the chair, wincing again. "I've shared my concerns with President Dreddle," she went on. "I was in his office for most of the morning yesterday discussing some of the more problematic departments, and I have to say philosophy was at the top of our agenda. Dr. Dreddle agrees that we need to come to a new understanding. Our charge to you, Ben, is to change the culture of the Philosophy Department."

Ben paused for a moment to consider his response. "I don't see my job as changing the culture of the Philosophy Department. The culture's just fine. We teach and we write and we think, and that's what we ought to be doing."

Mitten-Kurz threw out a jiggling arm. "We all share that view, Ben. Philosophy doesn't have a monopoly on those values. It's just that we have to find ways to foster them, to bring them into the world. The university isn't the cloistered place it was when we were young. It's part of the world now, like it or not, and the way it presents itself to the community and the wider world matters. It's not as if the university is a collection of individuals sitting in their offices dreaming of spires or whatever. It's an organism, a complex organism whose parts are interconnected and when one part isn't functioning the others are affected all the way down the line. And that's not all. The university is connected to the larger organism of the world. What happens outside is felt inside and what happens inside is felt outside. Think of what happened yesterday afternoon."

What? Was she saying that this was the way the university *should* be, or only that this was what it was becoming? If the former, why? What was so inspiring about this notion of the university as a buzzing, clanking, whirring Rube Goldberg contraption contained by and subordinate to a still larger Rube Goldberg machine? And what could it mean to bring philosophy (or the humanities generally) into the world? If the humanities become part of the world, they become useless to the world. But there was no point in discussing any of this with Mitten-Kurz. She had all the advantages: an indifference to reason, a copious supply of administrative jargon, a facility for fogging up the room with demagogic nonsense. Better to bring this interchange back to earth.

"So we teach and write and think," he said. "We can agree about that."

A little nonplussed, she nodded.

"My question is: How can we do those things when we're constantly distracted by task forces and study groups and useless committees and endless memos? How do we find time to discover what's true when—"

"Ah well, *truth*," said Mitten-Kurz, tossing her chin. She was too sophisticated, she'd have him know, not to ironize *that* word.

"And how can we get anything at all done with a secretary—"

"Oh no no no, Ben," she cut in, as if remonstrating with a madman who would revert to the same delusion over and over if not sternly checked. "I already told you that's entirely outside our considerations here . . ."

But now one of the dogs was whimpering, trotting distract-edly back and forth in front of the door. "Oh dear, Big has to go again," said Mitten-Kurz. "It's the medication," she confided in a stage whisper. Picking up the phone, she summoned Marcy. "Big needs the facilities. Right away, please." Instantly, Marcy padded in on the balls of her feet. The dog pranced and capered, and as Marcy squatted to attach a leash to its collar, Mitten-Kurz con-tracted her brows, compressed her lips into a tender moue, and let loose a barrage of animal baby talk. Ben stiffened and stared down at his knees. He was humming inwardly, doing his best not to hear, the theory being that what he didn't hear he wouldn't remember. Nevertheless, the endearments reached him in blips: "Her is such a sad sad girl . . . her has got side effects . . ." When he looked up, the dog was dragging Marcy out the door, but even so she managed to fling her head back flamenco-dancer style and shoot him a significant look. It was a gesture of solidarity, and it gave him the courage to remember how purely and devotedly he hated Mitten-Kurz.

The door closed. For a moment they sat in silence. Soon Mitten-Kurz had begun to speak again in her fluty contralto, but Ben was no longer listening. Instead, he was looking out the window. Marcy and the dog had taken only twenty seconds or so to get down the stairs and around the corner to a patch of yellowed grass immediately beneath the rain gutter on the east end of the Business School building. The dog really must have been in some distress, because its haunches were already quivering and its back had assumed the shape of a C. Marcy was holding the leash slackly and staring off into the distance. Even from this distance he could see that for the moment she felt free. Not joyfully free, just free to drop the valiant perkiness and return to the brooding self she left at home when she went to work every day in the dean's office. A long, loosely spiraling tube—not a good color, too pale—was extruding itself from the dog's hindquarters. Ben got to his feet.

Ruth lay sprawled in front of the TV, contemplating a restaurant scene from a forties black-and-white movie with the sound turned off. A ferret-faced man in evening clothes had barged past the maitre d' and was menacing a table of champagne drinkers. A rangy young woman in a long sequined gown rose and strode away, tossing a disgusted look over her shoulder. An older woman spoke reprovingly to an older man, who followed the young woman out to the balcony, where they exchanged what looked like heated words.

Enough of that. She switched to the shopping channel and turned up the volume. All the charcoal-gray ones had gone in the first five minutes, one woman was saying to another, and the navy had nearly sold out. These red ones are really great, said the second woman, shrugging on a jacket and executing a twirl to display its front and sides and back while the first woman stood a little distance away, her hands thrown up in admiration. Who knew red denim could have so much impact? And yet it's really very neutral. You could throw it on over anything and you'd be all set for the mall, the post office, the grocery store. It's just great basic gear for the way we live now.

I want that, Ruth thought. No, she corrected herself, I don't, really. I want to be the kind of woman who requires gear. She switched back to the forties movie, where the angular young woman in the sequined dress was standing under a streetlamp, her face tipped up into the gaze of a man who was neither the ferret-faced intruder nor the avuncular defender. She switched the channel again, this time to another shopping channel where another pair of women were selling jewelry. The pearl earrings were gone and the square-cut zirconium rings were going fast and the diamond watch . . .

The watch. Of course. The olive-green enamel watch, the tiny, essential focal point of Ricia's memoir. Now what object from her own childhood might represent the equivalent, for Ruth, of the olive-green enamel watch? Could it be the embroidered black satin shawl she'd kept in the dress-up box, the one her grandmother had bequeathed to her? No. She'd always found it alien, with its patchy crusts of seed pearls. Could it be the pink net crinoline petticoat of uncertain provenance that one day had appeared, bunched up, in the back of her closet? No. She'd used it as a cage to trap a chronically runaway parakeet, and that had spoiled any iconic glamour it might otherwise have held for her.

Could it be the ceramic Staffordshire dog? She'd owned it ever since she could remember; it was the only surviving relic of her childhood. She kept it right over there, on a low brick-and-board bookshelf where she also stored twelve remaindered copies of *Getting Good*. She got up from the chaise, picked up the ceramic dog, sat down, examined it. She hadn't held it in her hands for years, but she'd have recognized it by feel even if she'd lost her sight. The ceramicist had given more attention to the ridges and runnels that suggested the dog's coat than to the actual shape of the thing. She turned it over, noting its remarkable crudeness. The front legs were fused into a thick column with a fluted base, ticked with black paint on the front-facing side to indicate claws. The hindquarters were only hinted at, though the head and the drapery of the ears were articulated a little more carefully than the rest.

She'd always assumed that the dog was meant to represent some English variety of spaniel. Its ears and nose and eyes had been rendered in black paint with a certain primitive verve, as had the splotches on its chest and legs. Or at least it had splotches in front; the maker had left it blankly white in back. As a child, Ruth had found this incompleteness a little shocking. Now, of course, she understood that its charm, and whatever small monetary value it carried, resided in its imperfections. The dog's undecorated rear aspect could even be seen as a calculated part of its appeal. I'm all for you, the maker might have meant it to say to anyone who bothered to pick it up and look into its eternally worried face. The part of me you can't see doesn't matter.

Its left ear had been chipped when four-year-old Isaac flung it against a wall, but otherwise the dog had remained intact for, what—a hundred years? Two? Longer? Ruth knew it was an antique of sorts, but she'd never thought to look into its pedigree. For a hollow statuette it was remarkably durable. It had been with her all her life, over here on a shelf, over there on a mantel under a mirror. Through all the wind and rain and sun and darkness transpiring outside the windows of all the rooms where it had been kept, through all the noise and silence of the life lived within them, the dog had sat, disregarded and unchanging. Its constancy was almost comic. Ruth turned it over again in her hands. The blankness of its back-facing side had begun to strike her as ominous, like the dark side of the moon.

It was hard not to imagine the ceramic dog as a silent witness, but that, of course, would be a mistake. It was an object meant to be sentimentalized, but it drew its totemic power from its inanimateness. It was like a boulder jutting out of a rushing stream, a marker by which Ruth could sense, for a moment, the continuity of time's passage. Even so, it seemed to her that while she'd been examining and contemplating the dog, its expression had changed from mute appeal to mute reproach. Its constancy was almost tragic. She thought of a line from an Auden poem: "Time will say only that I told you so."

She carried the dog back into her study, logged on to the Internet and consulted the Google oracle, which reported that it knew nothing of this line. She tried again, changing the search terms to "W. H. Auden" and "time." Now she was led to the poem, which was entitled "If I Could Tell You," and to the line, which she had slightly misremembered. It was the second stanza she'd been thinking of:

> If we should weep when clowns put on their show,
> If we should stumble when musicians play,
> Time will say nothing but I told you so.

She found a place for the dog on her desk, between a photograph of Isaac at age nine and the small pottery bowl where she kept paper clips and rubber bands. Then she leaned back in her chair and returned to the contemplation of the empty screen.

The decision had made itself in his muscles, not his mind. He'd simply risen from his chair in Mitten-Kurz's office and announced it and walked out the door and down the hall, where he was intercepted by Marcy and Big, just emerging from the stairwell. Dangling from her pursed fingertips was a knotted-off plastic bag containing the product of their excursion. "What happened?" she whispered. "I quit," he answered.

"You *quit?*"

"I did."

"Just now? In there?"

"Just now in there."

A look of doubt came into Marcy's shining eyes. "You quit your *job?*"

"No no. Just as chair."

A little crestfallen, she gave him her usual game smile. "Ah well, good for you," she said, and then she was headed down the hall, walking rapidly in her duck-footed way, pulling the depleted Big after her.

Now he was out in sultry daylight. Buildings and Grounds— what busy beavers they'd become lately—had spent the half hour he'd been closeted with Mitten-Kurz hanging a long line of Lola banners from the ceiling of the breezeway between the Administration Building and Horace Dees Hall. These were forked brown-and-orange things, emblazoned with Dreddle's new university motto, "TAKE THOUGHT." For a moment, Ben's eyes were tricked into seeing them as an endless regress—"TAKE THOUGHT, TAKE THOUGHT, TAKE THOUGHT."

Now he was in Horace Dees Hall, climbing the back stairs with their familiar trapped-toxin smell, and in a moment he was walking down the hall that led to his own office, glancing as he passed into the offices of a few of the department's most vulnerable denizens. There they were, as always, engaged in innocently characteristic behaviors. Ben thought of the Early Man dioramas he'd seen on elementary-school field trips to the Museum of Natural History—shaggy hominids behind glass, squatting to rake the coals of a fire or flay the hide from an antelope.

Muriel Draybrooke was sitting at her desk, holding the *Australasian Journal of Philosophy* three inches from her nose and steadily pushing a boulder of angel food cake into her mouth. Two offices down Stuart Dilbert was standing at the window with his back turned. He was thinking, Ben happened to know, about voting schemes. This was a practice he pursued for hours at a time. Nothing much had come of this thinking—he hadn't written a word in decades—and Ben suspected that he didn't do it particularly well. Even so, it was remarkable that he did it at all.

Active thinking—thinking as an activity, structured and directed toward an end—was a rare ability, growing rarer. Watching Stuart Dilbert as he thought was like prowling the alleyways of a carnival and catching a glimpse of an off-duty sword-swallower, rehearsing his act in solitude.

And there, on the other side of the hall, sitting in a monk's cell of an office playing video blackjack on his computer, was Banyan Naparstak. He was a young metaphysician, the department's most recent hire. In his first year of graduate school he'd written a seminal paper called "Parts of Parts," which had been the subject of mereological symposia in Reykjavik, Vancouver, and Bled. He would be up for reappointment next year, and Ben had been assembling a collection of arguments for retaining him. Each of these would have to follow a strategic concession: Yes, Banyan's teaching left much to be desired, but with supervision it would no doubt improve. Yes, he hadn't published much since he'd arrived at Lola, but he was only thirty-two and with patience and support, he could still be expected to realize his early promise. Yes, his social skills were underdeveloped, but Bruce and Sissy Federman had been taking him in hand, referring him to their dentist, helping him assemble a suitable wardrobe, offering him pointers on table manners.

What would happen to Banyan's reappointment case now that Ben had quit? What would become of Dilbert and Draybrooke? Would the dean install some lackey, as she had in the case of the English Department? Would Muriel be named graduate director? Would Banyan be appointed to the hospitality committee? Hard days would be in store for the hapless. But no doubt Hayley would be instantly reassigned. That, at least, would be good for the department.

He was coming into the anteroom of his office now. Hayley, of course, had not yet arrived, but the light on the desk phone was still blinking, reminding him that he couldn't in good conscience simply pack up his briefcase and leave. He sat down at Hayley's station, elbowed aside a few desk-dwelling fairies, picked up the receiver, hit the button. A long silence ensued, interrupted by a scatter of soft hiccuping sounds Ben took to be a disturbance on the line. Just as he was about to hang up he heard a faint voice—Hayley's voice. "Professor," Hayley said, "I am so terribly . . . terribly . . . *terribly* sorry." Her voice gained volume on each "terribly" and on the third, it broke. She began to sob and continued to do so for thirty seconds.

"I'm here," she said at last—now she'd switched to her dead-prophetess voice. "I'm in a motel in Meridian. Mississippi. I was trying to make it to Birmingham, but my kids were wiped so we stopped. I'm on my way to Harrisburg, Pennsylvania, where my sister lives."

In Ben's mind, a map of the eastern half of the United States unscrolled itself. A Matchbox-toy version of Hayley's gold Oldsmobile skidded across it, fishtailing from Meridian to Birmingham to Harrisburg.

"I'm so tired. I've been on the road since eight o'clock last night and I *know* I've got to get some rest but first I had to call you and let you know . . ." Another silence, broken only by a ragged intake of breath. "I feel so awful about this. I feel so guilty about leaving you and Rhoda there with no support . . ." More sobs. Ben held the phone six inches away from his ear, wagging his head from side to side and doing things with his tongue and facial muscles he hadn't done since latency. He looked down to see that his feet were moving jig-wise on the carpet. He stood, reached up, grasped a fairy by its slender plastic ankles and tore it from the ceiling.

"I hate it, Professor. I absolutely hate this. I like to think I'm not the kind of person who just . . . bails . . . when things get tough. My kids could tell you how I get when the chips are down. But after what I saw out there in that hallway . . . It brought everything back. I was so frightened. I was crying and shaking and I couldn't stop and I walked right over to the Counseling and Testing Center and they took one look at me and bumped me up to the front even though the waiting room was full. It was a gentleman who helped me, a tall gentleman with a mustache."

That would be Brett Something-or-other, C&T's chief facilitator and glad-hander. Ben had momentarily forgotten his last name. Ruth called him Mr. Butterscotch.

"He was so kind. I'll never forget. I told him I felt so guilty about just walking out of the office in the middle of the day and he said, 'Now, hold on a minute, Hayley. Don't you go beating up on yourself. I'm sure you had your reasons,' and when I got into my history he said to me, 'Hayley, you are absolutely doing the right thing. Your first duty is to yourself and your kids.' You see, I have to stay away from violence because witnessing violence can trigger a recurrence of my PTSD. For me, it's poison. He told me I shouldn't go to the movies. I shouldn't even watch certain shows on TV. He said I needed to pack up my kids and get myself to safety right away. So that's what I'm doing, and I hope you understand."

Another pause, a faint click and whirr. Hayley was lighting a cigarette. "So I guess it's goodbye, Professor. Just a minute. Can you hang on just a minute?" A series of flutterings and scratchings followed and then Hayley's voice, low and soft, a little distance away. "BJ, get back in that bed right now. I said *now*. Count of three, young man, and I will come in there and tear a new one for you. I said one. I said two . . .

"Hello, Professor? Where was I? I was going to ask: Would it be too much trouble to mail me my fairies once I get settled? And will you tell Rhoda I'll miss her? Are you there, Rhoda? I hope you hear this message because I want you to know I'll never forget you, and Professor, it's so sad and it's so ironic because the Philosophy Department is the gentlest place in the world and it's just about the safest place I ever found in my whole life . . ."

Gently, Ben hung up the phone. He rose and left the office, neglecting to lock it, walked down the hall and jogged down the stairs. He was out of the building before he realized that he seemed to be gripping a plastic fairy in his right hand. He jammed it into a trash basket and continued along the breezeway. He'd left Mitten-Kurz's office what, eight or ten minutes ago? Surely it wasn't too late to say that he'd thought better of his decision. Surely she hadn't had time to inform the provost.

There they were, one hundred and fifty words suspended in the blue medium. Were her tired eyes deceiving her, or was the paragraph pulsating on the screen?

Was it good? Impossible to judge, but somehow it struck her as promising. She had an intuition that left overnight it might reveal itself to be something that would grow like a culture of cells in a petri dish. She'd check on it tomorrow morning. Waiting, after all, was the true job of writing.

In the meantime she retreated to the screened-in porch and lay back on her chaise. She felt relaxed and dilated, content just to look out on the afternoon. What time was it? Two? Three? She had misplaced her watch and had no idea. For all she knew it might be close to five, time to think about starting dinner. Odd that the light gave her no clue. Strange color, wasn't it? Greenish.

Something was happening. As he approached the Administration Building, he saw that B&G workers were emerging from the propped-open back door in a steady stream, carrying large objects. When he got closer he understood that these were office furnishings. Great potted plants passed in review, hoisted on burly shoulders. Ben stepped aside to make way for the monstrous fern-thing that had menaced him every time he'd sat in Mitten-Kurz's visitor's chair.

On they came. Now they were carrying minor plants and hangings and paintings and coffee tables and wicker chairs and rolled-up rugs and humidifiers and dog beds and Mitten-Kurz's portable refrigerator and microwave. How much longer could this emptying-out go on? *Sic transit gloria mundi.* So it must have been to witness the barbarian lootings of ancestral hoards. Ben wouldn't have been surprised to see a Buildings and Grounds man emerge from the building leading a bedizened elephant on a golden cord.

But instead it was Mitten-Kurz who brought up the rear, hobbling along haltingly on a single crutch, clutching her brass samovar to her stomach, her face slack and vacant. Ben approached her, but she struggled past him without giving a sign of recognition. Marcy was standing in the doorway, holding one of the dogs by its collar and speaking softly but vehemently into a cell phone. Ben edged over to her. "Wait a minute, Tracy," she said—she'd been talking to her counterpart in the president's office. To Ben she said, "Would you believe it? He fired her. He holds her responsible because she hired Charles Johns. He sent a crew over to move her out. No heads-up, no phone call." Into the phone she said, "She's absolutely in shock. You should see her color. She's not a well woman. I may have to call an ambulance. Excuse me, Tracy, I think I'd better—"

Just then, Baby—Ben assumed it was Baby, because Big was not a well dog—began to pull away from Marcy's restraining hand, shaking and tugging violently. In a moment he'd popped out of his collar like a cork from a bottle. Marcy lunged, but Baby was whipping across the green. Soon he'd made it past the two great oaks in the center of the quadrangle and now he'd taken a turn toward the West Oak parking lot. Beyond that were the hedges and beyond that, humming continuously even if everyone had learned not to hear it, was the freeway. Ben and Marcy stood rooted in place, watching in helpless dismay as Baby diminished to a traveling dot. Mitten-Kurz, still clutching her samovar, still moiling along the breezeway, hadn't noticed.

CHAPTER NINE

⌒

T hose outer bands'll just keep rolling on in for a while," Roush Spanier was saying. "Rolling rolling rolling. We've got landfall estimated for just about seven o'clock tonight, and we're projecting her arrival as a Category Four."

Ben and Ruth were sitting in wicker chairs on the screened-in porch, watching televised coverage of the approach of Hurricane Heather. The light was even greener today than it had been yesterday. Early that morning Ben had stepped out to pick up the paper and noticed that several of his neighbors were standing on their front steps in bathrobes, sniffing the still air like domestic animals.

"Like we've been saying, that's based on the very very rapid decrease in pressure in the eye that frankly came right out of the blue and upset all our projections and got us scrambling to adjust our models. That's why we all woke up to a brand-new story this morning. Not a good story for the folks on Survivor's Island . . ."

Roush Spanier was seated on a high stool across from Mirielle Poirot, who had opted not to display her cleavage today, though her long crossed thighs were visible through the clear Lucite of the anchor pod. Roush Spanier had made his own concession to the occasion by leaving off his trademark red beret and smoking jacket. He was a small, roosterish man with an advanced case of tonsorial baldness. In shirtsleeves he looked diminished, but also authoritative, like a somber doctor called to a late-night bedside. The studio lights seemed to be troubling his eyes; wincing smartly, he took off his dark-rimmed glasses and massaged the bridge of his nose.

"So how does it look right now, Roush?" asked Mirielle. "What's the take-home for our viewers?"

Roush Spanier hopped nimbly from his stool and strode over to the illuminated weather map. "Well, as I say, we're seeing those outer bands coming in to Survivor's Island, rolling in, rolling in." He made rowing motions with his arm. Ruth reminded herself that the outer bands meant bouts of high wind and rain, punctuated by lulls.

"They've got some feisty folks down there," said Mirielle, "and we love them for it, but those folks have got to understand this is not one to try and ride out."

"Let me underscore that, Mirielle." Roush removed his glasses again and squinted directly into the camera. "I can't overstate the seriousness of the situation. This is a catastrophic storm. No amount of plywood is going to keep a structure standing in a Cat Four, so Survivor's Island folks can forget the trip to the lumber yard. Forget the bottled water. Forget the portable generator. Now, we've been hammering at this message for the last eight hours, but it bears repeating: Do not attempt to shelter in place. Anybody left on the island needs to listen up and pay attention to the compulsory evacuation order and get on out of there."

"Amen to that, Roush."

"Don't you have Martinez's cell somewhere?" asked Ben. "There's got to be a way to get in touch—"

"We've never had his cell," said Ruth. "I keep telling you. We asked and he said he doesn't give it out. Don't you remember?"

"We know it's major bad news for Survivor's Island," said Roush Spanier, "which is very sparsely populated. It's going to mean trouble here in the greater Spangler metropolitan area as well, but as yet we don't know what kind. Cat Four trouble? I doubt it. Hurricanes have a way of losing steam over land, thank the Lord. Cat Three? Very possible, and Cat Threes are nothing to fool around with—"

"Just a moment," said Mirielle. "Sorry to interrupt but I'm just getting word that the evacuation order has been extended to Spangler and the whole of Gingris County. It's not mandatory yet. But it's strongly advised."

"Try him at his office," said Ben. "It's ten to the hour."

"I called an hour ago exactly," said Ruth. "He's not seeing patients. He's probably fleeing. Like everyone."

As if to illustrate that point, the television screen switched to an overview of snarled freeway traffic. "That's our Doug Bandicot, manning our Channel Nine chopper," said Mirielle. "How's it going, Bandy? Can you see any break up ahead?"

The only answer was the noise of the helicopter's engine and the thwack-thwack of its blades. The voiceless din continued, finally overridden by Roush Spanier. Perhaps because the dead air had panicked him, he'd slipped out of his tone of high seriousness and back into character as Channel Nine's Ragin' Cajun Weatherman. "Lotta folks don't need a 'vacuation order," he shouted. "They jes' grab the dog and the cat and the mother-in-law and they pile in the car and go. When the goin' gets tough, the tough get goin'. I'n that the truth, Mirielle? I'n that the way?"

Another ten seconds of empty, flapping roar.

" 'Course that *can* be a problem. 'Specially if the dog and the cat and the mother-in-law all got their own cars. Hoo! That makes for a whole lot of traffic, I gar-rawn-tee."

Ben muted the TV and stood up. "I'm going to take the car out right now and look for him. Maybe I can spot him, if he hasn't found someplace to go."

"Good luck," said Ruth. "Two years of trying, and today you're going to find him. He's going to hop in the car and come home with you. Thanks, Dad!"

But Ben was walking past her as she said this and now he was collecting his keys from the kitchen counter. In another moment he was out the door and she was left alone to ask herself why she seemed to feel it a matter of honor to scoff at his anxiety about the hurricane and even his anxiety about Isaac. Somehow she felt she had no choice but to occupy the ground of obstructionism, as if Ben had seized all the territories of worry and concern that had once belonged to her.

She walked into her study, sat down at her desk, called up her document, which for lack of a better designation she'd given the file name "Newthing." There it was, and there, reassuringly, were the two paragraphs it grew late last night when she approached it with a glass of wine. The second was more than a page long.

On this reading she saw that the opening passages were tight and awkward, like most beginnings. But the second paragraph was better and the last long paragraph was good—rough, but alive. The piece was gathering energy, picking up rhythm and urgency, the sentences knocking one another along like the suspended balls of a perpetual-motion machine. Newthing was a keeper, or at least it would be if she kept up the momentum—precisely what she wouldn't be able to do if Heather paid them this visit that the television had been going on about all day.

Leaving the document on the screen, she returned to the porch and took her place on the chaise. Why was she failing to worry about Isaac? She made a deliberate effort to imagine him on the street, pushing through wind and rain, his head lowered, his long coat blowing. Did that picture alarm her? Not really. Perhaps because he lived in daily extremity, she'd come to think of him as invulnerable to the elements. If cockroaches could survive a nuclear holocaust, Isaac could survive Heather. He'd find a place to hide. He'd be the first to stir and rise when the waters receded.

She tried substituting the child Isaac for the adult. There he was, a toddler, wailing in the slashing rain. She felt an instant rush of adrenalized pity and terror; in her imagination she was sprinting toward him, scooping him up, spiriting him to safety. She'd conducted these thought experiments many times before, trying and failing to reconcile the vanished infant, for whom she continued to feel an unhealed ache, with the adult, for whom her feelings seemed to have dried up as surely as milk dries up after weaning. After a lifetime of feeling too much, it seemed now she felt too little, and her feeling about that was not the flare of guilt she would have felt in early motherhood but a small inward shrug of acknowledgment. At this stage it hardly mattered how she felt. Like her love, her guilt was no longer necessary.

Glancing at the silent TV, she noted that Channel Nine's wet and windblown Darren Doggett was clinging to a palm tree on Survivor's Island. Then it was back to Roush and Mirielle at the anchor desk, and on to the weather map, where the progressive encroachment of Heather was illustrated and then back to the Channel Nine whirlybird's aerial view of freeway gridlock. How irritated she was by all this, irritated at Darren and Roush and Mirielle and Bandy and the National Weather Service and—especially—at Heather herself, that petulant valley girl of a storm, barging into Ruth's study just as she was starting to get a grip on her writing.

It seemed she was increasingly incapable of appropriate reactions. She felt no fear of this rapidly approaching hurricane; instead she found herself harboring an odd conviction that it was a fraud. She knew quite well that evidence for its reality was mounting—it wasn't some flunky just out of camera range who was splashing buckets of water on Darren Doggett. It wasn't a wind machine that was causing him to stagger and sway. Even so, she couldn't shake a primitive suspicion that Heather was a lot of hooey. Hurricane? What hurricane? She'd never been in a hurricane. But now she was beginning to feel alarm, not at the hurricane but at her own sclerotic thinking. It was as if some squint-eyed crone had taken control of her mind for a moment, some elderly harridan who shouted at neighborhood children when they knocked at her door.

The hurricane was real. "Real," she said aloud. She got up from the chaise and paced the porch, trying to assimilate the idea that this real hurricane was on its way to do real damage to Spangler and her house and perhaps to her and Ben and Isaac. Returning to her computer, she called up and printed out the three and a half pages of Newthing, folded them into a rectangle, and dropped them into her medium-sized canvas carryall. Moving around her study, she collected a few other items as well—a yellow lined notepad and two felt-tip pens, a tiny framed snapshot of Isaac in a bumper car at age seven, the ceramic Staffordshire dog.

SEE YOU AFTER THE BIG BLOW. These words had been scrawled on a piece of lined yellow paper and Scotch-taped to the door of the Cosmos Club Coffeehouse. Through the window Ben could see that somebody had forgotten to turn off the lazily revolving ceiling fans, and with his presbyopically acute middle-aged vision he could make out the list of specials listed in various shades of Day-Glo pastel on the blackboard above the counter:

HOMEMADE GNOCCHI WITH WILD MUSHROOMS
TRIO OF RED PEPPER, LEEK, AND SUMMER
    SQUASH SOUPS
GIANT FUDGEROO BROWNIE

Giant Fudgeroo Brownie, he thought. How Pompeian.

He walked around to the far side of the property, where the flagstone patio had been cleared of tables and chairs. Except for the moldering maroon school bus with four flat tires that the owner had once used to transport his now-defunct jug band, the parking lot was deserted. Behind the dumpster at the far end was a derelict aluminum parking shelter. Ruth had always maintained that Isaac spent some of his nights here in a small colony of homeless men, and Ben did find evidence of habitation—a filthy rucked-up chenille bedspread, crumpled fast-food wrappers, a generalized urine reek, six empty fortified-wine bottles. Was Isaac a wino now, like his bum confreres? That would be a sad irony, because the teenaged Isaac had had such a horror of alcohol that he wouldn't allow Ben to drink a beer in his presence (though for some reason he ignored Ruth's wine consumption). At first Ben had been proud of Isaac for his purity of mind; it seemed of a piece with his aptitude for math and music and his fastidious indifference to the opinions of his classmates. A few years later he'd come to understand this aversion as a symptom, the herald of a proliferating swarm of contamination fears—tobacco-smoke residue in motel drapes, milk within a week of its sell-by date, little girls who might not be wearing underpants.

He kicked the bedspread back a little with the toe of his shoe, as if hoping to uncover some kind of forensic evidence. Nothing but weeds and pebbles. People slept here? What must it be to be a bum? What must it be to leave the world of elevators and credit cards and clean towels? It made Ben's bones ache to think of it. This was a familiar train of thought, and it always ended in anxious ruminations about his own frailties; his hemorrhoids and how maddeningly they would itch after a few days without bathing, his carefully reconstructed teeth and how they would loosen without the quarterly attentions of his periodontist. There was Isaac's youth to mitigate the discomforts a little, he supposed, and the unimaginable compensations offered by his mental illness. Perhaps he'd decided that the only way to escape his fears was to become one with them—no dirty person fears dirt. Perhaps he was also less lonely now: bums, after all, were the only group who had ever admitted him to their society.

Back in the car, he took a turn around the Museum District. Like the rest of Spangler, it was almost entirely deserted. The only vehicle he encountered was a police cruiser driving very slowly down the middle of the street. He passed Martinez's old office building. Farther along that renovated red-brick dead-end block, a couple in a driveway were struggling to tie a kayak to the roof of an SUV. He turned the car around and headed down Tyler Street to Madison, where he turned right and drove around the block occupied by the low-slung, high-modernist Dufour Museum, with its spread of lawns and salaaming live oaks. He'd caught a glimpse of Isaac on the grounds here a year ago, sitting on the very same marble bench facing an architecturally celebrated ecumenical chapel that he was not sitting on now.

He swung back onto Madison, turned left, and drove west along Ferris Avenue, where the gentrified environs of the museums gave way to a scruffy district of head shops and tattoo parlors and sex-toy emporiums. He could see that Isaac's favorite anime bookstore was closed, but even so he parked and got out and peered through the darkened window. The woman who ran the shop had known Isaac for years. For a moment it had seemed plausible that she might have offered him the closed store as a refuge.

Back in the car and continuing down Ferris, he saw a wild, dirty young woman with blond dreadlocks and a missing shoe limping along the sidewalk. He slowed the car and pulled over, meaning to offer help and to ask—if she seemed lucid—whether she knew Isaac. "Excuse me, miss," he said. The girl kept her head down and slightly turned; her profile was obscured by bobbing clots of matted hair. "Are you all right? Is there something I can do?" Silence. She continued to hobble along, but more rapidly.

He continued to cruise at her side. He was sounding and behaving—he knew—exactly like the kind of predatory creep young girls are warned to avoid, but if anyone should feel an obligation to persist in trying to help a person like her, it was he.

"Do you have a place to go to get out of the storm?" No answer. He tried again. "Maybe you could help me. I'm looking for Isaac Blau. He's big. Very tall. He wears a long coat and a wizard's hat. He's my son." The girl turned with a look so dazed and puzzled that he felt a stab of simple social embarrassment. Just then, the median-straddling cop, who seemed to have nothing better to do than to trail him at a distance, drew up alongside and eyed him. Ben drove on.

Where do fish go when the lake freezes? Where do bums go when the wind blows? Was there some kind of public shelter around here? Not that he knew of, but now he remembered the Shining Star Ministry, where bums were said to be catechized before they were hosed down and fed and offered a cot. It was not a place that Isaac, with his adolescent contempt for religion, would ever have willingly gone, but in these circumstances he might have been shunted there by Martinez. It wasn't far, on a side street a few blocks down, next to the Lotus, a former Walgreen's drugstore that housed the best Vietnamese restaurant in Spangler. Just last spring he'd been there eating pho with a visiting epistemologist from Stanford, a pleasant, assertive woman with a young family who asked the inevitable chain of questions:

Any children?

Yes, a son.

How old?

Mid-twenties.

Out of grad school then?

Never went, actually.

Ah! Yes! She knew of many such. Didn't Dennis O'Donnell at Penn have a son who kicked over the traces and became a furniture restorer? Very skilled, she'd heard. Made all kinds of money. The conversation trailed off, the epistemologist nodding and re-folding her napkin. She was sitting with her back to the window, so it was only Ben who took note when one of a huddle of derelicts who'd been smoking and sharing a wheezy laugh in front of the Shining Star suddenly jackknifed at the waist and deposited a wad of phlegm the size of a robin's egg on the sidewalk.

Today there was no such gathering. The Shining Star was dark and bolted. A note taped to the chicken-wire-reinforced porthole in the aluminum door read: BUS FOR HONEYCUTT HURRICANE SHELTER LEAVES 2 PM. Perhaps he could hope that Isaac was on it. He could also hope it had left early enough to escape the gridlock on 117. Alternatively, he could hope—this had been his ace in the hole all along—that Martinez had somehow gotten him to safety.

What now? He'd canvassed all the places Isaac had been known to frequent in the past two years. All he could think to do was to get back into the car and retrace his route, east on Ferris, right at the Dufour. The sun was sinking now, and the light was the color of unfiltered pineapple juice. When he thought to turn on the car radio it was a voice from another era that he heard— not the light facetious tenor of today's radio announcers but a deep calm baritone, like Edward R. Murrow's on the *I Can Hear It Now* records that had so impressed and frightened him when he and his father listened to them in the late 1950s. The voice was interrupted every few seconds by an alarming double beep, and it informed him that the voluntary evacuation advisory for Gingris

County had been canceled. As of 4:45 PM, a new advisory had been issued: shelter in place.

Every Lola building constructed in the last six years had been designed to withstand a Category Four hurricane. Horace Dees was one of these, and it had other features that made it suitable for use as a shelter—an auxiliary generator and showers in both the men's and women's restrooms on the third floor.

And so it was that campus security opened the doors to Horace Dees (and three other campus buildings) at six thirty on the evening of September 24. Ben and Ruth were among the earliest arrivals. They brought with them only Ruth's canvas satchel and a small suitcase containing changes of underwear, toilet articles, Ben's altruism manuscript, a light thermal blanket, and a flashlight. At the last minute Ruth added two novels and a flask of single-malt scotch. As they locked the house, a soft drizzling rain was beginning, and as they walked through their neighborhood past houses boarded up with plywood (a useless precaution, according to the special Hurricane Heather edition of the *Spangler Advocate*) a capricious breeze kicked up. The sky, Ruth observed as she took Ben's arm, was as deep a shade of charcoal gray as she'd ever seen, and it gave the dying light a peculiarly intimate radiance. By the time they reached the outer parking lots of Lola, true dusk was spreading and the breeze had become a tree-tossing wind. The campus was so absolutely flat that they could see all four lighted shelter buildings, shining like passenger ships plowing through a darkening sea.

A few cars had been left parked on the access road, their hazard lights blinking. As Ben and Ruth walked toward Horace

Dees, a pack of undergraduate males came barreling past them, whooping and shouting, their eyes and teeth gleaming in the gloaming. Were they drunk? No, just excited, as Ruth herself (but not Ben) would have been at their age. The steadily gathering wind, the creaking trees, the skittering leaves: what anarchic joy she'd have felt at nineteen, out on a night when a hurricane was starting to blow. How she would have identified with this wild Heather—"Be thou me, impetuous one!" But now she saw that the rowdy boys were turning into the driveway of Dryden Commons, one of the lit buildings. They were Lola students after all, sensible at heart.

When they arrived at six fifty, the lobby was nearly empty. Barbara Bachman seemed to have imported a stack of coolers and baskets full of food; she and three of her children were setting up a sandwich-making beachhead at the other end of the room. They seemed very far away, their chirruping voices swallowed by echoes. The only other person present was Jean-Henri Deslauriers, a gouty bachelor who'd been teaching entry-level French conversation for thirty years without a promotion. Sitting just outside the foyer on a flimsy folding chair, his cane on his lap and an old-fashioned valise at his feet, he looked the part of a refugee. The lobby was dim; only the wall sconces were lit. That and the echoes and Jean-Henri's stoical presence gave the room the feeling of a vast, shadowy European train station.

By seven thirty, Heather was making landfall on Survivor's Island (Category Four, 151 mph winds, gusts up to 170, storm surge 18 feet) and the lobby was swarming with academic life. Faculty and staff were arriving steadily, carrying suitcases and backpacks, blankets and pillows, board games and bags of provisions. They'd brought children too, of course—eye-rolling adoles-

cents, scampering preschoolers, wailing toddlers, sleeping infants
in front packs. And they'd brought pets: five cats vocalizing in
carrying cases, two squawking cockatoos, assorted mice and
guinea pigs and hamsters quivering under piles of cedar shavings,
one unblinking iguana, four nervously prancing dogs. Of these,
two were Big and Baby, chaperoned by Bobby Mitten-Kurz, who
circulated through the room accepting good wishes for Roberta.
She was resting, he explained to anyone who asked, at the Pavilion of the Pines Hospital. Yes, that was an officially designated
hurricane shelter. They'd had quite a scare on her account and
on Baby's as well, but all seemed to have ended happily. He'd
picked up Baby at a vet's office all the way over in Sharp City
this morning and he was fine, just a little shaky and spooked.
Bertie's confusion had been alarming at first, but it turned out
the problem was really only that her blood-pressure medication
needed adjustment. They'd kept her in the hospital for a night's
observation, just to be sure the new dosage agreed with her. He'd
be there himself, he said, if they'd allowed it.

It was odd, Ben thought, to look around him and see in the
flesh what he'd so often heard lauded in the abstract. This was
the Lola community—or at least the humanities part of it—flowing into the lobby and milling about as if awaiting orders, its
multiple faces flickering with anxiety and confusion. He'd seen
this group assembled before, but only to mark the ceremonies of
the academic calendar, never for atavistic reasons of safety and
survival. There was Dolores and her husband and two of their
older grandchildren, divesting themselves of hats and raincoats in
the foyer. And there was Muriel Draybrooke in her damp tweeds,
doggedly pushing her way through the crowd toward the sandwich table. There were the Federmans, back from Majorca, Sissy

smiling gamely and waving at acquaintances, Bruce looking exasperated. He was relieved to see that Rhoda was present, standing over by the glassed-in shelves where faculty books were displayed, talking to a young couple from the History Department. He saw Beth Mapes and the doctor in scrubs who was said to be her partner. He spotted the timid young Philbys and a few of the other current graduate students and wondered where the missing ones might be: they could have joined the evacuees, he supposed, or found shelter elsewhere. Was he responsible for them? With graduate students, that was always the question.

He knew nearly everyone here, if only by reputation, but in some cases he had to adjust for the effects of aging or make inferential guesses. The hurricane had flushed out people who hadn't shown themselves in decades. It took him a moment to recognize a famous emerita, the author of a definitive history of the Spanish Civil War, now inching along with the help of a walker, her elderly son clearing a path. For the first time he laid eyes on the legendarily anorexic daughter of the History Department secretary. He spotted a reclusive poet with multiple chemical sensitivities and a young ethnomusicologist who'd been on medical leave since exposing himself to a group of Korean middle schoolers in the parking garage of Crossgates Mall. He witnessed some particularly stiff encounters between rivals who for years had been arranging their schedules to avoid meeting one another. He saw two scenes of joyful reunion.

He hadn't gone far in his wanderings before an eddy of shop-talking gossipers formed around him, all demanding to know the latest about the fallout from the Charles Johns incident. Was the SCAC inspector still in the hospital? (No.) Was the inspector suing the university? (Not as far as Ben knew.) Was Ricia Spottiswoode leaving the university now that Charles had been fired? (Yes.) And who would take over as dean? (It hadn't yet been announced, was Ben's evasive answer, although Marcy Bainbridge had told him unofficially that it was Josh Margolis.) Excusing himself from his questioners, he was surprised to find a number of them stepping forward to shake his hand, as if somehow he'd been credited with the vanquishing of Mitten-Kurz. Dorit Rubenfeld, a dark and bosomy Israeli anthropologist, pulled him toward her and planted a moist kiss on his left ear. Where was Ruth? He'd have given a lot for her to see that.

Ah, there she was, leaning against the far wall, paging through the *Lola Lantern,* isolating herself in her beckoning way. Striking out in her direction, he saw that a crowd of school-age children had been allowed to gather in one of the lecture halls adjoining the lobby to watch cartoons on an overhead monitor. Adults were drifting in and out of another such room, checking on Roush and Mirielle's continuing coverage. (Heather was weakening slightly, but still a strong Cat Three, clocked at 119 mph as she came through Old Prison Farm Corners.) Ariel Bachman snaked through the crowd with pen and notepad, offering a choice of sandwiches in her piping, tremulous voice. Ben ordered a turkey and cheese on sourdough for himself and hummus with tomato and onion on pumpernickel for Ruth.

But now, just as he was approaching her, Ruth put down the *Lantern* and moved away. In a moment he saw why: Ricia and Charles had just arrived; they were standing in the entryway, surveying the scene. No doubt Ruth had been watching for them. Josh Margolis was signaling to him from another quarter of the room, but now Ben was waylaid again, this time by Dwight Alsop of the English Department, demanding to know his opinion of

Dreddle's new core distribution requirement proposal. He hadn't given it much thought, Ben confessed. Well, it had to be stopped, Alsop said. It was quite mad, quite unreasonably restrictive, and it would mean a drastic reshuffling of the curriculum and a serious decline in the number of majors. Behind Alsop's head, a window pulsed with lightning. Was that the wind, that high, faint keening he kept thinking he was hearing over the shoptalk jabber?

Baring his teeth apologetically, Ben backed away, pointing to the sandwiches he was carrying as if they constituted a self-explanatory excuse. He had hoped to be swallowed quickly by the crowd, but just in the last few moments some critical mass had been achieved and a diasporizing impulse had begun to break the aggregation into constituent couples and groups. These were rapidly moving away from one another and drifting up the stairs and down the hallways to offices and lounges and other private places where the parts could escape the whole.

It wasn't the first time," Charles was saying, "I'm sorry to say. I seem to have a penchant for it. I had a job in a paper factory, just before I met Ricia, working the night shift. There was a person there, a foul-mouthed fellow who simply could not restrain himself from baiting me. I ignored him for months and then one night I picked him up and carried him out the back and dropped him off the truck ramp." He passed the flask to Ricia, who took a quick pull and offered it to Ruth, who took a longer one. "It's a switch that gets thrown. I can't anticipate it. I can't guard against it."

"He doesn't know his own strength," said Ricia. "This has always been a problem." She ran her fingers lightly over Charles's shoulder. Charles leaned into the caress, his eyebrows rising slightly, as if in puzzled recognition of something he'd forgotten. "I think he needs taming. Do you think he needs taming, Ruth?"

"No," said Ruth. The flask had traveled around several times now. "I think he's perfect," she added. The three of them were sitting in a pond of soft light at the far end of Ricia's otherwise darkened office. Ricia had inherited a sagging foam-rubber couch that had been doing the rounds of faculty offices for years. She'd festooned it with pillows and throws and pulled up a pair of university-issued chairs to make a conversational grouping and set it all off from the rest of the room with two rice-paper screens. The effect was provisional and theatrical and it brought Ruth back to the days of her youth, when she spent many hours in settings and situations like this—often bored, always excited. It was amazing, she was thinking, how little she felt excluded by Charles and Ricia's intimacy. Not excluded at all, in fact. Welcomed into it, rather.

"Thank you, madam," said Charles, toasting her with the flask. "I only wish Dr. Lee Wayne Dreddle shared that sentiment."

"Oh, do you care?" asked Ruth. "I'd have given a lot to have you stay, both of you, but I didn't think you—"

"I don't really," said Charles. "It's just that I'd been banking on having something to put on my résumé. I'd been looking for some kind of academic work in Providence. I was hoping for an adjunct position at Brown, but I'd have settled for a community college. We don't need the money, strictly speaking, but I don't feel quite right about being a kept man—a completely kept man. I'd like to contribute to the common weal, but I'm too arthritic for heavy labor now. Do you think I could take advantage of this temporary state of anarchy and smoke a cigarette here, Ricia? Would it set off some kind of alarm?"

Ricia got up and ventured into the darkened end of the office, returning with a shallow, speckled ceramic bowl. Charles lit a cigarette and offered one to Ruth, who declined it and found herself saying, "Ben could write you a letter." But what was she thinking? Ben couldn't write a letter for Charles.

"Ben's a good man," said Charles. "I wouldn't put him on the spot. I'm sorry I caused him so much trouble. What happened to the chairmanship? Has he quit for good?"

"No no," said Ruth. "He reinstated himself after Mitten-Kurz was fired."

"Ah," said Charles. "Good of him to stay on. Is that what he wanted?"

Ruth hesitated. "I think it was, really. He complains about losing writing time, but he has an impulse to take care of things—of people."

"He takes care of you," Ricia interjected. "I've noticed that. Every time I see him, he's looking for you."

"They certainly need taking care of in that department," said Charles. "I never saw a more bewildered bunch. I think of preschool children on an outing, all holding on to a rope. Someone needs to keep a grip on the front end."

"So, Ruth," said Ricia. "Have you been writing?"

"In fact I have," said Ruth. "Just a start. Just a few pages, but it has the feeling of something that could go on."

"Wonderful! Do you have it here? Read it aloud. Give us a reading."

"No," said Ruth. "I left it at home." In truth it was there in her purse, at her feet. She'd transferred it when she stopped at Ben's office to get the flask from their suitcase, but suddenly it seemed the better part of valor not to show it off. "So," she said, addressing Ricia, "what will you do when you get back to Providence?"

"Let's hope we do get back," said Ricia. "Listen to the wind. It's howling, just the way they say it does."

Charles got up and went to the window. "That old oak out there is swaying like a Balinese dancer," he reported.

"You know, I've had the hardest time taking this hurricane seriously," said Ruth. "I just can't get the idea into my head. It doesn't seem real."

"It's real enough to me," said Charles. He remained at the window, his arms crossed over his paunch. "Any possibility of calamity seems real to me."

The flask circulated once again. "I'll miss you both," said Ruth. "It's been so wonderful having you here. I was looking forward to getting to know you better. Actually, I feel I've known you for years, and what's it been, three weeks?"

"Ah, well," said Ricia, reaching across the coffee table to squeeze her hand. "We'll stay in touch. You'll come visit. We'll have a party for you."

But Ruth was too full of feeling not to go on. "The two of you," she said. "It's as if you opened a window in a stuffy room. I can't tell you how much of a difference you've made. The years go by in circles and the only change is that I sink into myself a little more. Ben does all right. He makes progress in his work. Sometimes I think he thinks he's only treading water, but at least he has the illusion of moving forward."

"At our age that's almost always an illusion," said Charles.

"Charles!" said Ricia. "That's a terrible thing to say to Ruth. She's just starting a book. That's no illusion."

"I'm not sure it's a book," said Ruth. "And I'm not sure it's not an illusion."

"I'm sorry," said Charles. He returned from his post at the window and sat down again. "I'm a terrible old cynic. Or maybe not exactly a cynic. Maybe I'm a terrible old stoic. I don't quite see this notion of progress. Not past youth. It only breeds discontent. You seem so discontented, Ruth, but from my point of view there's much to be said for the life here. I wouldn't mind sticking around, though I know Ricia would. There are some very kind and admirable people here. There are old attachments and loyalties. You need a protected place for bonds like those to form. You need to get out of the wind and rain . . ." He gestured at the window. "I think I could content myself with life here. Of course that's just my own view. I suppose I'm looking back at Paradise after the expulsion."

"Yes you are," said Ricia. "You exactly are. You couldn't tolerate Paradise any more than I could. Any more than Ruth can. Some archangel would get on your nerves and you'd be shoving him off a cloud."

Charles shrugged and smiled. He shook the flask. "I believe we've killed this," he said.

Ricia got to her feet. "I've got a very nice bottle of pinot noir in my desk drawer. Somebody left it in my mailbox last week, along with a manuscript. What I don't have is a corkscrew."

"Ah," said Charles, tilting to one side to dig a hand into his pants pocket. "Never fear, my dears. I've got my Swiss army knife."

Just then they were startled by a tattoo of sharp raps on the door. Charles rose. "Who's there?" he demanded. "Joel Bachman," came the answer in a cracked adolescent voice. "We're doing a head count. How many people in there? Do I smell smoke?"

T he Margolis era," Ben was saying. "Sounds good to me. Sounds like progress." He and Josh were walking down the dimly lit third-floor hall toward Ben's office.

"You understand it's only interim. They'll have to do a national search next year, but in the meantime I'll have a chance to get a few things done."

"Yes," said Ben. "Eliminate committees. Cut back on university service. Reduce teaching loads. Actually . . ." He stopped and turned to Josh, who was four inches taller than he and twenty-five years his junior. "Actually, there's something quite serious I'd like to ask you. Could you get Dolores back? Do you think you could arrange that?"

"I don't see why not," said Josh. "All in a day's work for a benevolent despot."

"It wouldn't be seen as some kind of cronyism?"

"I don't think so. She had no business stealing Dolores in the first place. People like to see the natural order of things restored." Ben switched on the outer-office light and they found themselves in the midst of Hayley's fairyland. He hadn't really taken account, he realized, of its advances over the last week. The walls were a montage of overlapping fairy posters and the ceiling was swarming; not a square inch had been left unsparkling or untwinkling or untwirling. "Good Christ," said Josh. "It's an infestation. I'd heard about this, but it's worse than I thought. You should have talked to me: I think there's some bylaw about defacing university property you could have appealed to. How did you stand it?"

The only possible answer was to reach up and detach a fairy from the ceiling. Josh did the same, and soon they were systematically dismantling the display. It was quick, pleasant work, but when it was done the fairies lay strewn across the carpet like battle casualties. That wouldn't do, so they gathered them up in handfuls and dropped them into a cardboard box Ben found in the utility closet. "Close it up," said Josh. "It makes me think of those mass-grave photographs. You know: 'Having no natural defenses against the diseases of civilization, the fairies were decimated.'"

Ben went into his office and rifled through the suitcase. "Sorry," he called. "No scotch. Ruth got here first." When he came back into the outer office, Josh was standing at the rain-spattered great window. "Look," he said. "See those headlights, way across the green? What is that? Some kind of amphibious Coast Guard vehicle?" Ben joined him, standing back a little; branches were tapping on the glass, and the wind was making it rattle ominously in its casing. "See? It's coming overland. It's headed straight toward us," said Josh. "It's crossing the access road." Ben could see the vehicle now; its headlights flaring and dipping. It looked like a small tank, and it was being driven with reckless, jerky abandon, jouncing over curbs and brick sidewalks and flattening plantings. "Oh yeah," said Josh. "That's Dreddle's Hummer. He's out riding the storm. Whoa! He's just as crazy as they say he is. I bet he's got his quail-hunting posse with him."

"How long do you think he'll last?" said Ben. "As president, I mean."

"The average these days seems to be about six years, but I

doubt he'll make three. I don't think the trustees expect him to stay longer than that. He'll raise a lot of money and he'll build some buildings and he'll be gone."

But now the lights in the office were flickering. The room was suddenly dark, and so, Ben could see, was the hall. The building's background hum had gone silent, and when Josh said, "Well, that was inevitable," his voice startled them both with its volume and intimacy. They stood at the window, watching as the taillights of the Hummer bounced out of view.

"The backup generator should be kicking in," said Josh. So it did, and the lights went on for a few seconds. Then it, too, failed, and the lights went out again.

"When night descended he went to seek out
the high house . . ."

Charles was reading from *Beowulf,* one arm draped around Ricia, the other around Ruth. He paused to refresh himself from the half-finished bottle of pinot noir, then continued:

". . . to see how the ring-Danes
had bedded down after their beer-drinking . . ."

When the lights went out the first time, he drew Ruth and Ricia closer. "Well, ladies," he chortled, "we are advantageously placed, are we not?"

"Power failure," said Ricia. "I love it! I'm such a Luddite."

The lamp flickered and went back on just long enough for Charles to say, "Ah, too bad!"

. . .

In darkness, people come together. A few minutes after the lights went out for the second time, the Lola humanities community began the process of reconstituting itself. It ventured out of offices and seminar rooms and trickled through hallways and down the central staircase, flashlight beams wavering along the carpet, adults laughing softly, small children lamenting loudly, dogs whining in inquiry, adolescents complaining in plangent adolescent voices. At the head of the stairs a quorum of flashlights convened to throw a dancing, uncertain light on the problem of the darkened stairwell. Ruth looked down to see the anxious up-lifted face of a little girl. "It's fun. Isn't it fun, Mom?" she asked. "It's *lots* of fun, honey," said the mother. "Don't let go of my hand."

Standing at the foot of the stairs, Barbara Bachman was dis-tributing lighted candles, long white tapered ones. (Had she actu-ally thought to bring them along, Ruth wondered. If so, what else: inflatable rafts?) Holding these aloft, parties of people launched into the lobby, and soon the great high-ceilinged space was fill-ing up with softly illuminated faces, making a bobbing clock-wise progress. Ruth was reminded of those Chinese ceremonies where lanterns are set afloat on rivers at night. She'd lost Ricia and Charles somewhere on the way down the stairs. Just as well, she thought; she'd hate to be remembered as a clinger.

Ben and Josh had parted ways when Josh caught sight of his wife and small son in the second-floor hallway. Now Ben was doing a solo turn around the lobby, moving against the current of the crowd. It was hard to judge distances in this watery light, hard to recognize people, difficult also to avoid them. He hadn't gotten far when the long patrician face of Bruce Federman hovered into view. "Hey, Ben," he called out in his ringing voice, fumbling to find and shake Ben's hand. "Great to see you. Sorry about the circumstances. This *would* have to happen the minute we get back!"

"How was Spain?" asked Ben. In a way, he was glad to encounter Federman. The evening had begun to feel like a dream, one of those swarming formless ones that drone on like an Indian raga. Federman's presence was a powerful dream-solvent; for him there was no world but the waking one of tenure decisions and racquetball and faculty-club lunches. "Fabulous," was the answer. "We were living on the beach. Very primitive. The food, the wine. So cheap, so good. Sissy says I've got a little gut. By the way, I know you've been waiting for my pages for the anthology. I got sidetracked in Spain, but I'm home now and it goes to the top of the agenda."

Ben nodded, and the lights went back on. The crowd ceased its slow circular movement and everyone stood in place, blinking. A moment passed. A few finger-in-mouth whistles could be heard above a growing murmur. "Hoo-ray?" some Bachman called out, a little tentatively.

"Well!" said Federman. "Maybe we'll get home yet. Have you seen Sissy? She was over with Dorothy Dixon, trying to calm her down." Dorothy Dixon was the nervous widow of a former chair of the department. Sissy was an old-style faculty wife of the Southern variety, always in the know about illnesses and family troubles, always the first to make a call or bring a casserole. Ruth could be very tiresome on the subject of Sissy Federman. Where *was* Ruth? He looked around. There she was, only a few feet away, her back turned.

Taking his leave, Federman leaned in conspiratorially. In a tone he might have used to disparage a job candidate with an inflated reputation he remarked, "I really don't see this Heather living up to her billing. She's been over land too long; I doubt she's even a two."

Just then the windows rattled. A loud, splintering, cracking noise followed. The lights went out and the crowd gasped as a limb from the live oak in the courtyard catapulted through a window. The room was full of the shriek of the storm and the cascading tinkle of breaking glass.

Children screamed. Ruth found herself shoved and dragged in a sucking human tide as the crowd contracted and migrated toward the corner farthest from the broken window. When it had come to rest, Barbara Bachman broke the silence by calling out in her flat, carrying voice, "Is anyone hurt? Is anyone injured?" There was no reply except the weeping of children; Ruth recognized the deep, hiccuping sobs of real terror. "We have first-aid supplies over here. Please make your way toward the sandwich table if you feel you've been injured."

It was too dark at first to tell if she had any takers, but now flashlights were being switched on and a cigarette lighter was being passed around to relight extinguished candles. Parents were able to assure themselves that their children had not been cut by flying glass. Ruth was able to make out the contours of the room and the shapes of the heads and shoulders of the people surrounding her. Was that Ben, just one body over to her right? Yes it was. She reached around the intervening one, found his shoulder, squeezed it. He edged next to her.

A long suspended moment ensued. People stood quietly, still pressed against their neighbors, listening to the whistling, soughing wind that had invaded the room, smelling the misplaced smells of rain and overturned earth. The unseemly tree limb itself was visible a few yards away, lying on the glittering floor like the severed hand of a giant. Nobody was inclined to move; no one was prepared to believe that something worse might not happen at any moment. When Janice Trumpeter of the French Department spoke up to suggest that everyone take deep breaths to reduce the general stress level, only a few complied. When Ariel Bachman and her mother launched into the first verse of "Itsy Bitsy Spider," they got only as far as "climbed up the water spout" before their quavering voices trailed off. Nobody, they seemed to realize, would want to hear the part about the rain coming down and washing the spider out.

Ruth found that her sense of interval had failed. She had no idea what time it was, or how long it had been since the power failed, or even how long it had been since she and Ben had arrived here at Horace Dees. But now something was happening: two candle holders were pushing their way toward the front. As they passed, Ruth recognized Ricia's curls and Charles's bulk. They were taking charge.

Charles and Ricia turned to face the crowd, Charles holding an open book in his hands. "I'd like to read aloud from *Beowulf*, beginning with the prologue." The assembly murmured its assent. Charles cleared his throat. Ricia moved in closer, took Charles's candle in one hand and her own in the other and held them so that they shed light on the book. She looked, Ruth was thinking,

like a medieval page. For a moment, Charles closed his eyes and
rocked back and forth on his heels, as though deliberately throwing himself into a trance. He began:

> "Listen!
>> We have heard of the glory in bygone days
> of the folk-kings of the spear-Danes,
>> how those noble lords did lofty deeds."

Charles's voice was a remarkable phenomenon in any circumstance, but in this breathing, flickering darkness it was exponentially more marvelous than in daylight. It was like the concentrated
meat jelly in the grooves at the bottom of the roasting pan, or the
mesmerizing burble of a distant Piper Cub on a summer afternoon. The voice commanded the crowd to obey the text's injunction: it listened, and people were called to themselves. The
older ones were reminded of what they'd lost; the voice brought
it back with a revivifying sadness. The younger ones were moved
to imagine what was yet to come; the voice promised miracles, or
disasters. Charles's voice made children see, against the screen of
darkness, just what it was that the story was telling them:

> "I have never heard of a more lovely ship
> bedecked with battle-weapons and war-gear,
> blades and byrnies, in its bosom lay
> many treasures, which were to travel
> far with him into the keeping of the flood."

The voice tamed and enchanted the crowd, made it an audience. Hardly realizing what they were doing, people sank to the

floor and sat transfixed, leaning into one another, their eyes wide and their lips parted. The power of the voice was such that most failed to notice that while Charles was reading the stanza that told of the sea burial of Beowulf's father—

"Then they set a golden ensign
high over his head, and let the waves have him,
gave him to the Deep with grieving spirits,
mournful in mind."

—the headlights of a van had come bobbing up to one of the unbroken courtyard windows.

B en saw the headlights, or rather felt them on the back of his head. He turned. The headlights were extinguished. Someone had arrived. Brigands? Dreddle? The missing graduate students? He got up quietly and wove his way through the seated listeners, still in thrall to Charles's voice. He could see that some complicated entity was moving slowly through the wind and rain outside, a human aggregation with several lowered heads. The double doors were pushed open and the company came trooping in. Reluctant to train his flashlight on their faces, he shone it on their advancing feet. They were a group of five, of indeterminate genders and radically varying sizes, wearing multiple layers of soaked clothing. Walking a few feet ahead of them was a sixth, a more tidily shaped person who seemed to be acting as their leader.

Now a murmur had gone up. Heads were turning. Charles's voice was faltering. He stopped. As the group approached, Ben slowly backed away, using the flashlight beam to guide them around the fallen branch and the spray of broken glass that surrounded it. As they came into the ambit of the crowd's candlelight, he was able to identify the leader. It was Martinez. Standing directly behind him, the largest member of this troglodytic band, was Isaac, though he was not wearing his trademark wizard's hat. And could it be that he was taller? He seemed to have grown a full, face-obscuring beard. *Was* that Isaac? Ben lifted the flashlight. Isaac threw up an arm to shield his eyes. Ah, a mistake, already.

Ben held the flashlight under his own chin. "Professor Blau," said Martinez, coming forward to shake Ben's hand, his teeth glimmering like a chain of moons. "Please don't be alarmed. Our little group has had nowhere to take shelter. We have driven here and there all evening, to no avail. The storm has grown stronger. We have a woman among us, a special circumstance. The campus security officer told us to come here. I would never have arranged it like this, but here, you see, is Isaac."

Martinez stood aside. Ben moved into the semicircle formed by the group. He smelled their combined smell. Isaac declined to acknowledge him. "And here," Martinez continued, "is Rosemary." A tiny Asian woman wearing a large hooded Lola sweatshirt stepped forward. At first she struck him as elderly, but after a moment he saw that she was only prematurely wizened. Perhaps she was forty, or forty-five. Tucked into her elbow was a small wrapped bundle, shaped like a blintz.

As Ruth approached, Martinez smiled brilliantly and threw his hands into the air, a frantically punctilious host. "Mrs.

Blau," he called out. "Please remain for a moment just where you are. Right there, please. Come no farther. Professor Blau, take your place with Mrs. Blau. We will make the introduction." As Ben joined her, Martinez removed the bundle from the small woman, placed it in Isaac's arms, propelled him gently forward to Ruth. The crowd had formed two blazing banks on either side.

Ruth found she didn't dare look into his eyes. Neither was she able to say anything except, softly, "Isaac." Keeping his head lowered, Isaac extended the bundle to her. Ruth took it in both arms, and looking down, saw that it had a face. What she was holding was a baby, very small but not quite newborn, perhaps four or five weeks old, wrapped tightly and artfully on the diagonal, like a papoose. She swiveled to show the baby to Ben, and just as she did so it opened its eyes. It was a girl. The baby let out a cry, or perhaps a trill, an emphatic "L" followed by a succession of vowels—"laaaah." A groan of adoration rose from the crowd, followed by scattered imitative coos. Ben took the baby, holding her awkwardly, just as he had held the newborn Isaac. This, Ruth understood, was Isaac's daughter. This was also, she couldn't help but infer, her grandchild, and Ben's.

"Drusilla," said Isaac, in his deep, hollow voice.

"Drusilla," said Ruth. (Drusilla?)

The baby's mother stepped forward and took her place next to Isaac. "Miss Rosemary Tran," said Eusebio Martinez, "Professor Ben Blau. Mrs. Ruth Blau."

This Rosemary was as much a street person as Isaac, Ruth could see—more so, perhaps, and a great deal older. But it was clear she had what Isaac lacked: manners. Presented to Ruth, she raised her eyes and smiled shyly, showing that she also lacked a number of teeth.

Ruth looked at Isaac. How tall he was, and how remote. The lattice of hair that overhung his eyes like a caul and the beard that had crept up his cheeks over the last two years obscured any expression. He might have been an apparition, were it not for his smell, which she'd been breathing through her mouth to avoid. But now she gave that up and took it—took him—into her nostrils. It was worse than she'd been able to imagine, but also quite tolerable, perhaps because in the context of this encounter it seemed more a confession than a challenge. What was the line from *Lear*? "It smells of mortality." That wasn't quite the case with Isaac. He was too young. Instead, she supposed, he smelled of humanity—of terror and need.

Were they a couple, Isaac and this Rosemary? Were they actually married, in some bummy way? Could it be that the imperative to mate for life had found an anchoring place in them, mad and dirty as they were?

Ruth looked down at the baby, who was yawning. Her eyes squeezed shut and her mouth opened wide enough to expose her cat-sized tongue and the delicately ridged vault of her palate.

The first to come out of the crowd was Barbara Bachman, Ariel in tow. "Look," she whispered, approaching on tiptoe. "Look how tiny. See how the fingers curl? That's a reflex. She'll lose that as she develops." The next was Fran Tevis, whose eyes seemed to be filled with real tears. She kissed Ruth on the cheek, struggled to speak, gave up, kissed Ruth again and moved on. Bruce Federman threw an arm around Ben's neck. "Life," he breathed hoarsely. "Full of surprises, old man. Full of surprises." Then came Rhoda, and Josh Margolis and his wife, and Beth

Mapes, and Daphne Porter and her husband, and, finally, Dolores. Ruth offered the baby to her for a moment. She took the bundle and turned it toward the light, dipping a little to examine the baby's face. "A beautiful child," she pronounced.

Now Eusebio Martinez was laying hands on Ruth's shoulders, shuffling her a few feet to the right. "You also, Professor," he said, escorting Ben across the floor so that he stood arm to arm with Ruth. He did the same to Isaac and to Rosemary, herding the family into a tight cluster. Meanwhile the crowd, understanding its part, began to shape itself into a long coiling line.

Outside, the wind continued to blow. Inside, the candlelit occasion had become a highly social and rather formal one, as decorous and rule-bound as a tribal feast or a shipboard reception. Ruth held the baby. Ben stood at her side. Eusebio Martinez hovered behind Isaac and Rosemary, whispering prompts. Unsummoned, Ricia and Charles moved in to flank the group on either side, holding their candles high. One by one, the members of the Lola Dees humanities community filed by, stopping to congratulate the family, to peer into the baby's face, to marvel.

ACKNOWLEDGMENTS

Thanks, as always, to Julie Grau and Elyse Cheney, editor and agent extraordinaire.

Thanks, more than ever, to my husband George Sher, who appreciated, criticized, and contributed to nearly every page of this novel, including the acknowledgments. He is a man obsessed with names, and out of his fertile and fevered imagination swarmed many of the names of characters, institutions, places, journals, and journal articles in the book. He came close to being a collaborator in this effort, and can thus lay claim to about thirty-seven percent of any credit or blame it accrues.

ABOUT THE AUTHOR

Emily Fox Gordon is an award-winning essayist and the author of two memoirs, *Mockingbird Years: A Life In and Out of Therapy* and *Are You Happy? A Childhood Remembered*. Her work has appeared in *American Scholar, Time, Pushcart Prize Anthology XXIII* and *XXIX, Anchor Essay Annual*, the *New York Times Book Review, Boulevard*, and *Salmagundi*. She lives in Houston and teaches writing workshops at Rice University.

mL

GORDON   Gordon, Emily Fox,
           1948-

           It will come to me..

DATE			

FICTION CORE
COLLECTION 2014   BAKER & TAYLOR

MAY 2009